Werewolf Academy Book 2

Hunted

By Cheree L. Alsop

ISBN: 9781500840242
Cover Design by Robert Emerson and Andy Hair
www.ChereeAlsop.com

ALSO BY CHEREE ALSOP

The Werewolf Academy Series-
Book One: Strays
Book Two: Hunted
Book Three: Instinct
Book Four: Taken
Book Five: Lost
Book Six: Vengeance
Book Seven: Chosen

The Silver Series-
Silver
Black
Crimson
Violet
Azure
Hunter
Silver Moon

Heart of the Wolf Part One
Heart of the Wolf Part Two

The Galdoni Series-
Galdoni
Galdoni 2: Into the Storm
Galdoni 3: Out of Darkness

The Small Town Superheroes Series-
Small Town Superhero
Small Town Superhero II
Small Town Superhero III

HUNTED

Keeper of the Wolves
Stolen
The Million Dollar Gift
Thief Prince

Shadows
Mist- Book Two in the World of Shadows

PRAISE FOR CHEREE ALSOP

The Silver Series

"Cheree Alsop has written *Silver* for the YA reader who enjoys both werewolves and coming-of-age tales. Although I don't fall into this demographic, I still found it an entertaining read on a long plane trip! The author has put a great deal of thought into balancing a tale that could apply to any teen (death of a parent, new school, trying to find one's place in the world) with the added spice of a youngster dealing with being exceptionally different from those around him, and knowing that puts him in danger."
—Robin Hobb, author of the Farseer Trilogy

"I honestly am amazed this isn't absolutely EVERYWHERE! Amazing book. Could NOT put it down! After reading this book, I purchased the entire series!"
—Josephine, Amazon Reviewer

"Great book, Cheree Alsop! The best of this kind I have read in a long time. I just hope there is more like this one."
—Tony Olsen

"I couldn't put the book down. I fell in love with the characters and how wonderfully they were written. Can't wait to read the 2nd!"
—Mary A. F. Hamilton

"A page-turner that kept me wide awake and wanting more. Great characters, well written, tenderly developed, and thrilling. I loved this book, and you will too."

—Valerie McGilvrey

"Super glad that I found this series! I am crushed that it is at its end. I am sure we will see some of the characters in the next series, but it just won't be the same. I am 41 years old, and am only a little embarrassed to say I was crying at 3 a.m. this morning while finishing the last book. Although this is a YA series, all ages will enjoy the Silver Series. Great job by Cheree Alsop. I am excited to see what she comes up with next."

—Jennc, Amazon Reviewer

The Galdoni Series

"This is absolutely one of the best books I have ever read in my life! I loved the characters and their personalities, the storyline and the way it was written. The bravery, courage and sacrifice that Kale showed was amazing and had me scolding myself to get a grip and stop crying! This book had adventure, romance and comedy all rolled into one terrific book I LOVED the lesson in this book, the struggles that the characters had to go through (especially the forbidden love)...I couldn't help wondering what it would be like to live among such strangely beautiful creatures that acted, at times, more caring and compassionate than the humans. Overall, I loved this book...I recommend it to ANYONE who fancies great books."

—iBook Reviewer

"I was pleasantly surprised by this book! The characters were so well written as if the words themselves became life. The sweet romance between hero and heroine made me root

for the underdog more than I usually do! I definitely recommend this book!"
—Sara Phillipp

"Can't wait for the next book!! Original idea and great characters. Could not put the book down; read it in one sitting."
—StanlyDoo- Amazon Reviewer

"5 stars! Amazing read. The story was great- the plot flowed and kept throwing the unexpected at you. Wonderfully established setting in place; great character development, shown very well thru well placed dialogue- which in turn kept the story moving right along! No bog downs or boring parts in this book! Loved the originality that stemmed from ancient mysticism- bringing age old fiction into modern day reality. Recommend for teenage and older- action violence a little intense for preteen years, but overall this is a great action thriller slash mini romance novel."
—That Lisa Girl, Amazon Reviewer

"I was not expecting a free novel to beat anything that I have ever laid eyes upon. This book was touching and made me want more after each sentence."
—Sears1994, iBook Reviewer

"This book was simply heart wrenching. It was an amazing book with a great plot. I almost cried several times. All of the scenes were so real it felt like I was there witnessing everything."
—Jeanine Drake, iBook Reveiwer

"This book was absolutely amazing...It had me tearing at parts, cursing at others, and filled with adrenaline rushing along with the characters at the fights. It is a book for everyone, with themes of love, courage, hardship, good versus evil, humane and inhumane...All around, it is an amazing book!"

—Mkb312, iBook Reviewer

"Galdoni is an amazing book; it is the first to actually make me cry! It is a book that really touches your heart, a romance novel that might change the way you look at someone. It did that to me."

—Coralee2, Reviewer

"Wow. I simply have no words for this. I highly recommend it to anyone who stumbled across this masterpiece. In other words, READ IT!"

—Troublecat101, iBook Reviewer

Keeper of the Wolves

"This is without a doubt the VERY BEST paranormal romance/adventure I have ever read and I've been reading these types of books for over 45 years. Excellent plot, wonderful protagonists—even the evil villains were great. I read this in one sitting on a Saturday morning when there were so many other things I should have been doing. I COULD NOT put it down! I also appreciated the author's research and insights into the behavior of wolf packs. I will CERTAINLY read more by this author and put her on my 'favorites' list."

—N. Darisse

"This is a novel that will emotionally cripple you. Be sure to keep a box of tissues by your side. You will laugh, you will cry, and you will fall in love with Keeper. If you loved *Black Beauty* as a child, then you will truly love *Keeper of the Wolves* as an adult. Put this on your 'must read' list."
—Fortune Ringquist

"Cheree Alsop mastered the mind of a wolf and wrote the most amazing story I've read this year. Once I started, I couldn't stop reading. Personal needs no longer existed. I turned the last page with tears streaming down my face."
—Rachel Andersen, Amazon Reviewer

"I truly enjoyed this book very much. I've spent most of my life reading supernatural books, but this was the first time I've read one written in first person and done so well. I must admit that the last half of this book had me in tears from sorrow and pain for the main character and his dilemma as a man and an animal. . . Suffice it to say that this is one book you REALLY need in your library. I won't ever regret purchasing this book, EVER! It was just that GOOD! I would also recommend you have a big box of tissues handy because you WILL NEED THEM! Get going, get the book..."
—Kathy I, Amazon Reviewer

"I just finished this book. Oh my goodness, did I get emotional in some spots. It was so good. The courage and love portrayed is amazing. I do recommend this book. Thought provoking."
—Candy, Amazon Reviewer

Thief Prince

"I absolutely loved this book! I could not put it down. . . The Thief Prince will whisk you away into a new world that you will not want to leave! I hope that Ms. Alsop has more about this story to write, because I would love more Kit and Andric! This is one of my favorite books so far this year! Five Stars!"

—Crystal, Book Blogger at Books are Sanity

". . . Once I started I couldn't put it down. The story is amazing. The plot is new and the action never stops. The characters are believable and the emotions presented are beautiful and real. If anyone wants a good, clean, fun, romantic read, look no further. I hope there will be more books set in Debria, or better yet, Antor."

—SH Writer, Amazon Reviewer

"This book was a roller coaster of emotions: tears, laughter, anger, and happiness. I absolutely fell in love with all of the characters placed throughout this story. This author knows how to paint a picture with words."

—Kathleen Vales

"Awesome book! It was so action packed, I could not put it down, and it left me wanting more! It was very well written, leaving me feeling like I had a connection with the characters."

—M. A., Amazon Reviewer

"I am a Cheree Alsop junkie and I have to admit, hands down, this is my FAVORITE of anything she has published.

In a world separated by race, fear and power are forced to collide in order to save them all. Who better to free them of the prejudice than the loyal heart of a Duskie? Adventure, incredible amounts of imagination, and description go into this world! It is a 'buy now and don't leave the couch until the last chapter has reached an end' kind of read!"
—Malcay, Amazon Reviewer

"I absolutely loved this book! I could not put it down! Anything with a prince and a princess is usually a winner for me, but this book is even better! It has multiple princes and princesses on scene over the course of the book! I was completely drawn into Kit's world as she was faced with danger and new circumstances...Kit was a strong character, not a weak and simpering girl who couldn't do anything for herself. The Thief Prince (Andric) was a great character as well! I kept seeing glimpses of who he really was and I loved that the author gave us clues as to what he was like under the surface. The Thief Prince will whisk you away into a new world that you will not want to leave!"
—Bookworm, Book Reviewer

Small Town Superhero Series

"A very human superhero- Cheree Alsop has written a great book for youth and adults alike. Kelson, the superhero, is battling his own demons plus bullies in this action packed narrative. Small Town Superhero had me from the first sentence through the end. I felt every sorrow, every pain and the delight of rushing through the dark on a motorcycle. Descriptions in Small Town Superhero are so well written the reader is immersed in the town and lives of its inhabitants."

—Rachel Andersen, Book Reviewer

"Anyone who grew up in a small town or around motorcycles will love this! It has great characters and flows well with martial arts fighting and conflicts involved."
—Karen, Amazon Reviewer

"Fantastic story...and I love motorcycles and heroes who don't like the limelight. Excellent character development. You'll like this series!"
—Michael, Amazon Reviewer

"Another great read; couldn't put it down. Would definitely recommend this book to friends and family. She has put out another great read. Looking forward to reading more!"
—Benton Garrison, Amazon Reviewer

"I enjoyed this book a lot. Good teen reading. Most books I read are adult contemporary; I needed a change and this was a good change. I do recommend reading this book! I will be looking out for more books from this author. Thank you!"
—Cass, Amazon Reviewer

Stolen

"This book will take your heart, make it a little bit bigger, and then fill it with love. I would recommend this book to anyone from 10-100. To put this book in words is like trying to describe love. I had just gotten it and I finished it the next day because I couldn't put it down. If you like action, thrilling fights, and/or romance, then this is the perfect book for you."

—Steven L. Jagerhorn

"Couldn't put this one down! Love Cheree's ability to create totally relatable characters and a story told so fluidly you actually believe it's real."

—Sue McMillin, Amazon Reviewer

"I enjoyed this book it was exciting and kept you interested. The characters were believable. And the teen romance was cute."

—Book Haven- Amazon Reviewer

"This book written by Cheree Alsop was written very well. It is set in the future and what it would be like for government control. The drama was great and the story was very well put together. If you want something different, then this is the book to get and it is a page turner for sure. You will love the main characters as well, and the events that unfold during the story. It will leave you hanging and wanting more."

—Kathy Hallettsville, TX- Amazon Reviewer

"I really liked this book . . . I was pleasantly surprised to discover this well-written book. . .I'm looking forward to reading more from this author."

—Julie M. Peterson- Amazon Reviewer

"Great book! I enjoyed this book very much it keeps you wanting to know more! I couldn't put it down! Great read!"

—Meghan- Amazon Reviewer

"A great read with believable characters that hook you instantly. . . I was left wanting to read more when the book was finished."

—Katie- Goodreads Reviewer

Heart of the Wolf

"Absolutely breathtaking! This book is a roller coaster of emotions that will leave you exhausted!!! A beautiful fantasy filled with action and love. I recommend this book to all fantasy lovers and those who enjoy a heartbreaking love story that rivals that of Romeo and Juliet. I couldn't put this book down!"

—Amy May

"What an awesome book! A continual adventure, with surprises on every page. What a gifted author she is. You just can't put the book down. I read it in two days. Cheree has a way of developing relationships and pulling at your heart. You find yourself identifying with the characters in her book...True life situations make this book come alive for you and gives you increased understanding of your own situation in life. Magnificent story and characters. I've read all of Cheree's books and recommend them all to you...especially if you love adventures."

—Michael, Amazon Reviewer

"You'll like this one and want to start part two as soon as you can! If you are in the mood for an adventure book in a faraway kingdom where there are rival kingdoms plotting and scheming to gain more power, you'll enjoy this novel. The characters are well developed, and of course with Cheree

there is always a unique supernatural twist thrown into the story as well as romantic interests to make the pages fly by."
Karen, Amazon Reviewer

When Death Loved an Angel

"This style of book is quite a change for this author so I wasn't expecting this, but I found an interesting story of two very different souls who stepped outside of their "accepted roles" to find love and forgiveness, and what is truly of value in life and death."
—Karen, Amazon Reviewer

"When Death Loved an Angel by Cheree Alsop is a touching paranormal romance that cranks the readers' thinking mode into high gear."
—Rachel Andersen, Book Reviewer

"Loved this book. I would recommend this book to everyone. And be sure to check out the rest of her books, too!"
—Malcay, Book Reviewer

The Shadows Series

". . . This author has talent. I enjoyed her world, her very well developed characters, and an interesting, entertaining concept and story. Her introduction to her world was well done and concise. . . .Her characters were interesting enough that I became attached to several. I would certainly read a follow-up if only to check on the progress and evolution of the society she created. I recommend this for any age other than those overly sensitive to some graphic violence. The romance was heartfelt but pg. A good read."

—Mari, Amazon Reviewer

". . . I've fallen for the characters and their world. I've even gone on to share (this book) with my sister. . .So many moments made me smile as well as several which brought tears from the attachment; not sad tears, I might add. When I started Shadows, I didn't expect much because I assumed it was like most of the books I've read lately. But this book was one of the few books to make me happy I was wrong and find myself so far into the books that I lost track of time, ending up reading to the point that my body said I was too tired to continue reading! I can't wait to see what happens in the next book. . . Some of my new favorite quotes will be coming from this lovely novel. Thank you to Cheree Alsop for allowing the budding thoughts to come to life. I am a very hooked reader."

—Stephanie Roberts, Amazon Reviewer

"This was a heart-warming tale of rags to riches. It was also wonderfully described and the characters were vivid and vibrant; a story that teaches of love defying boundaries and of people finding acceptance."

—Sara Phillip, Book Reviewer

"This is the best book I have ever had the pleasure of reading. . . It literally has everything, drama, action, fighting, romance, adventure, & suspense. . . Nexa is one of the most incredible female protagonists ever written. . .It literally had me on pins & needles the ENTIRE time. . . I cannot recommend this book highly enough. Please give yourself a

CHEREE ALSOP

wonderful treat & read this book... you will NOT be
disappointed!!!"

—Jess- Goodreads Reviewer

"Took my breath away; excitement, adventure and
suspense. . . This author has extracted a tender subject and
created a supernatural fantasy about seeing beyond the
surface of an individual. . . Also the romantic scenes would
make a girl swoon. . . The fights between allies and foes and
blood lust would attract the male readers. . .The conclusion
was so powerful and scary this reader was sitting on the edge
of her seat."

—Susan Mahoney, Book Blogger

"Adventure, incredible amounts of imagination and
description go into this world! It is a buy now, don't leave the
couch until the last chapter has reached an end kind of read!"

—Malcay- Amazon Reviewer

"The high action tale with the underlying love story that
unfolds makes you want to keep reading and not put it down.
I can't wait until the next book in the Shadows Series comes
out."

—Karen- Amazon Reviewer

"Really enjoyed this book. A modern fairy tale complete
with Kings and Queens, Princesses and Princes, castles and
the damsel is not quite in distress. LOVE IT."

—Braine, Talk Supe- Book Blogger

". . . It's refreshing to see a female character portrayed
without the girly cliches most writers fall into. She is someone
I would like to meet in real life, and it is nice to read the first

person POV of a character who is so well-round that she is brave, but still has the softer feminine side that defines her character. A definite must read."

—S. Teppen- Goodreads Reviewer

"I really enjoyed this book and had a hard time putting it down. . . This premise is interesting and the world building was intriguing. The author infused the tale with the feeling of suspicion and fear . . . The author does a great job with characterization and you grow to really feel for the characters throughout especially as they change and begin to see Nexa's point of view. . . I did enjoy the book and the originality. I would recommend this for young adult fantasy lovers. It's more of a mild dark fantasy, but it would definitely fall more in the traditional fantasy genre . "

—Jill- Goodreads Reviewer

Love- the secret of the Universe.
Without it, we are lost.
With it, we are unstoppable.

I love you, Michael.
I love you my children,
Myree, Ashton, and Aiden.

HUNTED

Chapter One

Alex's paws drummed across the earth in a cadence few wolves would have been able to match. A train whistle sounded in the distance. He pushed himself harder, ducking branches and leaping the stream that babbled merrily along, unaffected by his haphazard flight. He reached the rise, but didn't slow down. With one final push, he leaped off the highest boulder. For an instant, it felt like he was truly flying. The wind brushed at his fur, beckoning for the werewolf to join its carefree dance.

Alex's paws hit a boulder. He leaped to the next, then a third. He hit the ground the same time that the train left the tunnel.

Careful to keep out of sight among the trees, Alex raced beside the steel beast. The horn sounded. It was faster than he was. He gritted his teeth and pushed himself harder, but it always slipped away, beating him to the edge of the forest.

Alex skidded to a stop at the fence. His heartbeat thundered in his ears as he watched the train continue its path oblivious of the race it had won. He was still fighting to catch his breath when another sound caught his ears. They were here!

Alex dashed back through the forest. He dodged a lightning-struck tree and ducked beneath a bush that turned out to be too low for his body. Breaking through the other side, he shook leaves and twigs from his fur as he ran.

He reached the road as the buses rumbled by. Accepting the challenge, Alex darted alongside, keeping as far into the forest as he could without being held up by the underbrush. He passed one bus, then the next. He ran alongside the limo at the front of the buses and glanced up in time to meet an icy blue gaze.

Alex's heart skipped a beat when Kalia's eyes widened in recognition. He tried to jump a log, but was a fraction too slow. His paw caught and he tumbled head over heels into nest of boulders. A poof of dust rose at the impact.

Alex stood slowly. Bruises would heal; he expected the pain to be gone by the time evening fell. He padded through the dust left by the vehicles to the point where they vanished between the tall gates that marked the entrance of the Academy.

Alex hadn't been sure if Kalia would return to the Academy. They hadn't left on the best of terms, to put it lightly. She had been mad enough at him that he doubted she would speak to him. Guilt flooded his conscience. It was his fault for accusing her of working with Dane Carso so he could kill the twins.

It had been Pip all along. Kalia was just a girl caught between two worlds. She hadn't phased, yet her eyes glowed golden whenever she was upset, which tended to be a lot around Alex. It wasn't her fault her parents feared werewolves and sent her to the Academy just in case she happened to phase. The fact that her brother Boris was an Alpha didn't help matters, and he wasn't especially pleasant. No wonder they were worried.

Alex ran to the back of the Academy and phased where he had left his clothes. He pulled them on and reached the courtyard just as Dean Jaze was addressing the new students. Alex walked to Jet's statue.

"Where were you?" Cassie demanded, her dark blue eyes worried.

"Just changing my clothes," Alex replied, giving his twin sister his most convincing smile.

She reached up and pulled a twig from his hair. "This is from a blueberry bush."

"Huh," Alex said. "They aren't very tall, are they?"

"What does that have to do with anything?" she asked, frustrated.

"Shh," Alex told her. "Jaze is talking. You don't want to be rude."

Cassie sputtered at him for a moment. She finally gave a shake of her head and turned back to the proceedings. "Boys," she muttered under her breath.

Alex smiled. He wanted to point out that he doubted human boys would have any success racing a train or buses, but decided not to press his luck. Instead, he folded his arms and leaned against the base of the huge black wolf statue. Jet guarded over the courtyard, watching the proceedings from his vantage point. If he had been alive, Alex knew no one would dare to go into the Academy with malice in their hearts; as it was, the Academy had been breached last Christmas. Alex was determined to never let it happen again.

"Mingle among yourselves," Mrs. Nikki Carso, the dean's wife, encouraged the students. "Get to know each other. We'll have the Choosing Ceremony in a few minutes, and the contacts you make now may very well determine how the rest of your term here goes."

A tall seventeen year old with brown eyes walked up to Alex and Cassie.

"Ready for another year?" Jericho asked, holding out a hand.

"I didn't think you'd take me back," Alex replied with a grin. "We had quite the year."

Jericho nodded. "Yes, we did. But I think that if you're not my Second, this next year is going to be quite boring in comparison."

"We wouldn't want that," Alex said with mock solemnity.

"No, we wouldn't," Jericho replied.

Both boys looked over the crowd of students.

"Fifteen more this year," a voice said beside Alex.

Alex smiled down at Trent. "Really? It looks like more."

"That's because they're extra loud," Terith proclaimed, standing next to her brother. She shook her head and her blonde curls bounced on her shoulders. "Don't they know Alphas like Grays who are quiet?"

Alex and Jericho exchanged a look. Terith was the most talkative of their pack. For her to be pointing out the noise was either ironic or showed how truly rambunctious the students were.

"Has anyone seen Pip?" Cassie asked quietly.

Alex shook his head. He had been searching the crowd for the small student with big ears who had almost cost them their lives. They had stayed friends until the end of the year, but it looked like the young Second Year hadn't returned.

"Too bad," Jericho noted. "He was handy at the first full moon challenge."

Cassie and Alex glanced at each other. Only a few others at the Academy knew Pip was the one who had been Drogan's contact. They planned to keep it that way and protect the little werewolf's name in case he returned.

"Time to go to the Great Hall for the Choosing Ceremony," Nikki announced.

Everyone filed into the Great Hall. As usual, Lifers and Termers sat on opposite sides of the hall, but this time the werewolves who had made up Pack Jericho stayed together. There really wasn't much doubt who was going to be in their pack. Alex didn't see any reason to mess with the camaraderie they had created, and everyone seemed content to stick together. With the addition of fifteen more students and Pip's absence, there might be two more spaces to fill, but the rest was pretty much settled.

"Sid Hathaway," Torin announced, choosing his Second for the year. Sid was always the Lifer Alpha's Second, so it came as no surprise.

Boris, the Alpha leader of the Termers, stood up next. Alex glanced at Kalia. She glared at her brother as if daring him to say someone else's name.

"Parker Luis," he called. Kalia gave a visible wince. Alex felt bad for her. It had to be hard getting chosen third by family.

The other Alphas took their picks. Jericho was last; even though he was seventeen, it was only his second year at the Academy.

"Alex Davies," Jericho called when it was his turn.

Alex took his place beneath the dais. If Trent's information was correct, the ten Alphas had one hundred and sixty-seven werewolves to choose for their packs.

Torin walked forward again. "Amos Jones," he called.

Alex stared. The huge Gray rose slowly from his seat with Pack Jericho. His expression was confused as he looked from Torin to Jericho and Alex. Alex nodded encouragingly, but his heart sank at the thought of losing the hulking Gray.

Alex glanced back at Torin. The Alpha smirked at him as Amos took his place below the dais. Alex clenched and unclenched his hands. He wanted to do something, but as a Gray, it wasn't his place. Jericho met his gaze and gave a minute shrug. There was nothing they could do.

Boris cleared his throat. "Matthews Johnson," he said.

Alex glanced at Kalia. She looked ready to cry or scream. Instead, she crossed her arms and glared at the floor as the other Alphas chose their pack mates.

"Cassie Davies," Jericho called.

Cassie hurried up to join Alex. She was excited to get out of the anxious crowd of students waiting to be picked. It was only the second year both she and Alex hadn't been chosen last. She stood next to him with a small smile on her face.

At the next round, Boris called Kalia's name. She stood up, but didn't move toward the stage.

To everyone's shock, she took a deep breath and said loud enough for everyone to hear, "I refuse the choosing."

Whispers erupted through the students. Professor Kaynan stood up from his seat with the rest of the Academy staff near the back of the stage.

"What are you doing? Don't be stupid." Boris growled, not caring that the rest of the students watched.

Kalia ignored the statement, her attention on Professor Kaynan.

The professor's red gaze traveled over the crowd. "It is Kalia's right to deny the choosing," he stated.

Kalia nodded and sat back down. She pointedly ignored her brother as he glared at her from the stage.

"Zach Mitchell," he finally called.

Maliki, Shannon, and Raynen made their normal choices. Drake hesitated. He glanced at Jericho, then out at the students.

"What's up?" Jericho asked the other Alpha quietly.

"I need a brainiac on my pack," Alex heard Drake reply. "Some of my guys are barely passing classes."

"Alex, what do you think?" Jericho asked.

Alex thought about it for a second. "Take Nate Smith. He's usually last on Shannon or Maliki's packs anyway. He'll be grateful for the bump up and probably become a strong member of your pack."

"But he's a Stray," Drake protested.

The word sent a surge of anger through Alex.

Even though he wasn't an Alpha, the expression on Alex's face made Drake quickly amend his word choice. "I mean a Lifer."

"It doesn't matter," Jericho replied quietly. "My pack was the most well-rounded last year. Can you argue against that?"

Alex could tell by the look on Drake's face that the Alpha wanted to, but he had no legs to stand on. All of the students were watching them, and with a room full of werewolves, there was no doubt everyone was listening. He finally nodded. "I choose Nate Smith."

The relief on the Lifer's face made Alex smile. The boy practically ran to Drake's area below the dais. He turned around with a big grin on his face, revealing the big gap between his two front teeth that gave him a bit of a lisp.

"Thanks, man," Nate whispered, leaning over to Alex. "I appreciate it."

"Anytime," Alex replied.

Jessilyn, Kelli, and Miguel made their selections from the normal members of their packs. It was Jericho's turn again. The Alpha asked quietly, "Who's next, Alex?"

Cassie spoke up, surprising them both. "Kalia," she pleaded.

Alex and Jericho both stared at her. "She hates me," Alex replied in a whisper. "That'd be a horrible idea."

"Please?" Cassie pleaded. "She needs a pack."

Jericho looked from Cassie to Alex. When the Gray met his gaze, the Alpha gave a slight shrug, leaving the decision up to his Second.

"Okay," Alex replied. "I hope I don't regret this," he muttered under his breath.

"You won't," Cassie promised with a huge smile on her face.

"Kalia Dickson," Jericho called.

Gasps ran through the crowd. Alex dared a glance sideways and met Boris' furious glare. Maybe it was worth it after all.

Kalia walked sedately to the front of the Great Hall. She stood next to Cassie, ignoring Alex entirely. While he felt relieved that she hadn't turned down their choosing, he wondered how the term would go with Kalia as a pack mate.

Chapter Two

"Shaking things up again?" Jericho asked as students left the Choosing Ceremony in packs.

Alex and Jericho walked slowly behind their new pack mates. The group was made up of mostly their regulars from last year, along with a new seven-year-old named Caitlyn, a Fourth Year named Steph, and Kalia. There was also a new fifteen-year-old Lifer named Tennison that Jericho had chosen at the end of the ceremony. It was unusual for new orphans to come to the Academy, but it was no secret Drogan and the General still waged their war on werewolves. Tennison had come in on the buses and nobody knew much about the werewolf, except that he wasn't an Alpha and he was going to be staying at the Academy with the rest of the Lifers.

Seventeen members made for a huge pack. Alex watched students stormed up the stairs anxious to get to their new quarters. Pack Jericho would be at the end of the hallway again because Jericho was the newest Alpha. They were in no hurry to fight the rush down the hall. Alex shook his head. The professors were going to have to figure something else out the next year if more Termers came in; the Alphas were going to have a hard time managing so many Grays.

"Could I share a room with you?" a small voice asked.

Alex glanced back to see Caitlyn, their new seven-year-old, clinging to Cassie's hand.

Cassie smiled down at her. "Actually, we all have our own rooms." Caitlyn's wide green eyes filled with tears. "But I'll make sure your room is next to mine, and you can visit me whenever you want," Cassie concluded quickly.

"Really?" Caitlyn asked.

Cassie nodded and the answering smile that broke out

across the little girl's face filled Alex with relief. His sister was making new friends. Besides Terith, himself, and Kalia, she hadn't really branched out over the last year. Perhaps Caitlyn was the beginning of something new.

"Alright, Pack Jericho, find your rooms, get situated, and let's head down to dinner. For those of you here for the first time, your belongings will be brought up while we eat," Jericho told his pack. He grinned at Alex. "Ready for another food fight?"

Alex laughed. "Always ready."

Alex held back as the packs hurried back down the stairs to the Great Hall. He wanted to make sure Cassie was alright because his sister hated crowds, but he spotted her in the midst of the stampede holding Caitlyn's hand and helping the little girl down. Apparently his twin had forgotten her own fears while assisting Caitlyn.

The door opened and Kalia ran straight into him.

"Oh, um, sorry," Alex stammered, even though he had only been innocently standing by when she practically bull rushed him.

"Sorry," Kalia mumbled, hurrying for the stairs.

"Kalia, wait," Alex called.

She paused with her foot on the top step. She didn't turn around. Reluctance to be up there with him showed in every line of her body.

Alex took a steeling breath. "I don't know how to apologize more than I already have. I was wrong and I'm sorry."

Anger flashed in Kalia's light blue eyes when she turned back around. Her blonde hair swished above her shoulders with the snap of her head. "Maybe you can't fix this, Alex."

"But you're in my pack," Alex pointed out.

She shook her head. "I'm in Jericho's pack, or have you

forgotten that you don't own it?'"

Alex held up his hands. "Whoa. Slow down. I'm not trying to fight with you. I'm just saying that since we're in the same pack, we should probably try to get along."

"Does that include accusing your friend of sending someone to murder you?" Kalia asked with true hurt in her voice.

"No, it doesn't," Alex replied quietly. "It doesn't at all. I was way out of line, and I am truly sorry. I hope you might be able to forgive me someday."

"I doubt that," Kalia replied. She walked slowly down the stairs.

Her footsteps paused and Alex heard a little muffled sound escape from her. Kalia bent over with her head in her hands. Her hair hid her expression from view. When he ran down next to her, he saw that her face was twisted in pain.

"Kalia?" he asked.

She didn't answer.

He put a hand on her shoulder.

"I'm fine," she said, though her tight tone said otherwise.

Alex took her by the elbow and helped her to a sitting position on the stairs. He crouched in front of her. "Do you want me to get Meredith or Lyra?"

She shook her head, then winced. "No. It'll go away." She pressed both hands to her forehead.

Alex didn't know what to do. He could hear Jaze's voice as the dean welcomed everyone to the first dinner of the term. He made a split-second decision and ran back up the stairs to Pack Jericho's quarters. He grabbed a hand towel from the bathroom and poured cold water over it. He then hurried back down and crouched in front of Kalia again.

"Here, try this."

She opened her eyes and saw what he was holding. He set

the folded towel in her hands. She pressed it to her forehead. A little sound of relief escaped her. "That's helps," she admitted.

Alex waited with her. The helplessness he felt to ease the pain made him pace the stairs, opening and closing his hands in frustration.

Kalia finally let out her breath in a sigh. She sat back against the wall and lowered the rag. "It's gone," she said.

"Just like that?"

Kalia nodded. "It comes on in an instant and leaves like nothing happened." She met his gaze and her eyes narrowed slightly as if she remembered who she was talking to. She stood up and wavered slightly.

Alex put out a hand to help her, but she took a firm grip on the railing. "I'm fine," she said, the chill back in her voice. "Thank you for your assistance."

Alex watched her walk down the stairs as if nothing had happened. He didn't move. He couldn't. As much as he wanted to join his pack in the first feast of the new term, too many emotions battled through him.

He had been Kalia's only friend last year and had thrown that away with the paranoia that she was leaking information to Drogan. Drogan and his father the General had destroyed too many relationships in Alex's life, and he had let the man with the mismatched eyes ruin yet another. Alex hated himself for how he had acted. He had been stabbed and shot during his battles to survive the last school year, yet the wound that hurt the most was seeing the loss in Kalia's eyes. He had betrayed her friendship when he questioned her loyalty and he destroyed her confidence in him.

Seeing her hurting and weak made his heart go out to her, yet she refused his help after she realized who was there. He walked down the stairs and turned away from the sound of revelry and laughter in the Great Hall.

Alex pushed open the backdoors and wandered outside.

"Not the social type?"

Alex jumped. He hadn't expected anyone to be outside with the dinner going on and had let down his guard. He schooled his face to a smile when he turned around.

"Oh, hey Tennison. I thought you'd be in eating with the rest of the pack," Alex said upon spotting the tall, lanky new Lifer.

Tennison shook his head. "I'm not much for that stuff."

"Uh, stuff like eating?" Alex said. When the werewolf didn't respond, Alex tried a different tactic. "So what do you think of the Academy?"

Tennison looked up at the spires that reached into the evening sky. He gave a small shrug of his bony shoulders. "It's alright."

Alex fought back the sudden surge of protectiveness toward the Academy. It might just be a school to the Termers, but to the Lifers, it was home. Alex suddenly realized that to Tennison, it was also home. He didn't know what had happened in the boy's life, but they were both orphans through whatever twist of fate had thrown them together.

"It's really not that bad," Alex said, his tone understanding. "It has a tendency to grow on you."

"It feels hollow," Tennison replied quietly without looking at Alex.

Alex breathed out quietly through his nose the way he would in wolf form to clear his senses. Tennison was obviously going through a loss. He was avoiding the crowd as much as Alex. That gave Alex an idea. "Want to go for a walk?" he asked.

Tennison gave him a searching look; Alex had the feeling

it was the first time the new Lifer had really looked at anything since reaching the Academy. His pale eyes were clear and contained a hint of surprise. "Uh, sure?"

"I'll take that as an answer instead of a question," Alex replied, leading the way to the gate. Alex opened it and stepped out.

Tennison paused at the wall. "Are we allowed in the forest?"

"Mostly," Alex said, pausing a few feet into the trees. He looked over his shoulder at the student. "Don't worry. I'm the Second of our pack. If anyone's going to get in trouble, it'll be me, and I don't get into trouble." He paused, then said, "Much."

"That's reassuring," Tennison muttered, following Alex through the heavy metal gate.

Alex stepped behind a tree. He turned around to take off his clothes when he found Tennison behind him.

"Uh, you might want to find your own tree," Alex suggested.

"To what?" Tennison asked.

Alex smiled. "To phase."

"Here? Now?" Tennison looked shocked.

"Werewolves were meant to run," Alex explained. "There are no rules here against phasing."

He went to another tree and left Tennison standing at the last one with his mouth open.

It only took a few minutes for Tennison to join him beneath the trees in wolf form. Tennison's gray coat was a shade lighter than Alex's, and he looked unsure of himself, as if he hadn't spent enough time as a wolf to be used to the form. Alex trotted a few paces away. He didn't turn back to look, but listened for Tennison to catch up before he took off running. The other wolf fell in beside him.

Alex had never taken anyone on his favorite run. He meant to just show Tennison the rise the Alphas liked to jump off of into the river, but something changed his mind. He led the way deeper beneath the trees, letting the muscle memory of a thousand such runs guide his paws.

The air cooled as the shadows grew deeper and Alex relied on his hearing and smell to keep on the right path along with his sight. The grays and blacks of the wolf's eyesight made it easier to pick out shapes amid the darkness. The scent of the thick pine needles that carpeted the forest floor tingled in his sensitive nose. He took a deep breath of the crisp night air and let it out with a wolfish smile. Forgetting the werewolf beside him completely, Alex stretched his legs out, pushing himself at his hardest run.

By the time he reached the junction where the train rounded the corner at close to seven o-clock morning and night, Alex felt his heart stuttering. He grimaced and slowed. Though he tried to push himself further in the hopes that strengthening his heart would fix the problem, it refused to go away. His breath caught in his throat as it stuttered again. Alex stopped running, knowing that if he continued and his heart gave one of its big jumps, he would fall and probably slam into a tree like the other times he refused to listen to his body.

Tennison was right behind him. Alex was shocked that the werewolf had kept up, but he shouldn't have been. Tennison had the same lanky build as he did in human form; his longer legs had probably allowed him to keep up easier than Alex thought. Alex wondered if the student used to run track at his last school; no human would have stood a chance.

There was a look of joy on Tennison's face. It was amazing how expressive a wolf could be, given that smiling revealed fangs and looked more like a snarl. Rafe highly discouraged the expression, saying that a smile could easily start a fight based on misunderstanding. Tennison must have known that, because he didn't smile. Instead, his ears were high and his pale eyes were bright as he looked around at the forest. He lifted one paw and then the other as if he couldn't stay in one place.

Alex gave a soft snort and began to trot down the decline. Tennison surprised him by racing past. The werewolf stopped and barked a challenge. Alex fought back a grin as he ran to catch up. Instead of stopping, he sped past the wolf. He heard Tennison fall in quickly behind. The two of them raced back to the Academy, their footsteps even and joy singing in Alex's heart at the run.

Chapter Three

"I've never run as a wolf," Tennison said after they had phased and were walking back to the Academy.

"Never?" Alex asked, amazed.

Tennison shook his head. "My parents thought it would draw too much attention to be outside as a wolf, so we stayed in the house." He looked like he wanted to say more, but then he closed his mouth, withdrawing.

Alex chose a different topic. "I thought I lost you back there."

Tennison gave a wolfish snort. "Like you could have. I had miles left in me."

"Me, too," Alex said, though his heart said otherwise. He pulled open the backdoor and led the way to the Great Hall. He opened the door, than quickly shut it again. "Don't go in there!"

"What's wrong?" Tennison asked. He reached for the door.

"Don't say I didn't warn you," Alex told him.

When Tennison pulled the huge door open, two rolls and a bowl of chili came flying through. He shut it quickly. "What's going on?" he asked.

"We apparently missed the feast, but made it in time for the annual food fight," Alex said, peeking back through the door.

Packs were huddled under tables while others ran around in groups. He grinned at the sight of Boris and Torin leading their packs like Jericho had done last year, taking down the others with precision attacks of vegetables and turkey legs.

"Annual? As in this happens every year?" Tennison asked. At Alex's nod, the new Lifer shook his head. "This place is strange."

"Well, we're supposed to be in there bonding with our pack," Alex explained.

Tennison looked at him like he was from another planet. "Throwing food at other students is bonding?"

"If you do it as a pack, yes," Alex replied. "I think this is one experience you need to participate in."

Tennison shook his head quickly. "No, thank you. I'd rather stay out here."

Alex grinned. "You have no choice. As your Second, I command you to participate in the food fight." He looked through the crack in the door again. "Our pack is getting pummeled. It's our fault for leaving them short-handed. I say we make up for the difference."

Tennison looked ready to argue. He crossed the hallway. Alex thought the werewolf was going to leave, but Tennison crouched and picked up the two rolls. "For Pack Jericho?" he asked.

Alex grinned and caught the roll Tennison tossed him. "For Pack Jericho."

Alex pulled open the door with Tennison right behind him. "Jericho!" they yelled. Immediately, every manner of food that had once occupied the tables sailed through the air toward them. Before the werewolves could do much more than duck, they were coated from head to toe in turkey, mashed potatoes, chili, and various types of steamed vegetables.

Tennison wiped potatoes out of one eye. "This is bonding?"

"Don't you feel it?" Alex said with a laugh. "I'm all covered in bonding."

"Defend our pack!" Jericho yelled from across the room.

"Pack Jericho!" the others replied.

The werewolves swarmed to their protection. Alex

grinned at the sight of Tennison throwing rolls with Cassie and Caitlyn. The little seven-year-old had gravy in her white-blonde hair, and took a bite out of a roll before she threw it.

"Die, you pack vermin you," the little girl yelled at the top of her lungs.

Everyone paused in what they were doing. Laughter began to bubble up from the crowd. Werewolves stepped from their hiding places armed with food in case the other packs decided to attack, but it was clear Caitlyn's battle cry had taken the heat out of the battle.

Chuckles followed as brooms were handed out. Alex mopped up a particularly stubborn spattering of cranberry sauce near the door. Tennison paused next to him. "This place is getting better," the new Lifer admitted.

"Just wait," Alex replied. "You might even start to like it."

Tennison smiled and pushed his broom in the other direction.

***

"I might not have Jaze's, uh Dean Jaze's, permission for a football team against other schools," Vance said as soon as Pack Jericho reached the gym, "But that doesn't mean we can't start training."

"Aw, man," Trent whined.

"What's wrong?" Boris demanded from the other side of the gym. "Scared?"

"Seriously?" Alex muttered under his breath. "First period and we're already paired with Pack Boris?"

"The guy's a troll," Trent whispered to Tennison.

"Hey," Kalia replied.

Trent's eyes widened. "I thought-I thought you were mad at him," the small werewolf stammered. He ran a hand across his buzzed head. "I didn't mean any offense."

"He's still my brother," Kalia replied.

"Are you sure?" Boris asked, glaring at her. "I think you forgot that during the Choosing Ceremony."

Kalia met his glare with one of her own. "I remembered it quite well, thank you."

Alex bit back a smile. Kalia had fire. At least with her on Pack Jericho, Boris' attentions were focused on her.

As if he had overheard Alex's thoughts, the Alpha's gaze shifted to the fifteen-year-olds. "I blame you," he mouthed.

A knot twisted in Alex's stomach.

"Alright, ladies and girls," Vance said, addressing the group as a whole. The girls snickered at the boys.

"You still have to play football," Trent reminded his sister.

"This stinks," Terith replied with a scowl.

Vance ignored them. "Get dressed and meet me out here in two minutes."

Everyone knew that the physical education teacher truly meant two minutes. They scrambled toward the locker rooms to change.

"Football is just another excuse to hit people and not get in trouble for it," Trent whined.

"It's not that bad," Marky replied. "I always watch football with my dad."

Trent gave the eight-year-old a pointed look. "I have a feeling this is going to be a bit different."

"I hope we get to pit packs against each other," Boris said loudly from the next row of lockers. "Pack Jericho's made of a bunch of scrawny wimps."

"Hey!" Steven and Marky said at the same time.

"He's right," Trent told them, his tone weak.

Alex fought back a wave of frustration. His pack might not have been made of the strongest members. Besides Don, Jericho, Tennison, and himself, their strengths were centered on more practical subjects like math and history. They were going to get killed.

Pack Boris laughed on their way past. "See you at the slaughter," Parker, Boris' Second, said.

"Listen up," Jericho told his pack as soon as the others were out of the locker room. "This isn't going to be easy, but we can learn from it. Alex, I want you to be the quarterback."

Alex stared at him. "I don't remember the last time I threw a football," he said.

It wasn't true. Alex remembered standing in the backyard with his dad when he was seven, throwing the football back and forth between them. His dad was proud of how tight Alex's spiral was getting, and Alex didn't drop nearly as many catches as he used to.

"It's alright," Jericho told him. "We'll probably have to hand it off a lot in the beginning anyway, but you need me and Don to protect you. I have a feeling Boris is going to send everything he can your way."

"What gave you that feeling?" Trent asked a bit snidely. "The target painted on his back?"

Jericho ignored him and looked at the other boys. "Who can run?"

"Tennison," Alex said into the silence.

Jericho glanced at the new Lifer and nodded. "Good. Let's make this happen."

"Two minutes has passed, ladies," Vance called. "Pack Jericho owes me ten laps at the end of practice."

"He's already calling it practice," Trent muttered. "Isn't it gym class?"

"Not anymore," Jericho replied over his shoulder.

Vance lined them up in packs.

"The girls are playing with us?" Boris asked skeptically.

Vance raised his eyebrows. The effect made the huge, hulking werewolf look even more like a bear. "Do you have a problem with that? Maybe we should pit boys against girls. They're already faster than you, and I've never seen an angry she-wolf I'd want to mess with."

Boris glanced at Pack Jericho. Alex realized the Alpha was worried about his sister. Since she hadn't shown any other traits of a werewolf other than her eyes changing colors, she didn't have the same strength and speed as the rest of the students.

"Uh, Kalia," Alex said. "Why don't you fall back? The front line looks ready to kill anyone in their path."

It was completely true. Pack Boris chomped at the bit; their monster-sized defensive line made Pack Jericho's look like preschoolers. Alex thought it was a good call, but Kalia gave him a look that threatened death as she fell back behind Talia and Trent. The siblings looked from Kalia to Alex.

"Do you want her to suffocate you in your sleep?" Cassie asked, her tone only half-joking.

"I'm trying to keep her from getting hurt," Alex argued. "I thought she would appreciate it."

Cassie shook her head. "You have a lot to learn about girls."

Alex met Boris' gaze. The Alpha gave a little chuckle. Alex was glad that Kalia's brother found the situation humorous. He only wished Kalia felt the same.

"Ready," Vance called.

Alex blew out a breath of frustration and hunched over behind Marky.

"Hike," Alex shouted. He caught the ball and backpedaled a few steps. Pack Boris' offensive line shoved aside Alex's defense like they weren't even trying. Within seconds, Alex was flat on his back with the ball clutched tightly to his chest and four of Boris' werewolves laughing down at him.

"Sorry, Alex," Amos said. The huge werewolf did indeed look sorry for smashing Alex into the ground.

Amos grabbed him by the shoulders and lifted him back to his feet as if he weighed less than a kitten. "No harm done," Alex said, though his ribs and bruised chest argued otherwise.

"Alright, alright," Vance said with what could almost be taken for a smile. "Let's try not to kill Alex. He may be a bit short for a quarterback, but I'm sure Jericho has his reasons for choosing him."

"So we can kill him," Parker called out. Everyone on Pack Boris laughed.

Alex set the ball back in the middle.

"Don't let them through this time," Jericho told his pack. "Protect Alex so he can throw the ball."

"Right," Don agreed.

He and Jericho looked formidable, but Steven and Max stood on either side of them like little twigs waiting to be broken. Alex heaved a sigh and called out, "Hike!"

In two-seconds flat, he was on his back again. Boris leered down at him.

"Might as well stay down there, Stray," the Alpha growled.

Jericho pulled Boris off and helped Alex up.

"Flick it to me," Tennison said quietly enough that only Alex could hear.

"What?" Alex asked.

"Flick it to me the second you have it. They won't be expecting it."

Alex nodded. It was worth a shot. He stepped up to the line again.

"Ready to meet the floor again?" Parker asked with a grin that revealed his yellow teeth.

"You really should use a toothbrush," Alex replied.

"Huh?"

Alex took advantage of Parker's distraction and called out, "Hike!"

Jericho tossed him the ball. As soon as it touched his hands, Alex flicked it to Tennison. The throw was off. He knew as soon as it left his hands that the ball would be short. It spun end over end toward the grass.

Suddenly, Tennison was there. He caught the ball against his chest and darted through Boris' shocked pack.

"Touchdown," Vance said with a hint of surprise.

Alex grinned at the huge professor. "You didn't think we could do it?" he asked.

Vance shook his massive head like a confused bear. "I didn't think you had a chance."

Alex shrugged. "We know we're the underdogs. We just don't know when to give up."

A true hint of a smile showed in the professor's brown eyes when he replied, "Those are the teams that win."

Alex smiled back and returned to the center of the line.

Now that Tennison had eyes on him, it gave Alex a chance to move. He called for the ball, sidestepped left, and tossed it before Boris and Amos could tackle him.

The throw wasn't pretty, but it landed in Trent's surprised arms.

Trent stared at the onrush of werewolves in terror.

"Run!" Jericho called.

Trent didn't need further encouragement. The only problem was that he was so scared of Pack Boris that he took off in the opposite direction.

"Other way!" Alex yelled.

"Turn around!" Jericho shouted.

Tennison reached Trent. "Throw me the ball," he commanded.

Trent was more than happy to give up the object that had made him Pack Boris' target. He tossed the ball and Tennison caught it. Spinning around, Tennison darted past Tomas and Brace. Parker and Boris were catching up. Alex and Jericho ran at an angle across the field toward their pack mate. They would only have one chance to stop the duo. Alex leaped.

He hit Parker and Boris so hard it felt like he slammed into a tree. Alex fell the ground and looked back in time to see Tennison run by with Jericho in front of him blocking others from the opposing team.

"Touchdown," Vance said.

Alex let his head fall against the grass.

"You realize this is just a game."

Alex glanced to the right. Boris was lying on his back.

The Alpha drew in a breath and winced. He met Alex's gaze. "It's just a game. You don't have to try so hard."

Alex knew moving was going to hurt. He gritted his teeth and rolled over to his hands and knees. "I don't know any other way to try," he told the Termer. He pushed up to his feet and limped back toward the line.

"Need a breather?" Vance asked. The football looked like a toy in the huge professor's hands.

Alex shook his head. "I'm good," he forced out.

Vance shrugged and tossed Jericho the ball.

"Last time I said it was your funeral, I got bawled out by the other professors."

Alex remembered the moment very well. He had been bleeding from knife wounds that wouldn't heal because of silver shards that had broken off of the blade. The walk through the forest had felt like the longest in his life, especially when Drogan's men attacked. Only the professors' fighting skills and the arrival of the werewolf packs had saved his life.

"I thought it was funny, in an ironic sort of way," Alex replied.

The comment brought a true smile to the professor's face. It looked out of place, as if uncomfortable there, and faded almost as quickly as it had appeared. "Huh," Vance said before turning away. "Play ball."

"Hike," Alex called.

Chapter Four

Alex shifted in his seat. He felt nervous, and felt silly because of it. Healing bruises from football the previous hour made his chest and arms ache, but above it all, an expectant chill ran across his skin.

"Think she's going to make it?" Cassie asked, her expression worried.

Alex nodded. "Definitely. And she's going to do great."

Cassie sat back in her chair, her gaze on the door.

The door opened and their aunt Meredith walked in.

"Good morning, class," she said with only a hint of nervousness in her voice.

"Good morning, Professor Meredith," the students replied.

Pack Jessilyn already looked bored, but most of the members of Pack Jericho sat up and smiled at the new professor. They knew about her relationship to the twins, and when Alex found out she was teaching their next class, he had asked his pack to be supportive and help her out.

Alex was amazed at the different person his aunt had become during her stay at the Academy. She was far different than the beaten, scared woman Jaze had rescued from Drogan's base. As much as she reminded him of her twin sister who had been his mother, the differences were now more pronounced.

Meredith's shoulder-length black hair was pulled back on one side by a light blue flower clip that matched her eye-color perfectly. His mother had always worn her waist-length black hair in a ponytail because she said it got in the way otherwise. When Meredith smiled, there was a dimple on one of her cheeks, while his mother had had two. She also had freckles across her nose while his mother's fair skin had been clear of

47

them.

Above all, the biggest difference was scent. To Alex, his mother had smelled like strawberries and the good things she cooked every day for them. She had loved to bake, and could make practically anything with flour and an egg. Her sister Meredith, on the other hand, smelled of pine and mint. She had confided to Alex and Cassie that Mindi had taken all of the cooking and artistic genes, and she was left with only a love of the outdoors and a good book.

Alex repeated these subtle differences over and over in his mind as he watched the woman who looked so much like his mother stand at the front of the class. She smiled at Alex and Cassie before opening her teaching manual.

"Welcome to Algebra," she said.

Groans answered.

Meredith laughed, then looked surprised she had done so. She glanced at the twins with her eyes slightly wider.

Alex gave her an encouraging nod.

"It's not so bad," she said, skimming through her book for anything useful. "It's only, um, math."

"Math is bad," Marky called out.

Alex gave the young werewolf a look that silenced him.

"It's not so bad if you follow the steps," Meredith continued. She seemed to warm to the topic. "It's like a language. Once you figure out the basics, it all falls into place."

"Learning math is learning a different language?" a member of Pack Jessilyn asked doubtfully.

"Yes," Meredith affirmed. "Exactly. I'll give you the basics."

"And the rest will be easy," Cassie finished.

Meredith gave her a grateful smile. She began to write equations on the board.

"My brain already hurts," Don said to Jericho. The big werewolf barely fit at his desk. Alex had already helped to extract him from a few last year; it looked like this year was going to require the same efforts.

"Don't worry," Jericho replied in a whisper. "Trent is our secret weapon. He's a math whiz."

At their attention, Trent gave them a calm smile. "I speak the language," he said.

Alex shook his head while Jericho rolled his eyes. Cassie smothered a laugh.

"What?" Trent asked.

"That was really lame," Terith told her brother.

Alex smiled and turned his attention back to the board.

***

"You did a great job," he told his aunt after the class was over.

"Are you sure?" she asked worriedly. "They seemed eager to leave."

He laughed. "They're always eager to leave. I think it's a werewolf behind walls thing. We have combat training next. Everyone's just looking forward to hitting something."

Meredith replied with a laugh of her own. "I think I can understand that." At Alex's surprised look, she gave a smile that was so like his mother's his chest ached. "There's got to be some way to let out teaching frustrations, right?"

"Maybe you should join us in combat training," Alex offered.

Meredith gave him a kind smile. "I would, but someone's got to teach algebra to restless werewolves, right?"

"Right," Alex agreed with a chuckle.

"Are you coming Alex?" Cassie called.

Alex looked over to see Cassie and Tennison standing near the door. "Goodbye, Aunt Meredith," Cassie said. "Good luck!" Meredith waved at the pair as they left.

"Who's that?" Meredith asked.

Alex looked back again to be sure he hadn't missed something. He realized she meant the werewolf with Cassie. "That's Tennison. He's a new Lifer here."

"Looks like Cassie's taking a shine to him," Meredith noted.

Alex stared at her. "They only met yesterday. She's just being nice."

Meredith nodded as though she wasn't quite convinced.

"Seriously," Alex told her. "Cassie doesn't like boys."

"You might be surprised," Meredith replied. The bell rang

and students flooded into the classroom. "Have a good day, Alex."

"You, too," Alex said before walking through the door after his sister.

He found Cassie and Tennison talking just inside the combat training room. Pushing his aunt's suspicions aside, Alex patted Tennison on the shoulder.

"Ready to fight?" he asked.

Tennison looked around as if he had just realized where they were. The training ring, punching bags, and practice dummies made it hard to miss. "Oh, uh, do we have to?"

Several members of Pack Jericho laughed.

"Everyone has to," Professor Chet said, walking into the room. He looked over Pack Jericho and Pack Miguel quickly. "Looks like we're pretty well matched. Alex, why don't you show some of the newbies a bit of sparring?" Chet met Miguel's gaze. "Why don't you join him?"

Alex heard Cassie gasp beside him. Her fingers dug into his arm.

After Alex's sparring bout with Boris last year, he was a bit more reluctant to take on another Alpha. Things with Drogan had quieted down, and Alex had fewer anger issues at the moment. Miguel also looked unsure as he accepted the sparring gear Chet handed to him.

Professor Dray entered the room. "What's going on?" the professor asked. His hair was light blond from all the time he spent in the sun working in the Academy gardens. He pushed it out of his eyes as he looked from Chet to the two getting geared up.

Dray gave Chet a stern look.

"What?" Chet asked, feigning innocence.

"Alex is a Second and Miguel is an Alpha," Dray pointed out.

Chet shrugged. "I really don't see the problem. Alex and Miguel are about the same size. They were just going to show the newbies what sparring is all about."

"You know packs are supposed to spar each other by pack rank, not size," Dray argued.

"Semantics," Chet replied. He took the sparring gear from Alex and tossed it to Jericho. "Fine. Gear up."

"They're really going to fight?" Tennison asked from behind Alex.

Alex nodded. "It's practice, but sometimes things get out of hand. I don't think Miguel and Jericho will be as ferocious as when Pack Boris was in our class last year. There were some pretty good bouts."

"Boris took cheap shots," Trent said.

"Don't talk about my brother," Kalia warned.

Trent turned with wide eyes. "Uh, s-sorry," he stuttered.

Alex watched Kalia closely. Her normally icy blue eyes flashed gold for the briefest second as she looked at the Lifer. The gold was replaced with pain and she grabbed her head.

"Kalia," Alex said. He caught her arm before she could fall.

Kalia hunched over with a moan of pain.

"What's going on?" Dray asked.

"I'm not sure," Cassie told him. "I think her head hurts."

"Please take her to Lyra," Dray told the twins.

Alex walked Kalia slowly to the door. Cassie rushed to open it. Kalia's eyes were closed and she held her forehead with one hand while the other gripped Alex's arm. Cassie ran in front of them to the medical wing of the Academy.

"It hurts," Kalia said in a barely audible voice.

"I'm taking you to Lyra," Alex reassured her. "She'll be able to help."

Kalia nodded, then winced as if the action hurt.

Footsteps hurried back up the hall toward them. "I've got a room ready for her," Lyra said. The little professor adjusted her large glasses as she turned to walk beside Alex and Kalia. "How are you doing, sweetie?" Kalia didn't answer. Lyra's gaze shifted to Alex. "Don't worry," she told him at the worry on his face. "I'll take care of her."

She led them to a room on the left side of the hall. Alex helped Kalia sit on the paper-lined bed. Her eyes were still closed at the pain. Alex wondered if she knew she still gripped his hand.

"You two can wait outside if you'd like," Lyra said kindly.

A wave of protectiveness rushed over Alex. He didn't want to leave Kalia in the room that smelled of sterile cleaners and lemons. If her headache eased, she might forget that they had walked there. She might be scared.

"Come on," Cassie encouraged him.

Alex pushed down the strange feelings and worked his hand out of Kalia's grip. Kalia placed both hands on her forehead, hunching over on the bed. Her shoulder-length hair hid her face from view. The sight sent a surge of sympathy through Alex.

"You've seen this before," Cassie guessed, speaking quietly as soon as they were out of the room.

Alex nodded. "Once, on the stairs. She said she gets bad headaches. They come and go without warning."

"Her eyes went gold when she was talking to Trent."

"I know," Alex confirmed. "That's why her parents sent her here. They're worried she may be a werewolf."

"Worried?" Cassie's confusion was clear in her voice.

"I think her parents are afraid of werewolves. Kalia said they were Extremists before they found out Boris was one."

Cassie let out a breath. "Man, that must have been hard to take."

Alex nodded. "Apparently, they hid the fact that Boris was a werewolf from his sister until her eyes began changing. They sent her here in case she phased."

"She doesn't like werewolves, does she?"

Alex was surprised at his sister's deduction. "Not really. What makes you say that?"

Cassie shrugged her small shoulders. "She avoids pretty much everyone, barely speaks, and I'm pretty sure the entire school heard her arguing with her mom about why she had to stay here when they arrived for the term."

"I missed that," Alex said musingly, his thoughts still on the girl hunched on the bed.

"It echoed off the building. I'm surprised you didn't hear it while you were changing," Cassie said in a tone that suggested she guessed more than he let on.

Alex gave in and grinned. "I might have been out for a run."

Cassie pushed his shoulder. "You're going to get in trouble. You know Jaze said to lie low. How is racing trains and running along the boundaries of the forest lying low?"

"I can't help it," Alex told his sister. At her doubtful look, he let out his breath in a rush. "Look. We know Drogan's still out there. I have to be ready." He hesitated, then said, "If I don't condition my heart, it's going to fail me again. I have to push myself if I'm ever going to have a chance at beating him."

The understanding in Cassie's eyes ate at him. "What if you're damaging your heart further?" she asked quietly, her gaze worried.

"I can't be weak," Alex told her. "I can't just sit by and know that if we meet again, he can best me." A hint of anger colored his voice. "No human should be able to defeat a werewolf."

"You said he wore Kevlar and had a silver knife," Cassie pointed out.

Alex shook his head. "It shouldn't matter. I've got to make sure I'm strong enough."

Lyra stepped into the hallway. She gave the twins a warm smile. "Kalia's resting. You can go back to class."

"I'd like to wait for her," Alex said. At Lyra's lifted eyebrows, he hurried to finish, "If that's alright."

She nodded. "I think she would appreciate having a friend nearby." She noted a couple of things on a clipboard before walking down the hall.

"You're Kalia's friend?" Cassie asked.

Alex nudged her with his elbow.

"Okay, okay," Cassie said. She rubbed her side. "Don't be so touchy. I'm going back to class. I'll let Professor Dray and Professor Chet know you're waiting for your *friend*."

Alex rolled his eyes. "Chet's probably waiting for me to fight Miguel."

A hint of laughter showed in Cassie's dark blue eyes when she said, "You're right. It's probably safer that you stay here."

Alex stepped forward as if to take off after her. She laughed and ran down the hall away from the medical wing. Alex shook his head. He crossed his arms and leaned against the wall, prepared for however long it would take for Kalia to recover.

Chapter Five

A smell touched Alex's nose. It wasn't unusual or particularly pungent, but it definitely didn't belong in the medical wing. He turned his head, searching for the source.

To his confusion, the scent seemed to come from the wall behind him. Alex walked along the tan striped wallpaper. In most places, it smelled sterile and clean like the rest of the medical wing, yet when he paused where he had been standing, he scented what he recognized as a meatball sandwich.

Curious, he ran a hand down the wall. His fingertips revealed the slightest separation hidden within the brown and tan stripes. Alex pushed on the wall. Nothing happened. He pushed harder. The panel refused to budge. Alex blew out a frustrated breath. He sighed and leaned against the wall again, content to give up the strange search until the flashing of a tiny red light caught his attention. He grinned up at the camera in the corner. He could imagine Brock's sigh as the human sat at his many computers in Dean Jaze's secret lair beneath the school.

All at once, the door panel slid away. Alex waved at the camera and stepped inside. The panel slid shut once more.

Alex expected to find yet another passageway to the lair. Instead, the cement tunnel seemed to go much deeper than the room beneath Dean Jaze's office. The smell of meatball sandwich intensified.

"What was it?" Brock's voice reached him before he turned the last corner. "How did you find this place?"

"The smell of your sand..." Alex's voice died away at the sight before him.

The secret of how the professors made it in and out of the school on their many missions for Jaze without being seen by the students was answered. Rows of cars and motorcycles occupied the left side of a giant cavern that took up what had to have been the entire foundation of the Academy.

Brock sat at a desk of computers similar to those in the room beneath the closet. He took a big bite of his meatball sandwich and smiled up at Alex.

"I know. Impressive, right?" he asked around the mouthful.

Alex nodded wordlessly. He walked down the wide ramp that led to the computers. Several other branches of tunnels met the ramp from various parts of the Academy. Alex wondered how he had lived so long at the school without knowing about the hideout.

"Your sandwich," Alex said vaguely as he reached Brock and stared up at the computers that turned out to be twice as large as he had first thought.

"What?" Brock asked.

"That's how I found you."

Brock looked down at his sandwich. "I have got to remember the whole sense of smell thing. You'd think after all these years I'd have it figured out." He smiled at Alex. "I used to wonder how your brother always knew where I hid my snack stash. He would've had a field day with everything I have hidden around here."

The mention of Jet sent a pang of longing through Alex. The same sadness showed on Brock's face.

"You guys were close?" Alex asked.

Brock nodded. "Mrs. Carso made me food; Jet ate it all before I could get there. It was a great relationship." He rubbed his stomach. "I sure miss Mrs. Carso's cooking. I'm wasting away without it."

Alex eyed the sandwich in Brock's hand dubiously.

Brock shrugged. "It's not nearly the same. Her cooking blew the socks off anything Cook Jerald makes." He lowered his voice. "Don't tell her I said that; then I really will starve."

"I won't," Alex promised, his gaze traveling the cavern.

What appeared to be random stacks of equipment turned out to be tracking devices, weapons, harnesses, and electronics. Some were collecting dust while others looked brand new.

"What do you do down here?" Alex asked.

Brock nodded toward the computer screens. "Same thing as I do upstairs, only on a bigger scale. I track all the werewolves we know of in the United States and other parts of the world. I monitor the packs of Alpha-less that hide in unsettled areas, and I alert Jaze whenever we find out about someone who needs help."

Interested, Alex pulled up a chair. "Help, how?"

Brock took another bite of his sandwich. "Well, you know," he said around the mouthful. "The Extremists are working very hard to wipe out the rest of the werewolves, and most of those left have banded together in large packs so they can protect each other's backs, but there are always lone wolves or those who get separated. There are still lots of orphans we're trying to locate, and for some reason, there's no shortage of scientists and other sickos who enjoy cutting up werewolves to either experiment on their healing abilities or try to capture the phasing abilities for themselves."

Alex's stomach tightened. "That's horrible."

Brock nodded. "I know, right?" He accidentally spit some sandwich on one of the screens. "Oops." He used a corner of his shirt to clean it off. "Anyway, Mouse and I rotate monitoring the computers, the Internet, and the cameras. It keeps us plenty busy. I could definitely use like ten of me down here."

"There wouldn't be enough food," Alex noted. His stomach growled at the smell of the sandwich, reminding him that lunch couldn't come fast enough.

Brock gave him a worried look and attempted to scoot his food out of Alex's sight. "There won't be if you stay down here. You should probably go before we both get in trouble."

"But I just found this place," Alex protested. "It's so cool and—"

"And you have classes to go to," Brock reminded him. "Combat training just got over. Vance seemed a bit annoyed that you never returned."

"I should have—" Alex paused. He gave Brock a searching look. "How do you know where I'm supposed to be and Vance's reaction?"

A touch of chagrin colored Brock's face. He ran a greasy hand through his spikey brown hair. "I, uh, I'm also supposed to be monitoring you."

Alex couldn't decide how he felt about that. "Show me," he demanded.

Brock pushed a button on the keyboard in front of him and the view on the screens changed from data files and maps to video surveillance. Images from each other classrooms at the Academy showed along with the hallways and the Great Hall. Alex searched them quickly until he found Cassie walking with Caitlyn to the Great Hall.

"You know my schedule?" he asked quietly.

Brock nodded without a word. He took a bite of the sandwich, then after one chew realized how noisy his eating had suddenly become in the silent cavern. He sat with his food motionless in his mouth as he waited for Alex's reaction.

"You keep an eye on me?" Alex asked.

At Brock's nod, he clenched and unclenched his fists,

unsure what to think.

"I'm monitored every second I'm in this school?"

Brock hesitated, then nodded again.

Alex let out a slow breath. "I know Jaze is trying to look out for me, but this is ridiculous."

"To be..." Brock choked on his food.

Alex slapped the human on his back until he swallowed the meatball.

"Thanks," Brock said. He cleared his throat. "To be honest, we keep an eye on both you and Cassie. We watch the rest of the students as well, but since there is a current threat, you are the focus."

"I know I shouldn't be upset," Alex said.

Brock held up a hand. "I understand. I told Jaze it was an invasion of privacy, but he argued that he had everyone at the school to watch out for, and he couldn't allow the threat to reach us again."

"I agree," Alex replied quietly.

"I also think, uh, you do?" Brock asked in surprise.

Alex nodded. "Cassie and I are a danger to the school as long as we are Drogan's targets. He almost succeeded in destroying this place last year. We can't let him try it again."

"Exactly," Brock replied. "I'm glad you get it."

"Is there any place I'm not monitored?" Alex asked.

"Well, the forest," Brock said. "It's so big, and the trees are so thick. We don't have nearly enough cameras to monitor every inch of it."

Alex took off for the ramp, his mind made up.

"Where are you going?" Brock called after him.

"The forest," Alex replied.

"Alex, wait!"

The werewolf stopped at the top of the ramp. He forced himself to turn around.

Brock was standing at the bottom of the ramp. Alex hadn't heard him leave the seat. "Do you know why I let you down here?" Brock asked. At Alex's silence, he said, "I could have left you standing in the medical wing searching for the source of the smell, but I buzzed you in. Ask me why."

Alex didn't want to. Frustration burned through him at the thought that every action he made was monitored. He understood that it was for the good of the school, but to know that his freedom was just a façade filled him with a need to get away.

Brock waited below. It was obvious the human wasn't going to tell him what he wanted to know without the question.

"Why?" Alex finally forced out.

"Because you need to know that Jaze is taking your safety seriously," Brock replied, his expression earnest. "What you went through last year will never happen again."

"I know Jaze cares," Alex said, though the words felt bitter in his mouth.

Brock shook his head. "You don't know how much he cares. You see cameras and an infringement of your personal space. What you don't see are the nights and nights Jaze stays up trying to figure out how to protect you. You don't see how much it kills him that Drogan was able to hurt you. He built this place to protect werewolves, and the two children he cares about the most in this entire school are under threat." His voice lowered. "You don't see how it kills him."

Alex shoved his hands in his pockets. He leaned against the wall, letting Brock's words sink in. "I know he cares," he finally made himself repeat.

Brock nodded. "Now you do."

Alex sighed and put a hand to the door.

"Alex," Brock called.

Alex waited, but didn't turn around.

"Just don't make him regret caring so much," Brock said.

Alex pushed the door open and walked into the dark tunnel beyond.

***

"Those of you who remember our full moon games last year won't be strangers to this class," Colleen said. Her violet eyes caught in the light of the sun that filtered through the trees. "Sense training is to ensure that you can rely on your wolf senses instead of just those you are used to using as a human."

"What's wrong with human senses?" Torin asked, his tone bored as he lounged in the grass with the rest of his pack.

"Nothing is wrong with them," Colleen replied with a smile. "But they are weaker than a wolf's. Even though your wolf senses carry over to your human form, they are much less strong than when you are in wolf form. Our goal is to help you work with your senses in both forms."

"What good is that?" Sid, Torin's second, demanded. He looked completely annoyed at being in the middle of the forest.

Colleen gave him a patient look. "Part of our goal at this school is to teach you academics; the other is to train you on what you need to survive in the world. In human form, would you be able to smell a man sneaking up on you with a silver blade? Would you hear the slight snick of a window as it opens in the middle of the night? Would you be able to protect your family by getting them to safety before danger arrives?"

"And how would we do that?" Sid asked.

His tone grated on Alex's nerves.

"Instincts," Colleen replied. "I'm going to teach you how to listen to your instincts."

"What, are they like a siren, telling us to run?" Sid's sarcastic tone made his pack mates laugh.

"They can be," Colleen replied. Alex could tell by her expression that she was trying to keep calm.

The professor with the violet eyes was one of only two genetically-created werewolves in existence as far as anyone at the Academy knew. Jaze had told Alex Colleen and Kaynan's story. Colleen had been unable to control her phasing, and had been confined to a rehabilitation facility until the General's men lit it on fire. Rafe, the golden-eyed, wild werewolf who lived in the forest, had saved her life and taught her how to control her phasing, though if she was extremely stressed, it still got away from her once in a while.

Alex knew Sid was trying Colleen's patience. She glanced at the trees around them, her eyes seeking the security of the forest.

"So my ability to protect my supposed family relies on if I can listen to imaginary sirens?" Sid pressed with a smirk.

"They aren't imaginary," Colleen replied, his voice tight. "They are as real as your ability to breathe."

"But if I stop breathing, the sirens will tell me to breathe again, right?"

"Shut up, Sid." The words were out of Alex's mouth before he realized he had spoken.

Everyone looked at Alex. Sid's eyes narrowed. He glanced from Alex to Jericho, then at Torin, his Alpha. Torin gave a slight lift of one shoulder. A small smile touched Sid's mouth. The Second stood. He towered above anyone in Pack Jericho besides Don, and even then, the Seventh Year was given deference.

"I'm tired of your know-everything attitude, Alex," Sid said, his voice steady and dangerous.

"Leave him alone, Sid," Jericho replied.

Torin met the Alpha's eyes. "Let them work it out."

A chill ran through Alex's veins. He realized what was

happening. There were very few fights at the Academy, mostly scuffles within packs or between the Lifers and Termers. The Alphas usually broke these up or let the dean handle them. Only one type of fighting was sanctioned within the school.

Rank duels, as they were called, were allowed because they played a very important part of pack life in the wild and in society. If someone felt a leader was unfit, the werewolf could challenge the leader to a duel. In the Academy, because so many packs were unnatural in such a small space, the duels were also allowed between packs as long as the ranks fighting were the same. Standing for Alphas and Seconds was very important in the way the entire structure held together. The fight Sid called for was sanctioned.

Sid gave a toothy smile as he loomed over Alex. "I'm tired of the way you are buddy-buddy with all of the professors, and the way Dean Jaze and Professor Nikki treat you and your sister. They may have considered you like their own kids, but they have their baby now. You're Strays again like the rest of us."

A growl sounded low in Alex's chest. Cassie grabbed his hand, but he shrugged out of her reach and rose. The linebacker built Second glared down at him from at a least a foot greater in height. He was two years older than Alex, but since they began at the Academy together when it opened, they were both Seventh Years. Even Professor Colleen couldn't argue that the fight was unfair, though Alex knew by her anxious expression that she wanted to.

"If you have a problem with me, say it. Don't wear out the professors with your meaningless babble," Alex said.

Everyone scooted quickly away from the two Seconds.

Chapter Six

Sid's eyes narrowed. Alex caught the slight shifting of the werewolf's weight a split second before Torin's Second threw a punch.

Alex leaned back just far enough for Sid's long arm to miss him. He grabbed Sid's wrist in his right hand and pulled as the werewolf was thrown off balance by his own momentum. Alex landed a quick jab to Sid's right kidney followed by an elbow to the back. He danced out of the way before Sid could retaliate.

The huge werewolf turned and glared at him. Though Alex had landed the punches, the Second appeared completely fine. Alex let out a slow breath and bounced on the balls of his feet, ready for the next round.

Sid wasn't about to make the same mistake twice. Instead of another blind attack, he circled Alex, looking for an opening. Alex chose to give him one. He lowered his right hand just enough that it would look like he was still on guard, but maybe wasn't paying attention enough to protect his face.

Sid took the bait. His jab glanced off of Alex's jaw hard enough to stun as Alex spun out of the way. Alex dropped to one knee and kicked, catching Sid behind the knees. When the huge werewolf fell, Alex jumped on top of him, but Sid was ready. He grabbed Alex's right arm and threw him to the side. Alex's elbow caught across a log and bent back further than it was supposed to. A shard of pain raced up to his shoulder.

Alex climbed to his feet holding his arm. Sid leered at him.

"Give up?" the Second asked.

In answer, Alex hit Sid on the jaw with a left haymaker, then brought his elbow back and snapped Sid's head the other way with the reverse. He kicked Sid in the stomach, then in the face. Sid staggered back and clutched his nose as it started to bleed.

"I'll accept your submission," Alex said.

Sid glared at him over his cupped nose. "I'll kill you," he growled.

To Alex's surprise, when Sid did move, it was to phase.

Usually rank duels were fought in whatever form the combatants started; breaking tradition, Sid ran forward and phased to his huge Gray wolf form. He caught Alex's wrist in his fangs as he loped past. Alex spun, freeing his hand. He landed on Sid's back, slamming both fists down on the werewolf's spine. Sid let out a yelp and shook him off.

Alex phased and hit the ground in wolf form. He growled at Sid. The huge Gray gave a mocking wolfish smile.

Rage burned through Alex. He made a dive for Sid's front paws, feinted to the left when the werewolf dropped his head to meet the attack, and latched onto the side of Sid's neck.

Sid let out a howl of pain. He reared up on his hind legs, yanking Alex up with him. When that didn't work, Sid slammed into a tree, effectively scraping Alex free. Alex darted away before Sid could reach him. He knew he had to use speed and swift attacks to defeat the stronger werewolf.

Alex ran a full circle around Sid. When the werewolf turned in an effort to keep him in sight, Alex leaped over him and slammed his head into the werewolf's ribs. Sid fell heavily onto his side. Alex took advantage of the opening and latched onto the huge werewolf's throat.

Every sense strained. Alex could hear the blood pulsing through the werewolf's jugular millimeters beneath his fangs. His own heartbeat gave a stutter from the strain of the fight. Alex held still, willing his muscles to obey.

The scent of the wolf's dirty fur filled his nose along with the smell of the pines and loam around them. Alex saw only red as he battled the instincts that told him to end the threat to his standing in the Academy. The rank duels never ended in death, but Alex realized at that moment how easily it could happen. The wolf's ragged breaths came out gasping as he held perfectly still, unsure what Alex was going to do.

Alex slowly let go of Sid's throat and backed away. He limped slightly on his front leg where Sid had hyperextended his elbow, but he could tell by the lessening pain that it was already healing. He grabbed his clothes in his mouth and carried them to a nearby pine. He phased and pulled them on. The shirt had been torn at the neck when he phased. Luckily, the pants had fared better. He settled the shirt the best he could, then made his way back to the clearing.

"Well done," Jericho said in a low voice. "That was perfectly executed."

Cassie hugged him tight around the neck before he even had a chance to protest. "I'm glad you're okay," she said. She stepped back and Alex followed her gaze to Torin.

The Alpha gave him a searching look. Alex couldn't tell if Torin was upset or pleased. Sid was nowhere to be seen. At Alex's questioning glance, Torin tipped his head toward the Academy. "I sent him back to have Lyra look at his nose. It didn't want to stop bleeding."

Alex nodded, unsure what to say.

Torin surprised him by holding out a hand. "I agree with what your Alpha said. That was well done." Alex held out his hand slowly and Torin shook it. "I honestly didn't think you could take Sid. I'm glad you surprised me."

Alex was taken back. "But Sid's your Second."

Torin nodded. "We've all grown up together. I've heard him say a million times that he could beat any Second at the Academy. When he chose to duel you first, I thought he was confirming his claims the easy way. Sometimes a little humbling is a good thing."

Alex stared at the Alpha. It was the first time Torin had cared enough to talk to him for more than a short answer, and he was congratulating Alex for beating his own Second.

Trent broke Alex's train of thought by slugging him on the shoulder. "Good job, man. That was awesome."

Alex thanked him and the other pack members who came forward to congratulate him. He looked at Colleen over Terith's head. "Sorry for fighting in class," he apologized.

She gave a smile of understanding. "Like I was saying, you've got to go with your instincts. That was an impressive fight."

"Thanks," Alex replied, feeling self-conscious from all of the werewolves watching him, especially the younger members of his own pack. Their wide eyes and awed expressions followed him as he took a seat at the base of the tree near where Colleen had been trying to teach. His pack fell in around him, and this time, no one interrupted Colleen.

***

Pack Jericho was ravenous by the time geography with Professor Thorson and English with Kaynan and Grace were over. They raced to the Great Hall in the hopes of beating the other packs.

"Seriously?" Trent complained when they pushed the doors open to find Pack Boris and Pack Miguel already eating. "What'd they do, skip class?"

"Football short," Amos replied. The huge werewolf smiled at his pack from the year before. "Parker broke arm."

"They don't need to know that," Boris snapped. He gave Jericho a steely look. "Just wait until we play you guys. It sounds like Vance is working on permission to start real games next year."

"We can't wait," Jericho replied steadily.

He sat down at the table with the others close behind.

"I don't want to play them in football," Cassie remarked quietly. "They'll kill us!"

"They'll try," Jericho corrected her. "We've been known to put up quite the fight."

Cassie smiled at him. "That's true. They better watch out."

Jericho winked at her. "That's the spirit. Sun Tzu said 'Every battle is won before it is ever fought.' In my way of thinking, we've already won."

Torin bumped into Pack Jericho's Alpha, sending his fork flying. "Quoting Chinese strategists, Jericho? I hope it pays off tonight."

Jericho chose not to answer. Caitlyn picked up his fork and gave it back to him. He smiled at the little girl and rubbed the fork with his napkin before stabbing it into his lasagna.

"Night games are going to be a bit intense," he told his

pack quietly. "Just stick with me. We'll figure it out."

After dinner, Jericho waited for Alex near the door.

"What's going on?" Alex asked.

The Alpha looked over the heads of the students going up the stairs to their pack quarters.

"Let's just say that Boris came back from the summer break with some extended plans for training, and I'm not exactly on board," Jericho said. His tone was normally level no matter what he was talking about; the edge of frustration in the Alpha's voice let Alex know just how much it bothered him.

"How can I help?"

Jericho shook his head. "I'm not sure. It sounds to me like the Alphas are trying to start an all-out war between the packs."

"They're tired of the peace already?" Alex asked with more than a hint of sarcasm. "At least pack against pack will be better than Lifer against Termer."

"They have that figured in as well," Jericho said. He leaned against the wall. "Apparently, it will be Lifer packs against Termers, but individual packs will strategize as a unit."

Jericho's concern became clear. "Then where do we stand?"

"Torin wants us to divide our pack."

Alex was speechless at the implication. "Uh, no!" he finally forced out. "That's not how packs work."

Jericho nodded. "Hence the part where I'm not on board."

Alex watched his pack weave between the others. Sid threw a punch at Trent when Torin wasn't paying attention. The Gray ducked, but tripped on the stairs and fell against Terith. Several other students tumbled down behind them. The werewolves started yelling at Trent.

Alex shook his head. "This is going to be interesting," he said under his breath as he followed Jericho between the few stragglers and up the stairs.

Chapter Seven

Alex leaned against the door frame. "How'd your first class go?"

At the sight of him, Aunt Meredith rose from where she had been making notes on a sheet of paper. She surprised him by giving him a hug.

"Sometimes it's nice to see a friendly face."

Alex fought back a wave of concern. "That bad, huh?"

She sighed and stepped back. "Let's just say that I'm not exactly used to dealing with so many werewolves in such a little space. It's a bit overwhelming."

"So's algebra," Alex countered.

Meredith laughed. "It can be," she conceded. She took a seat back at her desk and motioned for Alex to take the one across from it. "How was your day?"

Alex gave a nonchalant shrug. "Oh, you know, the usual. I threw a few touchdowns in football and surprised Vance that our pack could actually score points, got in a rank duel with Sid and beat him, found out that there is more to Jaze's underground lair than I thought, realized my sister may possibly be in love, and just got told that the Alphas want to split up our pack for night games training because they are intimidated by the fact that we mixed Lifers and Termers." He let out a dramatic sigh. "Again, the usual."

Meredith smiled, her light blue eyes sparkling. "Sounds boring."

"Totally," Alex agreed, grinning at her sarcasm.

"Guess algebra's not so complicated, huh?"

Alex laughed. "I guess not. I suppose I should assert myself more. Trent's the real math whiz in our pack. He can build practically anything." He smiled, remembering. "One summer a few years ago, he told Jaze he was bored and wanted to make something. Jaze brought in an old engine. By the time the term started, Trent had it running." He met his aunt's gaze. "And he didn't have instructions or anything. He said he could see it all in his head."

"Impressive," Aunt Meredith replied.

Alex nodded. "So the next summer, Jaze got him an engine that was completely in pieces. Trent put that one back together, too."

"What did he do this last summer?" Meredith asked.

"He built a helicopter engine. Jaze said he thought it would be a challenge, but Trent had it done a month into summer. I don't know what Jaze will come up with next." He smiled. "I think it's great that he tries to challenge Trent, though. Trent appreciates it."

Meredith smiled back. "You really like Jaze, don't you?"

Alex nodded with his gaze on the desk in front of him. "He's been so good to me and Cassie. He didn't have to take us in like that, you know?"

Meredith was quiet for a few minutes. She finally said, "It must have been hard losing everyone in your life."

Alex nodded again, but he couldn't speak. He thought they really had lost every person in their family. To have his mother's sister at the Academy was more than he ever could have hoped for. The twins went from only having each other to having an aunt who cared about them. She had spent time over the summer getting to know them. She cared about little things like their favorite colors or what kind of food they liked. She had even surprised Cassie with a box of chocolates one night. Apparently, they had the same tastes.

"I lost everyone," Meredith said in a voice so quiet Alex wasn't sure she knew she had spoken out loud.

He let out a slow breath as the realization hit him hard. He hadn't really thought of the fact that no one came for her or looked for her after Jaze rescued her from Drogan. Even though his parents had died, there might have been someone else who cared. "Did you ever get married?" he asked.

Something flickered in her gaze, some spark of emotion that she smothered quickly before it burned out of control. "I'm not the marriage type," she answered.

"I wished we'd known you when we were younger," Alex said.

Meredith nodded. "Me, too, but it wasn't to be."

The sadness in her expression made Alex ask, "Why not?"

She gave him a small smile, her eyes sad. "When the werewolves first started getting killed off, it wasn't safe for us to be in big packs. We split up and my sister and I visited each other only once in a while. Then Jet was taken." She took a shuddering breath. "Mindi and Will were beside themselves. They looked everywhere. I had never seen my sister look so lost. I tried to help in any way that I could, but he had vanished."

She rubbed her eyes as if the memories were painful. "So many werewolves were being killed. It was a dark time for our race, and nobody was safe. There were a lot of horrible things that happened. When you and Cassie were born..." She swallowed and continued, "Mindi and Will decided the best thing was to move away. I couldn't go."

The pain in Meredith's voice held Alex. His heart gave a slow thump. "Why not?"

She opened her mouth to speak, then shook her head. After a minute, she tried again, blinking back tears that she refused to let fall. "It wasn't safe. Bad people were looking for me. I couldn't let them find my family."

Alex nodded. With Drogan's attacks, he knew exactly how she felt. "I'm glad we're together."

She gave him a watery smile. "Me, too."

Familiar footsteps walked to the door. Alex and Meredith both looked up with expectant expressions. Cassie appeared from the hallway. Surprise colored her expression at the sight of both of them.

"I, uh, just..."

"Wanted to see how Aunt Meredith's first day went?" Alex guessed.

Cassie nodded, her cheeks touched with red.

Meredith crossed to the door and gave Cassie a big hug. At her motion, Alex joined them. "All I know," Meredith said. "Is I couldn't have a horrible day with you two checking on me."

"I'm glad," Cassie replied.

"Me, too," Meredith said.

***

When the howl sounded, Pack Jericho was the last to the courtyard. Per their Alpha's instructions, they hung back near the north wall away from the other packs who jostled each other for space.

"I don't like this at all," Cassie whispered. Her nervousness at the crowd showed in the way she couldn't stop moving her feet. Alex knew she wanted nothing more than to dart into the forest and not look back until sunrise. He felt the same way.

"It's okay," Alex reassured her. "Jericho will work things out."

"Don't be so sure," Kalia muttered.

Alex glanced at her. She pointedly ignored him.

"About time," Boris commented when Jericho joined them on the steps.

Alex clenched his hands into fists. He hated uncertainty, and it felt as if everything was changing again. The night games had once been just for fun, the way students blew off steam and relaxed after long hours of school. Last year, with Drogan's attacks on the Academy, Alex had made the suggestion to change the night games into training sessions so that the students would be prepared if the Academy was ever attacked again.

Their training had paid off several times before the term was through. Apparently, Boris' creativity had gone to his head during the summer months that the Termers were away from the Academy. He barked out orders as though he was in charge of every pack.

"Termers, to the steps, Strays," he grinned and corrected himself, "I mean Lifers, to the gate. Torin is going to take charge of the Lifers." He turned to the Alpha and said in an undertone, "Good luck."

Torin lifted his lips in a silent snarl even though he was still in human form.

Boris glanced at Jericho. Annoyance showed in his expression. "Since we have one pack that is neither Lifers nor Termers, the mutt pack," several members of Pack Boris laughed. "We'll have to split you up."

Whispers of 'mutt pack' traveled through the packs with laughter.

"I don't want them on our team," Alex heard Shannon say to her sister Shaylee where the Alpha twins stood near the gate.

"I know, right?" Shaylee replied. "Any student who hangs out with a Stray for so long must have something wrong in the head."

"We're not splitting up." Jericho's answer carried across the courtyard.

Boris glared at Jericho. "We talked about this."

"No," Jericho corrected him. "You talked and I listened. You never once asked for my opinion."

"I didn't feel like I needed it," Boris replied. "I'm in charge of the night games, and now we're at night games. Split up your pack."

At Jericho's silence, the Termer Alpha leaned closer. Alex heard him say in a lower voice, "Look, man. It's only a couple of Lifers. I already got rid of Amos."

Alex followed Boris' gaze to the Lifers gathered near the gate. Amos towered above them, but he refused to look in Boris' direction. Instead, the huge Gray stared at his feet, a sulking giant who clearly wasn't happy about the arrangements.

"If you choose to abandon your pack mates, that's your choice," Jericho replied. His gaze roamed over his pack who watched the discussion from near the wall. "But my pack is not splitting up."

"Do we need to fight about this?" The deadly tone in Boris' voice said he wasn't messing around.

To Alex's relief, Torin set a hand on the Alpha's shoulder. "Let him take charge of the mutts," Torin encouraged him. "I don't want to deal with them, and neither do you."

"Jericho would be a big asset on a team," Boris argued.

Torin nodded. "Yeah, but is it worth babysitting the rest of them? They're worthless."

Neither Alpha bothered to lower their voice. Alex glanced at his pack. Hurt showed on several faces. There were tears in Cassie's eyes that she refused to let fall. She and Terith held hands, leaning on each other. Alex couldn't take it anymore.

"When did students come to regard each other as lesser members of this school?" Alex demanded.

"Alex, no," Trent whispered behind him. "They'll kill you."

"Don't do it," Cassie pleaded.

Both Boris and Torin turned to glare at Alex. He felt the full force of the Alphas' disapproval. It was all he could do to meet their gazes against his instinct as a Gray. He clenched and unclenched his fists. His heart stuttered. He willed his legs to hold.

"You are a lesser member of this school," Boris said steadily.

"Boris," Kalia replied, her tone filled with dismay.

Boris ignored his sister. He took a step toward Alex. "You have no family, no one who cares whether you live or die. You have no real pack but the mutts who make up the pathetic group you dare to call Pack Jericho." He looked out over the students who watched in stunned silence. "We allow you to stay and play your little games, but you are nothing but dust, waiting to be blown away and forgotten."

Alex wasn't sure when he left the pack. The next thing he was aware of, Boris had him flat on his back on the top step with a tight grip around his throat.

Alex struggled to breathe.

Boris glared down at him. "You are not an Alpha, Alex. You never will be." His eyes narrowed. "The sooner you realize that, the better for your health."

The Alpha hefted Alex by his neck and the front of his shirt. He then threw Alex down the stairs.

Alex hit every cement step on the way down to the courtyard. He lay there stunned for a moment. No one in the courtyard moved. Alex took a ragged breath. His heart skipped, then skipped again. Alex gritted his teeth and willed his body to obey. He pushed up to his hands and knees, then climbed to his feet.

A glance to the side showed his pack. Shock was clear on their faces at the Alpha's boldness. Cassie met Alex's gaze. Tears streaked her cheeks. Only Terith's tight grip on her hand kept his twin sister from running to him. Alex was glad for Terith's intervention. He didn't want his sister involved.

He clenched his hands into fists. "I am nothing?" Alex's voice rang within the walls.

The Alphas had been discussing something from the top step, Alex's presence apparently forgotten. Only Jericho waited at the edge to see what Alex would do. When their gazes met, Jericho gave a slight nod, willing his Second to continue.

The Alphas turned, amazed that Alex had dared to speak again.

"I am nothing?" Alex demanded louder. He pointed at the statue near the middle of the courtyard. "Jet was my brother."

Gasps and sounds of surprise ran through the crowd. It was obvious with a glance at the Alphas that only Jericho had been aware of the fact.

Alex speared Boris with a look, his passion fueled by the dark statue that watched over the moonlit courtyard. "If it wasn't for Jet, none of you would be here. He fought and killed hundreds of Extremists intent on wiping out your families." Alex's voice lowered. "He sacrificed his life for you."

Alex climbed slowly up the steps. His knees ached from hitting the cement, but he didn't let it show. He stopped a few feet from Boris.

"If anyone doesn't deserve to be here, it's a bigot who feels that those who lost family members during the genocide are lesser werewolves." Alex's gaze swept over the crowd of students. "We're not Termers or Lifers." He glared at Boris. "We're not students with families or Strays." He met Cassie's gaze. Her dark blue eyes glistened with moisture in the starlight. "We each deserve to be here for our own reasons." He looked at the Alphas waiting on the top step. "I may not be an Alpha, but I'm no coward. I'm not going to stand by while you judge my pack mates as inferior and make them feel less than equal. If that's the way it is going to go, then we'll hold our own night games."

Alex met Jericho's gaze. It was a bold statement, and would only hold if his Alpha stood behind him.

Jericho gave a small smile. "I agree with my Second. You all know what Jet did. His sacrifice will never be forgotten, and the hundreds upon hundreds that he saved will forever be in his debt." He pointed at the Alphas and then at the students below them. "You are in Jet's debt. Don't soil the ground dedicated in his name by defiling the very lives he died for. Jet gave up his life to protect our families from those who hated us because they saw us as inferior. I'll not stand by and watch you do the same thing here." He joined Alex on the top step. They began to walk down together.

"Come on," Alex heard Torin whisper behind them.

"Alright," Boris muttered. He lifted his voice. "Hold up, Jericho. We'll make it work."

Jericho turned. Alex stopped beside him on the step, but refused to look back.

"We'll work it out," Boris continued. "It'll end up best if we're all together on this."

The silence that filled the courtyard pressed in as the students waited with abated breaths to see what would happen.

"Fine," Jericho finally agreed.

Pack Jericho walked over to join their Alpha and Second. Alex was proud of the way they accepted what had happened without a word, though Trent put a hand on Alex's shoulder, and Cassie leaned against his arm as though the event had exhausted her. He knew how she felt.

"Let's begin the training," Boris said.

Chapter Eight

After night games, the Alphas and Seconds met in a classroom to run through strategies. Boris' new system called for the teams to split so that they would be prepared to face larger groups of enemies if the Academy was ever attacked again. Though the Alpha ignored Alex entirely, the suggestions Jericho gave after listening to his Second had been well received. Secondary leaders were to be trained in case Alphas and Seconds were compromised.

Eventually, Boris dismissed everyone saying that if they stayed much longer, they wouldn't be any use the next night. By the time Alex fell into bed, he was exhausted.

He had just closed his eyes when a set of familiar footsteps caught his attention. He walked to the door and peered out in time to see Cassie close the door to the hallway. Concerned, Alex hurried after her. She was halfway down the stairs when he reached her.

"Where are you going?"

"Look," she said, gesturing down the hall.

Alex spotted Tennison near the back doors to the Academy. The werewolf pushed them open and went outside.

"He's going for a midnight stroll?" Alex guessed.

"He was asleep," Cassie replied. At Alex's confused look, she explained, "We were talking on the couch, and we eventually both fell asleep."

It was a sign of how exhausted Alex was that he hadn't even noticed them when he walked through Pack Jericho's common room. He knew he should be concerned about the fact that Tennison and Cassie were so close, but he pushed the thought aside to concentrate on the matter at hand.

"Then he decided to take a walk?" Alex asked, following Cassie down the stairs after Tennison.

She shook her head. "He sat up, but he didn't look like he was seeing anything. I asked him if he was going to bed. He didn't answer, and headed for the door. He opened it as if he was doing it by habit, not thinking about it. And so I followed him to the stairs."

They left the Academy in time to see Tennison walk through the back gate. Alex could see what Cassie had been talking about. There was something strange in the way the werewolf was walking, as if something was propelling him through the trees, not that he actually saw them. "Do you think he's sleepwalking?"

Cassie shrugged. "I guess."

"We'd better follow him." At Cassie's glance, Alex shrugged. "If he's asleep, I don't want him to get hurt. We need to follow him and make sure he's okay."

The twins hurried to catch up to the werewolf.

Alex waved a hand in front of Tennison's face. "Hey, Tennison. You in there?" The boy's blank stare was unnerving.

Alex was about to shake him when Cassie put a hand on Alex's arm. "I've heard you're not supposed to wake a sleepwalker. They can be violent."

"I'm not afraid of Tennison," Alex said.

She rolled her eyes. "I'm not worried about you."

"Oh, thanks," Alex replied dryly.

They fell silent and dropped back a few feet behind Tennison. The Gray took them deep into the woods. The ground rose at the base of a cliff.

"I don't like this," Cassie said worriedly.

Alex climbed silently beside Tennison, wondering where the werewolf was taking them.

"Maybe he likes a good view?" Alex hazarded.

They reached the top of the cliff Alex had only been to a

couple of times. The forest spread out below them on every side. The small, winding road that was the only entrance to the Academy from the rest of the world showed as a lighter ribbon of gray among the shadows of night. The eastern horizon was lit by a pale strip where the sun had begun its ascent.

Alex took a deep breath of the crisp night air. The scents of evergreens, early dew, and a hint of rain tangled on the breeze.

Tennison had stopped beside him and stood staring out at the dark landscape without appearing to see it.

"Maybe he just likes the exercise," Alex guessed.

"I don't think— Alex!" Cassie shouted as Tennison stepped off the edge of the cliff.

Alex leaped after Tennison. He grabbed the student's shirt with one hand and scrabbled for the edge of the cliff with the other. His hand snagged an outcropping of rock just before the vast empty space led to the trees far below.

Alex let out a grunt of pain as Tennison's weight slammed both of them into the side of the cliff.

Tennison jerked awake. "Ow, what the—" He stared down at the fall below them.

Alex felt the boy stiffen in fear. "Don't move," he forced out. His fingers were slipping, both on Tennison's shirt and on the cliff. Cassie was trying to crawl down to help, but the cliff was steep to the place where they hung. He wasn't sure if she would make it in time.

Tennison looked up. "Alex?" he said, his eyes wide with fear.

"Grab my hand," Alex commanded.

Tennison reached his arm up. The movement pulled the remaining cloth from Alex's grip.

"No!" Alex shouted as he felt the werewolf slip free.

Tennison flailed. His hand hit Alex's. Alex grabbed the werewolf's fingers. Tennison's hand tightened in his. They hung for a second in absolute silence.

Alex's heartbeat thundered in his chest. He willed his heart to slow. One skip, and they would both be done for.

"My fingers are slipping," Alex said in as calm a voice as he could manage.

"Let me go," Tennison replied.

Alex met the boy's pale eyes. "Never."

His fingers were cramping. The rock he had grabbed was crumbling from the strength of his grip. The image of Jet's statue filled his mind. He wouldn't give in. He wouldn't let Tennison die if he could save him.

"I'm going to heave you up," Alex told Tennison. "Be ready to grab the cliff."

"You might fall," Tennison said, his voice close to panic.

"Better one of us than both," Alex replied, forcing a tight smile.

He was about to swing Tennison up when a hand grabbed his wrist.

"Don't be stupid," Cassie said, peering over the edge at them. "Better both of you than one."

"Cassie," Alex breathed in relief.

With her holding his wrist, he was able to lever Tennison up. The werewolf grabbed the rocks and pulled himself to the top. Free of the other student's weight, Alex grabbed the rocks with his other hand and was able to pull himself over.

He lay on the cliff's edge willing his heart to calm. It skipped a beat. He gave a breath of relief at the timing. He closed his eyes at the memory of exactly when his heart had begun to fail him.

Jet was the one who had saved them the day their parents had been killed. He had taken out the guards. Only Drogan had escaped, but not without wounds. Jet had put a blanket over the still bodies of their parents, then carried the twins away, one in each strong arm. Alex remembered the feeling of his big brother's tears as they fell on top of his head.

"They're gone," Jet had said. "But I'll be here for you."

Yet Jet was gone, too. Within the next few days, Alex and Cassie had lost everyone in the world who cared about them; only a gaping hole in Alex's soul proved that they had once lived, laughed, and dreamed. The day Jaze told them Jet had died was the day Alex's heart had started to stutter. He had been broken and lost. Only the statue in the courtyard remained of those he loved.

"I knew what I was doing, but I couldn't stop myself," Tennison said, his voice breaking through Alex's memories.

"Why would you try to kill yourself?" Cassie asked.

Tennison was quiet for a few minutes. Alex didn't press. He knew the werewolf had been through a lot. Those who had seen such haunting things carried it in the depths of their eyes. Alex knew it showed in his.

"I should have saved them," Tennison said finally, his voice cracking slightly.

Alex looked over to see tears streaming down the werewolf's face as he looked up at the stars. Tennison threw an arm over his eyes, blocking out the sight.

"When the Extremists came," he continued, his voice wavering, "We had a plan. My dad was worried every day that they would find us, and so the plan was if anyone rang the bell, we would run to the hideouts." He sniffed. "We lived on a farm. My parents had hideouts all over our land."

He took a calming breath. Crickets began to quietly chirp around them, taking up their song where it had been interrupted by the werewolves' plight.

"I was in the barn when I heard the bell. I don't know

who rang it." Tennison swallowed. "It rang and rang and rang, then suddenly stopped. I knew someone in my family had died." He took a shuddering breath. "I hid under the floorboards where the cows walked when we milked them. There was a little ditch Dad had dug. The boards fit back down and you could hardly tell. The cows stood on top, so the Extremists had no idea."

Movement caught Alex's eye. He saw Cassie's hand slip into Tennison's.

As if her touch gave him courage, Tennison continued, "They killed the cows. It was horrible, hearing them moo in pain and kick out the last of their life. Blood dripped through the boards." He stopped talking for a few minutes. Pain colored his voice when he finally said, "I'm not sure how long I stayed in that hole. The blood got sticky, then dried to me, making my arms and legs itch, but I didn't dare move. Dad told us to wait two days before trying to find each other. I waited for as long as I could. It must have been at least a day because when I came out, it was dark again."

Tennison closed his eyes. Alex could feel the pain radiating from him.

"It's okay; we're here for you," he heard his sister whisper.

"It was horrible," Tennison replied, his voice tight with tears. "I made it to the house, and they were there, all of them." He sobbed. "My mother, my dad, my three brothers, and my two sisters. None of them had survived."

"That's horrible," Cassie gasped.

Tennison nodded. "I didn't know what to do. I just sat on the floor with their bodies and waited."

"Waited for what?" Alex asked into the silence.

Tennison's gaze drifted to the stars. "I'm not sure. I don't even know how long I was there. The light changed outside, but it didn't matter. Nothing mattered after that."

Tennison sat up slowly. Cassie helped him up the rise where he could sit more securely.

Alex remained where he was. Hearing Tennison talk about losing his family members made the pain of losing his own parents so much more real. Alex remembered the blood, the smell of iron in the air, the way it felt to look at someone you loved and see the light leave their gaze. He shut his eyes tight, forbidding the tears to come.

"Jaze Carso found me," Tennison said softly. "I don't know how they knew, but I heard sounds. When I looked up, Jaze was there with a blanket. He set it over my family, and helped me walk away."

"Where did he take you?" Cassie asked.

"To a safe house. I stayed there until school was ready to begin. He felt it would be easier for me to start with the rest of the students. He said I could begin a new life."

"It doesn't work that way, does it?" Alex asked. He sat up slowly and found both of them watching him. "You can't start over, not with that hanging over you."

Tennison shook his head. "It won't go away. Does it ever?"

When he looked at Alex, Alex knew Tennison guessed their story. Jet was the twins' brother, and the entire werewolf world knew what had happened to him and his parents. "Not for me," Alex said quietly. "We were eight when our parents were killed, and the memories still attack me when I least expect it."

Tennison turned his gaze on Cassie. She gave Alex a small, grateful look. "Alex covered my eyes. He kept me from seeing everything. He protected me."

Tennison nodded. "You're a good brother. I wish my older brother had made it."

"You're not alone," Cassie told him. "You have us, and you have the pack."

"It's not a real pack," Tennison replied.

Alex knew the words were true, but the truth of them still hurt. "It's better than nothing," he replied a touch defensively.

Tennison stood. "If this is all I have, why try?"

He took two steps toward the cliff's edge before Alex barred his way.

"You jump, I'm jumping after you. Again," Alex said.

Tennison took a breath, then let it out slowly. "You're crazy, you know that?"

Alex nodded. He didn't want Cassie to guess just how crazy he felt sometimes, how on edge and out of control, but if it kept Tennison from jumping to his death, it was worth it.

Tennison finally gave in. "Fine. I won't do it."

"Promise?" Cassie asked behind him. The tremor in her voice let Alex know just how hard the experience had been on her.

"I promise," Tennison agreed quietly.

Cassie surprised them both by giving Tennison a hug. She stepped back quickly, her cheeks red with embarrassment.

"I just, I, uh, I want you to know you're not alone," she stammered as she retreated back up to stable ground.

Alex knew it was more than that. As twins, they shared a lot more than most siblings. It was a feeling, perhaps instinct, that let him know the truth of what was going on. He realized that Cassie loved Tennison.

He followed them numbly as his sister and Tennison walked side-by-side back to the Academy. From what he knew of the human world, and what the professors had told him, love was different with werewolves. For humans, it could be a fleeting thing, an attachment of sorts that sometimes faded.

Werewolves were like wolves in the wild when it came to love. They chose a mate and stayed with their chosen love for the rest of their lives. If a wolf lost a mate to one of the many accidents that came with living in the wild, the wolf often chose to live a solitary life, helping out with the pack, but staying alone in remembrance of the loved one.

Cassie's feelings for Tennison weren't just a simple infatuation. He saw it in the way she looked at him, the way she listened to his quiet words, and the expression on her face when he had almost chosen to jump over the cliff. He owned her heart. Alex wondered if Tennison knew it.

Chapter Nine

"Anything I should know?"

Alex crossed back to Jericho's room and leaned against the doorframe.

"What's up?" Jericho asked from his bed. The half-light of dawn spilled through the window, casting the room in gray shadows. Jericho's knowing brown eyes watched him steadily.

Alex nodded. "Tennison went sleepwalking. He's weighed down by guilt and sadness from when his family was killed. He almost threw himself off a cliff."

"A cliff?" Jericho repeated. He sat up.

Alex ran a finger down the rough wooden fibers of the doorframe. "Cassie and I stopped him. I think he's just trying to figure out how to cope."

Jericho watched him with an expression that said he guessed more than Alex was saying. "You're the right one to help him," the Alpha told him quietly.

"Thank you," Alex replied, touched.

"Thank you for saving him. I should have been there," Jericho said.

Alex shook his head. "If it wasn't for Cassie, I wouldn't have known either. I think..." He hesitated, wondering how much to tell the Alpha. He rushed on, "I think she likes him."

Jericho nodded. "I guessed as much."

"You knew?" Alex couldn't contain his astonishment. "When were you going to tell me?"

"I thought it was obvious," Jericho replied. "They're always together, eating, talking, not talking." He smiled. "It's cute."

"Cute?" Alex demanded. "Cute is for puppies or baby cougars. Not my twin sister."

Jericho held up both hands. "Slow down. I know it's a lot

to take in. But she deserves to be happy, and so does Tennison."

Alex pushed his forehead against the frame. "I know," he gave in reluctantly. "It's just so soon."

"She's fifteen," Jericho reminded him. "Love doesn't have a calendar, especially with werewolves."

Alex glanced at him sideways. "What are you, some sort of philosopher?"

Jericho rolled his eyes. "Get some sleep, Alex." He glanced at the clock. "You have an hour. Better make it count."

Alex groaned and turned back to his room. He paused in the hallway. "Jericho?"

"Yeah?" the Alpha answered.

"Next time, don't assume I know. I'm not so good at the social stuff."

He heard Jericho chuckle. "I'll keep that in mind."

Alex was almost to his bed when Jericho called, "Alex?"

"Yes?" he responded tiredly.

"You do better in the social stuff than you probably know," Jericho said.

Alex gave a small smile and fell onto the blankets.

***

Voices woke Alex up less than an hour later. He glanced out the door to see Cassie and Kalia on one of the couches. They had chosen to bring their breakfast back upstairs instead of eating with the rest of the packs in the Great Hall.

"He almost jumped?" Kalia was repeating.

Cassie nodded. "He did, actually. Alex jumped after him."

Alex wished in that moment that he could see Kalia's face, but she had her back to him.

"I almost saw them both die," Cassie said with a tremor in her voice. "It was horrible."

"Thank goodness you and Alex followed him," Kalia said with shock in her voice.

Cassie nodded. "It was scary. I'm just glad they're both alright." She hesitated, then said, "I really like Tennison."

"I can tell," Kalia replied.

Alex rolled his eyes. Apparently, it had been obvious to everyone but him. He definitely needed to pay more attention.

"Is, uh, is Alex alright?" Kalia asked.

Alex held perfectly still. The concern he heard in her voice surprised him. It made his heart stutter, but in a different way than he was used to. He put a hand to his chest to calm it as he listened.

"He's fine," Cassie told her. "He's pretty tough, though not as tough as I think he wants to be."

Cassie's comment made Alex's cheeks burn. He closed his eyes against the embarrassment.

"What do you mean?" Kalia asked.

Cassie sighed; her spoon chinked against the bowl as she took another bite of oatmeal. "He wants to be like Jet so badly, and Jet was an Alpha. I think sometimes Alex pushes

94

himself so hard because he thinks it's the only way to fill Jet's shoes."

The statement was true enough to make Alex feel exposed. He hated that Cassie knew it. The hate vanished immediately because he knew so much about her that he couldn't hold it against her. Cassie was just speaking from her heart. She had no guile; she was simply being honest.

Cassie fell silent, then said, "I really worry about him."

"It sounds like somebody should," Kalia replied, her tone unreadable.

Alex couldn't take it anymore. He pushed his door open all the way and crossed the room intent on the hall door.

"Hi, Alex," Cassie called.

He paused and acted surprised to see them there. "Oh, hi Cassie; hi Kalia."

Kalia's name tasted strange, as if it was different than the other times he had said it. He realized he was staring at her; he opened the door and hurried into the hallway before he could make a bigger fool of himself. He shut the door and leaned against it, filled with frustration.

"He looks tired," Kalia noted on the other side of the door with a hint of concern.

Alex hurried down the stairs before he heard anything else.

***

"I'm glad you visited us for breakfast," Nikki told Alex with a warm smile.

She held baby William in her lap. He had a tight grip on his mother's long black hair. She beamed down at him. "We like company, don't we, Will?"

She ran her hand through his shock of blond hair that reminded Alex so much of Jaze. The hair refused to stay down, sticking up all over in cowlicks. Nikki sighed and gave up. "Just like his father's. I guess I can't complain."

The baby gave a small gurgle that made Alex laugh. "Do you miss running the school?" he asked.

Nikki grinned. "Technically, Jaze runs the school." She gave Alex a wink. "But we both know who manages the details when he's off saving the world."

Alex nodded. "With your help, I never knew when he was gone. You two make a pretty good team."

She smiled, her blue eyes twinkling. "Like you and Cassie. I think you two really run the Academy behind the scenes."

The comment would have filled Alex with happiness a few days ago, but it only brought his concerns to the forefront. "Used to be," he said quietly. "Now I think Cassie's a bit distracted."

Nikki's eyebrows rose. "She likes someone?"

Alex nodded. "Tennison. He's a new kid in our pack."

"He's the new Lifer," Nikki replied. "Jaze said he was glad you guys took him in. He's gone through a lot."

Alex wondered how much Nikki knew. The events from the night before were still fresh in his mind. "What if he's gone through too much?" Alex blurted out.

William held Nikki's finger in his chubby hand. "You mean what if what he went through still affects him?" she asked perceptively.

Alex nodded. It was too late to go back, so he rushed forward. "What if he's not safe for her to be around? What if he's a danger to himself and others because he's unstable?"

Nikki's gaze was understanding when she replied quietly, "What if what he needs more than anything are friends who know what he's gone through?"

Alex was quiet for a few minutes. He thought of last night and all they had experienced together. The look on Tennison's face when he was about to jump the second time stayed in Alex's mind. When he spoke again, it was in agreement. "I think that's exactly what he needs."

"But it's hard to trust," Nikki guessed. "After all you went through with Pip last year only to find out he was the one leaking information to Drogan, it must be hard to let someone else in."

Alex nodded. He couldn't put into words how it was harder to see his sister fall for someone. He knew the connection they had as twins wouldn't ever go away completely, but already she spent more time with the girls in the pack and preferred their company to the adventures she and Alex used to have. Growing up was hard; he just hadn't expected to handle everything on his own.

"Tennison's a good guy," Alex admitted. "He deserves a break."

"As do you," Nikki replied with a kind smile. William began to get fussy.

"Can I hold him?" Alex asked.

Surprised by Alex's offer, Nikki nodded. "Of course."

Alex had held William a few times. When school wasn't in session, Alex and Cassie had spent a lot of time with Nikki and Jaze. The two had pretty much taken over as their parents when the orphaned twins arrived at the Academy seven years ago. With William's birth, Nikki had been much busier, but she always took time when the twins needed her, a fact for which Alex was grateful.

She positioned the baby in his arms. William quieted immediately, staring up at Alex with wide blue eyes.

"I think Jet would be happy you gave William his name," Alex said, smiling down at the baby. "I used to wish it was my name, too."

"You did?" Nikki said. "I didn't know that."

Alex met her gaze, forcing his tone to be happy when he said, "I can't think of anyone more deserving of it than the son of my brother's best friend. He would be honored."

"I hope so," Nikki replied; sadness filled her gaze.

"He would," Alex told her with confidence.

She nodded. "I'm glad. I think William has big shoes to fill."

"We all do," Alex said, but the melancholy didn't come. With Nikki, he couldn't be sad. She knew what the twins had gone through, and had been there for him when night terrors kept him up during their first year at the Academy. She had never been upset when he woke her up crying; she used to read him stories or sing him songs to help his mind calm down and to chase away the memories.

Sitting with her in their quarters felt like that again. She always had a kind smile or the right things to say to help him feel better. With Nikki, he always knew she believed in him. It wasn't so much in what she said, but in the way she looked at him and Cassie. She loved them; that much had always been obvious. Even though they had been orphans when they came to the Academy, she made them feel like they had a home.

"Thank you for all that you've done for Cassie and me," Alex said.

Nikki gave a surprised smile. "Thank you for being such a wonderful boy," she replied.

Baby William's fingers found his shirt. He smiled as the baby watched him with clear blue eyes.

Chapter Ten

"Welcome to this year's full moon games!" Dean Jaze announced to the anxious students gathered in the courtyard. He glanced at the sun setting below the trees. "As you all know, the moon isn't too far away."

Chuckles sounded through the crowd. Not only had the professors let the students out early again for restlessness, they had promised to join the students at the games this year as their own pack. Alex exchanged a smile with Professor Grace. Kaynan stood next to her already in his red wolf form, allowing her to see. She looked as excited to participate in the games as the rest of them.

"This year's games will be hosted by Professor Thorson, the only other human here besides my wife who is with our baby boy tonight and will be unable to join us." Jaze nodded at Professor Thorson who stood near the doors. "Thank you for your bravery in putting up with us."

The professor hefted a handful of medals on ribbons that chinked together from the movement. A breeze sent his wispy white hair waving. "If any of you act up, you won't be earning one of these," he said sternly. His usual smile broke through his attempt at a stern demeanor. "I'll probably just lock the doors and leave you all out here running amuck."

Jaze laughed and the students echoed the laughter. "That really will cause trouble." The dean smiled down at them, his brown eyes bright. "The full moon games this year will emphasize the traits of a wolf. Feats of stealth, speed, your ability to track, protect your pack, and your strength will be tested. There are five medals." He winked at Alex who waited near Jet's wolf statue. "We haven't quite figured out another task for the sixth, so you can relax this year, but don't relax too much!"

A shudder ran down Alex's spine. The full moon was rising. Alex set a hand on the cold metal of the statue to center himself.

"I guess I'd better speak quickly," Jaze said. "To all of you seven year olds who are phasing for the first time, stay with your packs, they'll take care of you. To the rest of you students, the race is on. If the professors return with all five medals, the entire group of you will be required to assist Professor Dray in building his new greenhouses."

A groan went through the students. It was no secret that Professor Dray was preparing to teach gardening and plant identification the next year. He had a sign-up sheet in the Great Hall asking for volunteers to help complete the building of the greenhouses. Apparently Jaze had found an answer to the lack of volunteers.

Another shudder ran through Alex's skin, harder this time. Students exchanged glances. Alex searched for Cassie. Instead of waiting on the outskirts of the crowd where she usually liked to avoid the masses, he spotted her curly brown hair near Tennison's tall form. Alex stifled a sigh. He then spotted the little girl next to her. Caitlyn held Cassie's hand as if terrified of being separated from her.

"It's going to be okay," he heard his sister say.

Caitlyn looked anything but reassured as she shook her head, her white-blonde curls bouncing back and forth.

Alex made his way through the crowd and stopped behind Caitlyn in time to hear the little girl say, "But I'm scared."

"Scared of what?" Alex asked.

Cassie threw him a grateful smile. "This is Caitlyn's first phase. She's afraid of what's going to happen."

Alex dropped down onto one knee so that he was eye-level with the little werewolf. "You're afraid of phasing?"

Caitlyn nodded wordlessly, her wide green eyes showing her fear.

Alex gave her a smile. "I was scared of phasing my first time."

"You were?" Caitlyn asked, her voice small within the excited crowd around them.

Alex nodded, his attention fully on her as if she was the only person in the courtyard. "I was, and I was glad to have Cassie with me. My big brother Jet was there, too, with his friends. Do you know who one of Jet's friends was?"

Caitlyn shook her head.

Alex pointed to the dean standing on the stairs.

"He was?" she breathed in amazement.

Alex nodded. "Dean Jaze was so nice to us. You're surrounded by tons of friends. It's the best possible place to phase."

"It is?" she asked.

Alex nodded again. "It is, and I'll bet Cassie wouldn't mind if you phased in her room with her so you won't be scared."

Caitlyn turned her gaze up to Cassie and Tennison who had been watching the conversation.

"Can I, Cassie?" Caitlyn asked. Her bottom lip trembled slightly.

Cassie smiled down at the little girl. "Of course you can phase with me. I'll be like your big sister."

Both of them smiled at the thought.

"Then I won't be so scared," Caitlyn decided. She surprised Alex by throwing her arms around his neck and giving him as tight a squeeze as her little body could manage. "Thank you, Alex." She took Cassie's hand again, her grip not so panicked this time.

"Thank you, Alex," Cassie repeated. "How do you always

know what to say?"

"I learned from my sister," Alex replied.

"Did she say you were also cheesy?" Cassie grinned at him.

Alex nodded. "Many times."

"Go phase," Jaze called over the group. "Enjoy the games!"

The students thundered up the stairs. Alex passed Kalia waiting near the doors. She looked almost sad that she was being left out. He remembered her comment from last year about how she couldn't relax when the full moon was out. She was caught in the middle; the only one Alex had ever known of.

He turned and pushed his way back through the crowd. The full moon was getting closer; he knew he was cutting his time short. He gritted his teeth and made his way to the door.

"Uh, hi Kalia," he said.

She looked surprised that anyone had noticed her. When she saw who it was, emotions he couldn't read crossed her icy blue gaze.

"Hello, Alex."

"Uh, what are you going to do during the games?" he asked.

She shrugged, her eyes flitting to the trees where the faint glow of moonlight already showed. "I'm not sure. Wait out here bored I guess."

"What about helping Professor Thorson?" Alex suggested on a whim. "He might need it since Nikki's with baby William."

She seemed surprised. "I hadn't thought about it. I guess I could." Though she tried to hide the fact that the suggestion sounded somewhat promising, Alex could hear it in her voice.

He smiled. "I hope you do." The next shudder ran

through him so hard he had to put a hand against the door to steady himself.

Kalia lifted a hand to help him. "Are you alright?"

He threw her a grin. "Yeah, but I'm going to phase into a wolf right here if I don't get to my room."

Kalia laughed. The sound was musical and light. She clapped a hand over her mouth and looked amazed that it had come out of her. "You'd better hurry," she said, her voice muffled behind her fingers.

Alex ran through the doors and upstairs. He remembered at the last minute not to shut the door to his room all the way. He tore off his clothes seconds before the moonlight spilling through his window forced him onto his hands and knees.

It felt good not to fight the phase anymore. He willed it to change him, pulling his joints in different directions, shortening his fingers, and sending dark gray fur up his arms and down his back. When it was over, he breathed a sigh of relief. It felt wonderful to be in wolf form again. The sound of wolves pacing Pack Jericho's common room filled Alex with joy. He pushed the door open with his nose and joined them.

He looked around for Cassie. It took the pair a few more minutes, but soon, his sister came down the hall in her cream-colored wolf form. The cute wolf pup that followed close behind made him want to smile. Caitlyn had the pure white coat of a female Alpha. When she was old enough, the little girl would be one of the leaders of the packs at the Academy. But right now she had the gangly legs and fuzzy fur of a pup. She pranced around Cassie and bumped straight into Jericho. The Alpha gave a soft snort of laughter and used his nose to help her back to the huge paws she would eventually grow into.

A howl sounded in the courtyard. Jericho pushed the door open with his nose. They were met by packs swarming down the stairs.

Last year, the packs had gotten stuck in their haste to hurry down. This year, it appeared as though the night games had paid off. Each flowed in order from Alpha to Second, to the rest of the werewolves who followed without shoving those in front. If the organization of the packs was any indication, the games were going to be close.

Alex was happy to see Kalia by Professor Thorson. She spotted him in the crowd of wolves and smiled her gratitude. His chest tightened and he ducked his head.

"Your first mission is one of stealth," Professor Thorson explained. "As a wolf, you may indeed require absolute silence when avoiding those who wish you harm, or in finding sustenance to fill your bellies. Last year, we created the challenges for you. This year, for the first challenge, you must rely on what you've been taught. Use Professor Colleen and Professor Rafe's training to catch a bird of your choice and bring it back to me."

The professor held up a finger. "But if the bird is harmed in any way, you forfeit the challenge. This is a test of your stealth as well as your ability to handle a delicate task."

Torin snorted behind Alex. A few members of Pack Torin snorted their echoed opinions of the professor's request. Alex didn't doubt they would rather just kill the bird to make it easier.

On the edge of the clearing a group of wolves stood calmly watching the rest. Alex recognized Jaze's black Alpha form at the head of the pack. As the rest of the students noticed them, the excitement increased. They were going to get the chance to pit their packs against the leaders of the school. Everyone was determined to win a medal for their

Alpha.

Professor Thorson smiled at them. "But as a twist, the last two packs in each competition will be eliminated. Bring the bird back to me. The first pack here gets a medal, as long as the entire pack is together. Stay close, use teamwork, and strengthen the way you work within your pack. These games can be very beneficial to you as you learn to use each other's strengths on these challenges."

The werewolves moved within their packs, anxious to be off.

"Want to say it?" Professor Thorson asked Kalia.

"Say what?" she replied, her tone nervous.

He smiled at her. "Begin the games," he whispered, though every wolf within the clearing heard.

Kalia lifted her voice. "Begin the games!" she yelled.

The wolves took off running.

Alex sniffed the air as they ran. Any birds close to the Academy would have been scared off by the ruckus the students made. Jericho must have had the same thought, because he led them through the bushes and off the trail deeper into the forest. Though they could hear the other packs behind them, they would soon be out of earshot.

A scent touched Alex's nose. He gave a little huff of warning. The entire pack paused. A surge of pride ran through Alex at how well they obeyed. Even Caitlyn froze at Cassie's side. The little white wolf looked like she could barely contain her excitement, but she glanced at Cassie and held perfectly still like her chosen mentor was doing.

Jericho followed the scent Alex had found. With soft paws, the black wolf made his way silently along the pine needle strewn forest floor. The pack stood behind Alex, watching their leader's every step.

The scent of grouse was strong beneath the pines. A quiet

cooing sound reached Alex's sensitive ears. His muscles tensed.

Jericho gave a low, almost silent bark of command. Alex crouched and stalked around the other side of the low-swept pine. He could hear the abated breaths of the rest of their pack as they waited for their Alpha and Second.

Another coo sounded. Alex made out the reddish-brown form of a male grouse as it pecked at the earth beneath the tree. Other sounds indicated that there were more of the birds deeper in the forest. If one spotted the wolves and called a warning, the rest would be gone before the pair could reach them.

Alex glanced to the right. Jericho's black coat was almost invisible in the deep shadows. The wolf was a few feet from the grouse and it hadn't noticed him yet. Alex took another step forward. The grouse paused. Alex froze with a paw in the air. The bird began to eat again. Alex gently set the paw down and took another step.

Jericho was almost to the bird. The animal's back was to the Alpha as it pecked at bugs hiding within the damp soil. Jericho inched forward. His paw found a twig. A slight snap sounded.

The bird's head lifted. If it looked to the right, it would see Jericho and fly away, warning the rest of the birds in the area of the danger.

Alex gave a soft cough to catch the bird's attention. The grouse's head turned. Its beady eye stared directly at him. It froze for the briefest second. Jericho took advantage of the delay and crossed the rest of the space between them. In less than a heartbeat, Jericho had his jaws around the bird's neck and a paw on its back. It squawked and flapped, trying to get away. The rest of the birds gave startled cries and took off; the beat of their wings said there were more of them than

Alex had guessed. Jericho put a bit more pressure on bird's back. The animal froze, terrified. Jericho shifted his grip from its neck to its back.

Jericho picked the bird up in his jaws softer than Alex had ever seen a wolf carry anything. Jericho gave Alex a wide-eyed look. Alex held in a laugh. Neither of them had been in that position before. He was glad he wasn't the one with a mouth full of feathers that could try to escape at any moment.

The wolves of Pack Jericho stared at them when they passed. They fell in behind their Alpha and Second and the pack made their way swiftly back to the Academy.

Alex couldn't believe any of the packs could have beaten their time. They had found birds faster than he had expected, caught the very first one, and were already on their return trip. No one could have been so lucky.

Chapter Eleven

They reached the clearing in front of the gate just in time to see Jaze with a mourning dove in his jaws. Professor Thorson accepted the small bird with great care. The dove sat quietly in his hand for a minute as though amazed it was still alive. The professor lifted his hand. Suddenly, the bird took flight. Within seconds, the animal was out of sight.

"Your bird was unharmed and you are the first pack to return," Professor Thorson said proudly. "You have completed the first mission." He picked up a medal on a ribbon and hung it around Jaze's neck. "Wait beneath the trees for the next competition."

Alex caught a gleam of competitiveness in the dean's eyes when the pack trotted past. Alex snorted and Jaze flashed a wolfish smile.

"Go ahead and get their bird, my dear," Professor Thorson instructed.

"Get the bird?" Kalia repeated, eyeing the grouse in Jericho's mouth with uncertainty.

"Go ahead," the professor urged. "I don't imagine either of them is enjoying the situation much."

Jericho shook his head. The grouse gave a squawk.

Kalia reached timidly for Jericho's mouth. He opened his jaws. Before Kalia could touch the animal, the grouse gave a flap of its wings and burst into the air. Its scolding call echoed over the forest as it flew away.

Professor Thorson laughed. "Well, at least we know it was alright. Well done, Pack Jericho. Take a place with your elders."

Though they hadn't gotten first place, Alex was proud of how well their pack had listened to commands and acted within the forest. Their pack settled on the grass a few paces from Jaze's. The dean gave them a nod of approval. Pride swelled in Alex's chest.

"Torin, really?"

The disappointment in the professor's voice caught Alex's attention. Pack Torin had reached the clearing. The Lifer Alpha carried a bird in his jaws that was clearly no longer alive. Blood coated the Alpha's muzzle and chest. The bird's neck hung at an unnatural angle. Neither the professor nor Kalia would take it. He deposited it at their feet.

"Pack Torin is disqualified," Professor Thorson said with a shake of his head.

Torin trotted over to the other two packs with a pleased expression on his face.

A growl sounded. It wasn't deep or loud, but the tone sent a shiver down Alex's spine.

Torin stopped in his tracks, his attention on Jaze. The dean stood a few feet from the packs with his gaze on the Lifer Alpha. No words needed to be spoken to express the disapproval in Jaze's gaze.

Torin's head and tail lowered. He glanced back at his pack. None of them would meet his eyes. He paced to a spot in the clearing a bit further from the other packs and sat down more subdued than when he had entered.

Pack Shannon reached the clearing next. Shannon carried a grouse as well, but it was smaller than the one Pack Jericho had found, and had the lighter coloring of a female. When she spotted the dead bird, Shannon immediately sought out Torin. The disgust and anger in her glare let him know exactly how she felt.

Memories surged forward of the time Alex had helped Rafe's wild wolf pack bring down an elk the previous year during wilderness education. Shannon had been the angriest about that, yet to Alex, it was different. The elk had fed

Rafe's pack. The animal was older, lame, and wouldn't have survived winter. The wolves had done what they were supposed to do, fill their bellies and ensure that only the strongest animals went on to produce offspring and further the strength of their species.

But the bird Torin had killed proved no such purpose. It hadn't died to feed hungry animals; in all appearances, it had been healthy and whole before Torin found it. The fact that the Alpha had killed the animal just because he found it humorous made Alex's chest tightened. Death wasn't something to be taken lightly. He knew the dean didn't take it lightly either. There was no doubt Torin would receive further punishment for his actions.

"Come back in," Professor Thorson yelled when Pack Miguel brought in a starling. Alex wondered where they had found the bird, but when the professor let it go, it flew haphazardly to the nearest tree, its wing whole but crooked as though it had broken it sometime not too long ago. He figured the bird probably found it easier to reach the lower branches close to the ground to rest; that was no doubt where Miguel had caught it.

Professor Thorson nodded at the group. "Well done, students. As some of you know, Pack Torin has been disqualified for failing to obey the rules of the competition and killing the bird they brought in. They will also be required clean the kitchen under Cook Jerald's supervision for the rest of the month." At the snorts and groans of protest from the pack, the professor speared them with a look. "Perhaps that will teach you to give more respect to life." He gave a small smile. "Or at least instruct you that the consequences of actions may not be worth the enjoyment you received while doing them."

Kalia whispered something to the professor that Alex

couldn't catch. A grin spread across the professor's face. "Good suggestion," he replied. He met Torin's gaze. "I'm sure Cook Jerald also won't mind preparing this bird as your next pack's meal as well."

Torin glared daggers at Kalia. She ignored him and glanced at Alex. He widened his eyes in a what-are-you-doing look. She gave a tiny shrug of her shoulders, her pale blue eyes sparkling in the moonlight.

Alex was glad that at least she was having a good time, but Torin wasn't a pleasant enemy. Alex made a mental note to warn her when he could talk again.

"Packs Drake and Kelli are also eliminated for having the slowest completion time," Professor Thorson informed them. The packs took up spots near Pack Torin to watch the rest of the full moon games. "Your next game is a race," the professor continued. "You will be running to that ridge and back." The professor pointed to the ridge students used to jump off into the small lake. It was about half a mile away. "The first pack to return here with all of their members wins the medal." He lifted a pair of binoculars. "I'll know if each of your pack members reaches the top." The professor nodded his head at Kalia.

She raised a hand. All of the wolves tensed. She dropped it and shouted, "Go!"

Alex ran behind Jericho. The rest of their pack flowed close behind, jumping logs and dodging bushes as one. They could hear the other packs on either side of them. The trail was too crowded. Wolves began to fall back as their Alphas took them on other routes. Pack Boris pushed ahead. They ran over the wolves who wouldn't get out of the way. Terith yelped when Boris shoved her with his shoulder into a tree trunk. Trent growled, but the Alpha and his pack was already past.

Jericho slowed just long enough for Terith to get her bearings, then he was racing again with the rest of them at his heels. Alex had no idea where Jaze's pack was. No doubt they knew the forest better than any of the students. He could picture another medal around Jaze's neck. The image spurred him to run faster.

The pack leaped another log of a tree whose trunk was colored black from the lightning strike that had killed it. A yip called behind him. He recognized Cassie's voice. A glance back showed Cassie still behind the log. A little white head poked over. Caitlyn was having difficulty making it.

Alex barked to notify Jericho of what he was doing before he turned and galloped back to the pair. He leaped the log and spun. Using his teeth as gently as he could, he grabbed Caitlyn by the nape of her neck and lifted her over. She took off running behind Cassie as soon as her paws touched the ground. Alex raced after them. They reached Markey and Max. Alex stayed behind to help Caitlyn. He had to give the little werewolf credit. Even though she was at a disadvantage with the huge paws she hadn't grown into yet, she pushed herself to keep up with Cassie.

Alex's sister gave barks of encouragement whenever Caitlyn faltered. Alex lifted her over another log. The path began to ascend. They could hear the other packs around them. A glance back showed Pack Shannon close on their heels.

Jericho gave a sharp bark and turned off the trail. Everyone followed without question. Alex had explored the forest since they had first been taken to the Academy. He knew exactly where the Alpha was going. The ridge could be reached by the trail that ran up the backside, but it wound north in order to avoid the denser areas. A faint path made its way up the boulders and shale that created the face of the ridge. It was a harder climb and more perilous, but shaved a good amount of time off the climb. Alex knew because that was the trail he always chose.

Alex fought back a grin at the sight of Jaze's pack above them. Of course the dean would know of the trail as well. Alex gritted his teeth. He was determined to help Jericho win the medal.

Caitlyn tried to leap the first big boulder. Alex slowed her with his shoulder before she crashed back to the ground. Cassie had reached the rock above. The rest of the pack scrambled up the path. Jericho was a black shadow on the boulders further up. It was a hard climb for even the larger wolves; there was no way Caitlyn would make it.

Alex grabbed Caitlyn gently by the scruff of the neck again. He was worried about hurting her, but he knew she would be heartbroken if her inability to climb made them lose the challenge.

Caitlyn hung quietly in his jaws as he made the first leap. His claws scrambled for purchase. He found a grip, and pulled himself up. He set her down and gave her a searching look. She gave an accepting yip, her green eyes bright in the moonlight. Alex grabbed her scruff again and jumped. It was easier the second time because he knew how the weight pulled. He set his paws more carefully, studied the rock above, and landed in the center.

By the time they reached the middle, Alex was exhausted. It was a hard enough climb without carrying a werewolf pup. But Caitlyn held still even though he knew his fangs must hurt no matter how gently he tried to carry her.

Howls came down to them from the top of the ridge. A shiver ran down Alex's spine. It was his pack, encouraging him and Caitlyn on their climb. He couldn't respond as he carried her, but the little wolf raised her muzzle and howled back. The high, sweet sound almost made him smile and drop her. He reminded himself that wolves didn't smile and leaped up the next boulder. The howls above him sounded louder.

Other voices mingled with his pack's. Alex recognized Jaze's voice among them. Jaze's pack was howling their encouragement as well. Even though they were supposed to be in a challenge against each other, his pack was cheering for Alex and Caitlyn. Alex jumped up the next boulder, then the next. His heartbeat pounded in his ears, but it was strong and didn't falter.

He took a deep breath and was about to leap again when a sound caught his attention. It was a high-pitched whining buzz that raced toward them. Jaze gave a bark of warning. Alex glanced over his shoulder in time to see a small object speeding toward them. He ducked to protect Caitlyn.

The missile hit the rock where his head had been. The force of the blow knocked Alex and Caitlyn from the side of the ridge. Alex managed to keep ahold of Caitlyn. He pulled her against his chest as they fell. He hit the ground on his back, the little wolf held tight against him.

Caitlyn's yips of fear pounded against his ears that rang from the impact of the missile. The fact that they were in danger sounded over and over in his mind. He needed to make sure Cassie was safe, but his shoulder throbbed with pain and he couldn't move.

Caitlyn huddled against Alex. He could feel her shaking. Her tiny tongue licked his muzzle as she tried to get him to respond. Alex forced his eyes open. When he met Caitlyn's green gaze, he could see the fear in her eyes. He tried to push himself to his feet. Putting weight on his right paw sent such fierce agony through his shoulder that he collapsed back to the ground.

The sound of paws racing toward them made Alex open

his eyes again. Though what had felt like centuries had passed after they hit the ground, it could only have been seconds. He saw wolves leaping down the side of the ridge, graceful shadows in hues of black, gray, and cream that flowed from one boulder to the next with effortless ease. They looked so beautiful in the light of the full moon.

Alex knew he was in shock. He could feel blood soaking through his fur. He willed his thoughts to sharpen through the haze. Someone had shot at them. That someone might still be in the forest.

Alex pushed carefully to a sitting position with his good paw. Caitlyn huddled against his chest. He lowered his head, giving her the wolf equivalent of a hug.

The cadence of paws neared. Alex looked up to see Jaze's black form burst through the bushes in front of them. He realized they were a short distance from the ridge. The force of the missile had blown them back pretty far. Only Drogan had such a motive, though it had never been stated fully why he wanted to kill the twins. Alex realized that if he didn't find out soon, the lack of information was going to be deadly.

Jaze looked Alex over quickly. He realized by the emotions in the dean's eyes that he must be worse off than he thought. Alex's face stung from the particles of rock that had blown into him like knives in the explosion. He had turned his head and ducked to protect Caitlyn. He could feel similar shards of pain all the way down his shoulder and side, though his shoulder hurt the worst. He wondered if the missile had clipped it.

Cassie ran past Jaze straight to Alex. She whined as she looked him over. She sniffed at his fur and her muzzle came away red with blood. Fear was stark on her face as she looked back at Jaze and whined. The rest of Pack Jericho drew up behind her. Jericho studied the forest around them. Drogan's men had missed. He wasn't one to let give up easily. Alex was worried about another attack.

Jaze gave a bark of command. The professors surrounded them. Kaynan scouted the forest ahead, his dark crimson form catching the moonlight like a demonic creature. Jaze lowered his ears back halfway and jerked his head toward the Academy, telling Alex they had to get moving.

Alex tried to rise, but Caitlyn pressed against his chest with a yip of fear.

Cassie crouched in front of Caitlyn. She gave an encouraging whine. Caitlyn's head rose. She looked surprised that all of the wolves were there. The little werewolf glanced back at Alex. He nudged her gently with his nose. Caitlyn licked Alex's muzzle. He pushed her again. She ran to Cassie as if she couldn't reach Alex's twin fast enough. Cassie led her to the side to clear a path for Alex.

Alex tried to put weight on his right paw. His shoulder gave such an angry throb that a yelp of pain escaped him. He almost fell back to the ground, but Jaze was there.

The dean leaned against Alex, putting pressure against Alex's shoulder that hurt, but helped him to rise. Alex stood for a moment on shaky legs. Jaze gave another urgent bark. Though Kaynan hadn't sounded an alarm, Drogan's men could be closing in. Alex couldn't let Pack Jericho or the professors put their life on the line for him.

Alex gritted his teeth. He took a step, then another. Jaze walked with him, using his shoulder to keep Alex up when his shoulder threatened to give out. The rest of the wolves fell in around them. Alex couldn't think past the pain. It blurred the edges of his vision so that even the moonlight was painful. He ducked his head and concentrated on the sound of wolf paws around him. Jericho and Vance ranged just in front of the pair, checking for anything Kaynan might have missed. It was a slow, painful trek back to the Academy.

Chapter Twelve

"Alex!" Kalia called when the wolves reached the Academy gate.

The other packs had found them on their way back from the race and had fallen in around Alex and Jaze. There was no sign of Drogan. Alex doubted the man would dare to attack with so many werewolves ready to fight back.

Kalia quickly pushed open the gate. Professor Thorson followed close behind as they made their way through. The professor didn't ask questions. The werewolves were captive by the moonlight until the full moon set. He would have no answers until they could phase back.

Jaze assisted Alex to the base of Jet's statue. Moonlight basked the courtyard in light brighter than the lamps that usually lit it but had been shut off for the games. Alex couldn't quite stifle a groan as he sank to his stomach on the grass.

A few seconds later, the doors to the Academy burst open. Brock came running out, his face white. An apparently forgotten half-eaten candy bar stuck out of his pocket as if it had been shoved there in his haste. Relief filled Brock's expression when he spotted Jaze and the other wolves near the statue.

"Drogan is in Haroldsburg! The cameras picked him up and I think—" He stopped talking when he spotted Alex next to the statue. "Oh, no," Brock breathed.

Alex lifted his shoulders in a small shrug. The action made him wince. He closed his eyes.

"What should I do?" Brock asked Jaze. "Does he need Band-Aids or a-a rabies shot?"

Jaze gave a snort that contained a hint of humor. Alex opened his eyes to see the dean sit down near the statue.

119

Brock nodded in understanding. "Oh, the moonlight. I see. Well, I, uh..." He looked around at the students who watched him. He seemed suddenly nervous to be the center of attention for so many wolves. He pointed behind him at the Academy. "I guess I'd better get back to monitoring." He gave a weak smile. "Don't want them sneaking up on us unexpected or something. Uh, again."

Alex closed his eyes and listened to the human make his way back to the Academy. The door shut with a slam. The thought that someone would have to phase again to open it after the moon set made its way through Alex's hazy mind. He remembered Pip running naked through the crowd of wolf students after the full moon games the previous year. He had laughed then; yet thoughts of all Pip had gone through chased the humor from his mind.

The little werewolf had betrayed Alex and Cassie to save his family. Drogan had held Pip's parents hostage. The only way Pip could free them was to tell Drogan of the twins' location whenever they left the Academy. They had survived, and Jaze had freed Pip's family and united them once again. Alex missed Pip's enthusiasm. The little werewolf hadn't deserved to live in fear for his family's safety. Drogan had that impact on people.

Alex settled onto his side so that his shoulder received the full impact of the moonlight while his back was warmed by the base of the statue. The grass beneath him was comforting and cool. It smelled like hope, he remembered Jet saying. Alex took a deep breath of hope and let it out slowly.

The moonlight pulsed against his skin. It felt like a heat lamp, warming its way through the wound in his shoulder and making it tingle past the pain. Alex could feel it healing, slowly closing from the inside. His face and the side of his neck tingled as well. He could feel the rock shards working free, sliding from beneath his skin. At least if his shoulder was healing, there wasn't silver in the wound. Perhaps it had only been the damaged from the rocks that had sliced it open instead of the missile. He had no doubt Drogan would use as much silver as possible in crafting such a weapon.

***

The ache in Alex's shoulder pulsed more strongly as the moon vanished behind the trees. He kept his eyes closed, knowing that any motion could open the healing wound and make it bleed again. He heard werewolves leave, and wondered who had been brave enough to phase and run naked to the door to let the rest of the werewolves inside so they could phase in their bedrooms and change into clothes. He hoped Caitlyn wouldn't hate phasing altogether after the attack.

Familiar footsteps hurried back to Alex's side.

"Just stay there with Jet," Jaze instructed. "Nikki and Meredith are on their way back out with supplies to get you patched up. Lyra went out with Mouse to survey the site. They'll be back with information soon."

Alex looked up at him. Jaze gave a half-smile despite the worry that showed on his face. The dean crouched next to the werewolf. "You were pretty tough out there."

Alex gave a soft snort of denial that rustled the strands of grass near his nose.

The dean's smile faded, leaving only the worry on his face. "You aren't supposed to be in danger in our forest, Alex. We've got to stop Drogan. I just can't figure out his motive." He ran a hand through his blond hair to push it off his forehead. "I have my men scouring the woods as we speak. It doesn't make sense to me that he is spending so much time and effort trying to kill you and Cassie. He has to have a reason. We need to find out what that is."

Jaze shook his head. "I hoped that the silence we've had up to now was a sign that he had given up. Drogan and the General have been busy down south. We've been hard-pressed to keep up with them."

Alex wondered why Jaze was confiding in him. The dean had never opened up to him about all they were doing to protect werewolves from the hate-filled General who was intent on wiping their entire race from the earth.

Jaze looked up at Jet's statue. The fading starlight bathed the dean's face. "We're trying our best to stop his efforts, but he's shifty, cunning. He likes pain." His voice lowered as he watched the statue above them. There was a look on his face as if he wished Jet was really there, that the statue would come alive and talk to him.

Alex knew the look. He had felt that way so many times since his stay at the Academy. He missed Jet as much as he missed his parents; it was clear by Jaze's expression that he felt the same way. They had both lost a brother the day Jet was slain.

"We keep trying, Jet. Don't give up on us," Jaze said. Though the dean's hand rested gently on Alex's side, Alex knew in that moment the dean had forgotten his presence. The sorrow that thickened Jaze's voice as he spoke to his best friend glittered in his eyes. "If you were here, I know we could figure it out together. You were so smart and so selfless. You were always willing to put yourself last." Jaze blinked and a single tear broke free. "You chose me over you that day. You chose to die so that I could live. You believed I could make something of myself, and of this." His voice fell to a whisper. "You trusted me."

Alex eased up to a sitting position. The pressure made his shoulder ache, but he didn't care. He wished he could tell Jaze the difference he had made in one young boy's life. Jaze had given him a purpose when everything else in his life had fallen apart. He had taken Alex and Cassie in and raised them as his kids; he made them feel as if they still had somewhere in the world left to call home.

Yet the look on Jaze's face was one of such loss and despair Alex realized the werewolf he had always looked up to hid his pain well. The hole in Alex's heart from missing his slain family showed in Jaze's eyes.

"He should be here for you, Alex," Jaze said, letting Alex know that he hadn't been forgotten. "He would be doing a much better job protecting you than I have."

Alex leaned against Jaze. The dean held onto Alex's good shoulder.

"Those you love are worth fighting for, Alex." Jaze looked down at the young werewolf he crouched beside. "There is never a price too dear to pay to protect those you love. It is the way of the wolf, and it was Jet's way. Help me keep you and your sister safe, because you, Cassie, Nikki, and baby William are my loved ones. I will find a way to protect you, I promise."

Alex nodded. Even if he could have spoken, his throat would have been too tight for words. He breathed in through his nose; the salt of Jaze's tears mingled with the cool night breeze that told him of Rafe wolves patrolling outside the wall. Jaze was doing his best, yet Drogan had found a way to attack him anyway. The frustration on Jaze's face was clear. He blamed himself for Alex's wounds.

But the wounds were healing. The moonlight had done more than ease the ache in his shoulder; it had sped his recovery. Alex could feel the muscles binding. Fresh blood no longer dripped down his front leg. The stinging sensation in his face and neck were gone. By morning, the worst of the pain would vanish.

Alex rose as the doors to the Academy were pushed open. Nikki and Meredith came running down. Aunt Meredith's arms were filled with supplies while Nikki carried baby William.

"Oh, Alex," Meredith said with heartache in her voice for his wounds.

Nikki handed the baby to Jaze; baby William gave a huge smile when his father took him. Meredith spread a clean blanket on the ground and Nikki began to set supplies on it.

Alex gave Jaze a pleading look.

A slight smile touched Jaze's face. "I think Alex would prefer to heal on his own."

Both Meredith and Nikki paused in surprise. Alex's cheeks heated under their scrutiny; he wondered if wolves could blush.

"Let me see what we're dealing with," Nikki said in a tone that allowed no nonsense. "Then we'll decide what's best for you."

Jaze shrugged at Alex's pleading. "I can't argue with her," he said.

Alex rolled his eyes in a thanks-for-leaving-me-to-the-wolves look.

Jaze merely chuckled. He bent his head and kissed William on one of the baby's chubby cheeks. William gurgled with happiness.

Alex winced at Nikki's prodding. Meredith's face was filled with worry as she looked at his bloody fur.

"It looks like things are healing nicely," Nikki noted. At Meredith's doubtful expression, she gave a reassuring smile. "His fur makes it look much worse. There is a lot of blood loss." She gave Alex a searching look. "I don't suppose you'll agree to phasing in the medical wing so we can look you over."

Alex snorted his disapproval.

Meredith smiled. "If he can make it up the stairs to Pack Jericho's quarters, I suppose he's not going to die."

Nikki shook her head. "You haven't seen what these

werewolves will put up with." She gave Jaze a level look that said more than her words. "If I counted the times Jaze told me he was fine and he ended up being on the verge of death, I would run out of fingers and toes."

Baby William grabbed Jaze's nose in a tight little fist. Jaze laughed. "Sometimes putting up with medical care feels worse than death."

Nikki slapped him on the leg before she rose. "You're just lucky your wife knows how to put you back together."

Jaze surprised her by shifting William onto his hip and pulling her into a hug. "Yes, I am." He planted a kiss on her lips.

When he stepped back, she smiled. "I'm just glad you know it."

"Let's get this wolf to bed," Jaze said.

"The corridors are packed with werewolves, no pun intended," Meredith said.

"Are you sure that pun wasn't intended?" Jaze asked.

She grinned. "Well, maybe just a bit."

"All the same," Nikki said, "The students are eager to make sure Alex is fine." She smiled at Alex. "It seems you've made a lot of friends."

Alex thought of Torin and Boris. While friends would definitely be pushing the definition of their relationship, given the attack from Drogan, he wouldn't consider them enemies. Perspective definitely shed things in a different light.

He limped up the stairs with Jaze, Nikki, and Meredith close behind. Healing took a lot of strength, and exhaustion made it hard to keep his eyes open. He paused at the top and looked back at the statue. The black contours of the metal caught the silvery light of dawn that peaked from the distant mountains. It made Jet look alive as he stood watching over the Academy. Meredith opened the door and Alex limped inside.

"Alex!" Cassie's shout rang over all the rest. She shoved through the crowd and dropped to her knees in front of him.

Alex winced as she wrapped her arms around his neck in a tight hug.

"Take it easy," Jaze said gently. "He's still healing."

She dropped her arms quickly. "Sorry, Alex. I was just so worried."

He licked her face before she could back up.

Everyone laughed as Cassie scrubbed at her slimy cheek.

"That's just gross, Alex. Grow up," she said. Tennison held out a hand. She took it and he helped her back to her feet.

"We're glad you're alright," Jericho said.

The rest of the packs crowded forward, asking questions and exclaiming about the missile.

"Alright," Vance's deep voice rumbled from the professors' end of the hallway. "Let's get to bed. You guys have class in the morning. Anyone late to football gets laps."

A groan went out through the students. They began to disperse up the stairs.

"We'll see you up there," Jericho said. "Take your time."

Alex was glad the Alpha didn't insist on helping him. Though his shoulder ached, he still wanted to save whatever reputation he had left.

"See you, Alex," Cassie said. She proceeded to humiliate him by kissing him on top of the head. "I'm glad you're okay."

Alex rubbed his head against his front leg in an effort to wipe away her kiss. She laughed and looped her arm through Tennison's. The pair walked up the stairs together.

"We're all glad you're alright," Nikki said as the last of the students reached the stairs. She leaned down and gave Alex a gentle hug. Baby William grabbed one of Alex's ears. Alex let out a quiet huff of laughter as Nikki extracted it from the baby's surprisingly strong fingers.

"See, even William's happy," Meredith said.

Instinct made Alex look up to see Professor Mouse standing next to Lyra at the door. His fingers were entwined with hers, but there was an anxious expression on his face.

Jaze followed Alex's gaze. He didn't look surprised at the small professor's silent entrance. "What is it, Mouse?"

Mouse's gaze flitted from Alex back to Jaze. Jaze nodded. "It's alright. Alex needs to know what's going on as much as I do. Tell us what you know."

Mouse pushed his big glasses further up his nose and kept his eyes on the ground as he said, "We found where the missile was fired." He cleared his throat, apparently uncomfortable at all the attention.

Lyra took over. "It appears to have been a precision guided missile launched from outside the forest boundaries. We're not sure what sort of tracking system guided it. Kaynan's gathering the pieces of the missile so that we can find out more about the technology they are using."

Mouse glanced at Jaze. "It might, uh, give us a better idea as to how they were so close to hitting Alex from that far away."

Jaze nodded. "Let me know what you find out. Until then, all students are required to stay within the walls. Let Colleen know we'll be moving the students from sense training to plant identification with Dray." Jaze winked at Alex. "He'll appreciate the extra help building the green houses."

Alex tried to fight back a yawn, but the exhaustion from healing was really starting to take a toll.

"You'd better get up to bed." Jaze looked him up and

down. "I'd recommend showering first."

"Phase in the shower," Nikki told Alex. She gave Jaze a warm smile. "You don't want a mess like the one we made at the Carso house."

Jaze nodded, but there was a hint of sadness in his eyes at the mention of the home he had shared with his mother and all of the werewolves they had rescued. "I wonder if the orange footprint is still in the hallway."

"We'll go see it again someday," she promised. "When it's safe."

Jaze slipped his hand into hers. "Yes, we will."

Chapter Thirteen

Alex rested his head against the tiles that made up the shower wall. He let the water run over his shoulder as it washed the dried blood from his skin. He was glad he had followed Nikki's advice to phase in the shower. Though the tiled floor had been slippery beneath his clawed feet, phasing had shed a lot of the dried blood onto the floor. It would have been a big mess to clean up in his room.

His shoulder ached. Prodding revealed that the wound had mostly closed, but it still bled enough that his fingers came back with blood on them. He sighed and turned, wincing as the water hit it more fully. Perhaps he should have listened to Meredith and gone to the medical wing to make sure there wasn't any debris left in the wound; but according to what he had learned from Nikki from her years serving as the Academy's medical director, as long as whatever was inside wasn't silver, the wound itself would push the contaminates free before closing.

His fingers revealed smaller wounds along his neck that had already closed. The one along his cheekbone didn't hurt anymore. Eventually, even the scar would fade to probably nothing.

Alex closed his eyes and let himself remember what had happened. He held Caitlyn in his jaws and was about to jump to the next ledge when the high-pitched whining buzz caught his attention. He heard Jaze's warning bark and ducked. He felt his shoulder be ripped apart when the missile struck the rock. The impact of the explosion threw him and Caitlyn backwards.

The whine of the missile repeated over and over in his mind until it sounded like the rush of the water from the showerhead. He slammed the handle down to turn it off. The slight buzz of the neon lights overhead took over. Alex put his hands over his ears and crouched in the shower, willing the sound to go away. He hated that he had been afraid. He hated the way his heart pounded and skipped beats at even the memory of the sound. He hated the sensation of falling through the air, and again heard Caitlyn's terrified cry before they hit the ground.

Alex grabbed the clothes Cassie had set out for him and pulled them on roughly. He ignored the way his shoulder throbbed at the treatment. He slammed his palm across the light switch hard enough to crack it. He winced when his shoulder protested.

"Alex, are you alright?" Cassie ran to meet him in the hallway.

Alex gave her a quick hug. "I'm fine, Cass. Thank you. I'll be back soon."

"Where are you going?" she asked in surprised.

"I told Jaze I'd be back down for Mouse's report," he lied.

She nodded, but he caught the hurt expression on her face before he left through the door. He shut it behind him harder than he intended.

He couldn't take it anymore. Being shot at, the helplessness, the fear in Caitlyn's voice, the hurt on Cassie's face; he couldn't take any of it any longer. He wanted to hit something, anything. His hands clenched into fists so hard his arms shook.

A hand caught his shoulder. "Why are you out here?"

"Get away from me," Alex growled. He shoved Boris against the wall so hard the Alpha's head dented the sheetrock.

"Calm down," Boris said, his eyes wide in surprise.

Alex couldn't remember if he had ever seen Boris

surprised before. He didn't care. Nothing mattered. None of it made sense anymore. He turned away and headed for the stairs.

Boris grabbed him by his good shoulder. "Slow down, Alex."

Alex's self-control vanished. He spun back around, grabbed the front of Boris' shirt, and pinned him against the wall. "Leave. Me. Alone." Alex said, forcing the words through his clenched teeth.

Boris lifted his hands. There was a touch of something in his eyes that caught Alex off-guard. He read shock along with the barest hint of compassion.

Alex realized he had just attacked an Alpha. By all accounts, he should be lying on the floor bloody or dead; yet, Boris was just watching him, waiting to see what he would do. The Alpha wasn't fighting back or defending himself.

Alex let out a slow breath. He lowered Boris down and took a step back. His chest heaved. Every-other beat of his heart was doubled as he fought to regain his control.

"I just wanted to know why you were out in the hallway instead of resting," Boris said in a steady voice.

Alex shook his head. He couldn't think of an answer because there wasn't one. He had flipped. He couldn't control himself anymore. He had to get out of the Academy.

He ran down the stairs. Every footstep sent a jolt of pain through his shoulder; the ache stole his breath.

"The dean doesn't want anyone leaving the Academy grounds," Boris called after him.

Alex shoved the door open with his shoulder. The sensation dropped him to his knees outside the door. He held onto his shoulder and fought back the tears.

The pain he felt exploded inside of him. It wasn't his shoulder. Physical pain didn't matter. He was doing nothing to defend himself. He was a sitting duck just waiting for Drogan to take another shot. He couldn't handle it anymore. He couldn't wait for Drogan to succeed with either him or Cassie.

Alex held his shoulder as he ran to the gate. He was about to open it when Boris' words echoed through his mind. Leaving the protection of the high Academy walls would be a direct violation of Jaze's orders. Up to that point, Alex had never blatantly disobeyed the werewolf who had taken them in. After all Jaze had done, obedience was the only thing Alex could give to repay him.

He paced along the wall. It felt like hours, as if his feet carved a path through the landscape. He looked down, almost expecting to see the grass worn away and dirt showing through; yet it remained green that was lightening as the sun rose in the early hours of morning. Dew covered his bare feet. His toes were dirty. He wondered if Cassie had left socks in the shower room and he had missed them. Knowing Cassie, she had even brought shoes because she knew him that well.

"Boris mentioned you were out here."

Jaze's voice startled Alex to the point that he spun with his hands up, ready to defend himself against Drogan.

Jaze didn't move. He merely nodded with a knowing light in his eyes that deflated Alex. "I know what you're going through."

"How could you?" Alex shouted. He punched the gate so hard the twisted metal rattled. The blow shook through his shoulder, reminding him as it stole his breath that it had been a very stupid thing to do.

His knees gave out and Jaze caught him. "Whoa, there. Take it easy." He lowered Alex to a seat on the grass with his back against the wall. "I think you've probably reached your limit."

"I think I reached it a long time ago," Alex mumbled. He hit his head back against the wall. "I just can't take it anymore."

"We'll find Drogan," Jaze promised. "I know it's slow, but there are so many werewolves and GPA agents out looking for him, I'm amazed he's lasted this long."

"What does he want from Cassie and me?" Alex asked. He met Jaze's gaze squarely without flinching. Grays didn't demand answers from Alphas, yet he had almost slammed a haymaker into Boris' jaw. Protocol had definitely fled out the window.

"I wish I knew," Jaze replied, meeting Alex's eyes. "If we knew, we could eliminate the problem and get rid of Drogan once and for all."

"Then let's find out. Let him take me."

Jaze stared at Alex. "That's being a little hasty."

"How else are we going to end this?" Alex asked. "He's not going to stop. He's proved that. Do we wait until one of us is dead?"

Jaze was silent for several minutes. He watched Alex, his gaze searching. The next time he spoke, he had made up his mind. "When I learned about all my uncle had done in killing off Alphas and attempting to take control of the werewolf packs, I was beside myself. I didn't know how to stop him." He gestured toward the Academy. "I didn't have all of this. It was just my mom and me." He swallowed, forcing down emotions. "So I found a way to fight back, and I built a team, a pack, around me that could fight at my side. I had to know that I wasn't alone. I needed to help others to help myself."

Alex rubbed his eyes with one hand. "So what do I do?" he asked; he hated the way his voice was so filled with despair.

"You help others," Jaze replied, rising.

Alex looked up; the dean held out a hand. "Come on."

Alex rose gingerly with the dean's help. Jaze led him back to the Academy without another word. Alex followed him down the hall to the hideout in the closet. The door buzzed when Jaze waved his thumb over the sensor in the middle. The room below was empty. Jaze didn't appear surprised to see it unmonitored.

"Brock mentioned that you found out about the rest of our surveillance capacity."

"You mean the bat cave? Yeah," Alex replied.

Jaze chuckled. "There aren't any bats down there." The dean crossed the room to a wall near the computers. "Open," he said simply. A panel sunk in and slid to the side.

"Is there an entrance from my room like that?" Alex asked, only half-kidding.

"There's one from the common room for each pack. I'll show you where they are if you take care that no one sees you using them," Jaze answered.

Alex stared at the dean's back as he followed the werewolf down a flight of stairs. "You mean you want me to come back here more than just now?"

Jaze looked at him. "How else are you going to help others?"

Something flamed to life in Alex's chest. He felt the slightest breath of relief, as if just the prospect of something to do in the fight against Drogan helped to relieve the pressure that had been building inside of him. He held onto the flicker of release, grasping it as if it was a lifeline.

"Ready, Brock?" Jaze asked.

Alex followed him around the corner to the huge surveillance cave. He couldn't help staring at the vast space before him. Even though he had seen it once before, it felt almost impossible to grasp the cavern that existed beneath the Academy. Cars, motorcycles, computers, tunnels, piles of equipment, and now a helicopter occupied the cement pads beneath Brock's seat in the midst of so many different screens Alex wondered how the human could keep it all straight.

To Alex's surprise, Brock wasn't alone. Another man stood next to him with the same spikey brown hair and slender build.

"Ready," Brock replied, standing as well. He smiled at Alex. "Alex, meet my cousin Caden. He's not a werewolf, but he makes up for it in his ability to shoot small things at large distances."

Caden walked down the stairs that led to the computers and held out a hand. "I'm a weapons specialist," Caden explained, rolling his eyes at the sandwich in Brock's hand. "At least it's better than a carbohydrate compost system."

Brock took a big bite and spoke around it. "You're just jealous you don't have my metabolism," he said.

"I do have your metabolism," Caden replied. "We're related, remember?"

"Then where's your sandwich?" Brock asked.

Jaze held up a hand. "Can we put the debate aside for a moment and get back to the sweep?"

"Sweep?" Alex asked.

Jaze smiled. "Ready for your first mission?"

Chapter Fourteen

Alex's heart pounded in his chest. He should have been in school, but instead, he was in an SUV with Jaze driving to the Haroldsburg suburbs where Drogan had last been spotted. Jaze had said it was doubtful that the Extremist leader would still be there, but any information they could glean from what he had left behind might be the means of saving other werewolves.

"You okay?" Jaze asked.

Alex nodded wordlessly.

Jaze smiled and nodded his head toward the street Mouse turned down. "Two more blocks over. We'll park in the driveway. Doing a sweep by," he checked his watch, "Ten in the morning doesn't exactly scream stealthy, so we'll give up any pretense of being where we don't belong and we own it."

Own it apparently meant three other werewolves dressed in black from head to toe barreling down the door and swarming the house when they arrived.

Alex followed Jaze. His senses screamed. He expected Drogan to pop out of every cupboard or door of the seemingly innocuous house.

"Take a breath," Jaze instructed quietly.

Alex stared at him in confusion.

Jaze removed the mask from his face and motioned for Alex to do the same. Alex held the cloth in his hands, attempting to keep his fingers from balling into fists in his anxiety.

"Breathe," Jaze said. The dean took a deep breath and let it out slowly. "Smell the air. No one has been here for at least a day. I smell Drogan; he was definitely here, but the scent is stale."

The smell made Alex want to bare his teeth, but Jaze's

assessment was right. According to Colleen's sense training, the sharper notes of Drogan's scent lingered, but the subtler whispers that came with activity like walking outside, eating food, or washing hands that made up a daily catalogue of a person's actions were gone. The tension in Alex's muscles eased.

"Clear," a werewolf called over the headset.

Alex was glad he had regained enough composure not to jump.

"Sweep the area. Let's see if Drogan's left us a trail," Jaze commanded.

Alex followed the dean from room to room. Jaze checked papers and searched through garbage cans. Alex was about to ask what they hoped to find when one of the men called over the headset, "Got something."

Mouse went immediately into the next room.

"What is it?" Jaze asked.

"Two phone numbers and a name," Mouse answered. "By the slant of the writing, they were written quickly."

"Good," Jaze replied. "Let's finish the sweep and head back."

Alex followed Jaze back to the SUV. With the adrenaline fading, his nerves were shot. He collapsed next to the dean in the vehicle.

"What'd you think?" Jaze asked.

Alex studied the house. "The fact that he was here gives me the creeps."

Jaze nodded. "Cameras will be set up, but Drogan's smart enough not to return to a place he's already used. That's why our surveillance has such a hard time catching him."

"Back to the bat cave?" Alex asked.

Jaze cracked a smile. "Yeah. We'll trace the numbers and name. Hopefully it'll give us the lead we're looking for.

Drogan's good at not leaving anything substantial behind, but this time he appeared to have left in a hurry. Perhaps he got sloppy."

Alex tipped his head back as Mouse started the vehicle. He dozed in and out on their way back to the Academy. He opened his eyes in time to see Mouse turn onto the train tracks he had ran beside many times. Mouse turned off almost instantly toward what appeared to be a rock wall that made up one side of the ridge. Alex let out a snort of amazement as the rocks fell to the side like the panel in the surveillance room and Mouse entered without slowing.

"This place just keeps getting better," Alex breathed.

Jaze chuckled and gave an approving nod. "Glad you like it."

"Do I get to go next time?" Alex was almost afraid to ask, but not knowing felt even harder. He was afraid to have it all taken away. He feared that Jaze had only invited him along because the dean knew the house was empty. If there was danger, he might not be able to go. But he needed it. The want to do more than sit by waiting for the shooter's accuracy to improve would drive him crazy.

"Of course," Jaze said, looking over at him. "You're in now. Just make smart decisions and try to keep up with school."

"I will," Alex promised. He fought back a smile, worried that too much enthusiasm would make Jaze second-guess his decision.

He climbed out of the SUV and breathed in the earthy, cool, metallic-tinged scent of the cavern. The prospect of the phone numbers and what they would find filled him with excitement.

Alex followed Brock up a path that led through the walls of the Academy. He could hear the students in the classrooms, and smiled at the fact that he was going to be able to help protect them and their families.

Alex wondered how Brock could make his way through the maze of paths as though he was able to see in the dark and smell the scents as good as a werewolf.

Brock pushed a panel open and motioned for Alex to step inside. Alex obeyed, and found himself next to the fireplace in Pack Jericho's common room.

"That's cool," Alex said.

Brock nodded. "It definitely makes keeping what you call the bat cave a secret."

Alex gave the human a tired grin. "As long as you don't have a meatball sandwich."

Brock laughed. "Yes. That's one I've had to keep in mind. You werewolves with your sharper senses make being sneaky with tasty food a bit more difficult."

"You've done a good job this far," Alex admitted.

Brock stepped back through the panel. "Get some sleep, Alex. You look like you need it."

Alex didn't have the strength to argue. He crossed to his room and was asleep before his head hit the pillow.

***

"Where have you been?"

Alex opened his eyes to see Kalia sitting on the floor with her back against the wall opposite from his bed.

"Uh, sleeping?" Alex said, rubbing his eyes.

"Is your shoulder feeling better?" Kalia asked.

Alex was surprised to realize he was using his injured arm without pain. He rolled it experimentally. "Yes, it is. It barely hurts," he said.

She gave a small smile. "Oh, to be a werewolf."

He sat up gingerly and pushed the hair out of his eyes. "Did you seriously just say that?"

"I was kidding," Kalia replied dryly. "You were just a target for a homicidal maniac. You think I want that?"

Alex nodded with mock severity.

Kalia rolled her eyes and pushed up to her feet. She headed for the door.

"Where are you going?" Alex asked, surprised by her sudden departure.

"I just wanted to make sure you were okay. Now that I know you are, I've got to get back to class." She gave him a level look. "Some of us actually have to go to school."

A thought occurred to Alex. "You missed me."

Kalia's mouth fell open. "Don't flatter yourself," she replied before storming to the door.

Alex stood up to go after her. The sudden movement made him lightheaded. He caught himself against the corner of the bed.

Kalia hurried back and ducked under his arm. "You're an idiot, Alex Davies. You know that?"

He nodded as she helped him sit down. "I was just going to class like you suggested."

She looked at him with her hands on her hips. "You stay there until morning. I don't want to hear of you moving from this spot."

Alex forced back the smile that threatened to cross his face. He watched her walk to the door. She hesitated and looked back at him as if certain he would be up again.

Something about the way her light blue gaze creased slightly at the corners made his heart jump.

"Stay there," she said.

"I will," Alex promised.

She disappeared through the door. He listened to her footsteps as she crossed the empty commons room and stepped into the hallway.

"Girls," Alex said quietly. He let his head rest against the pillow for a few minutes. Though he still felt lightheaded, his stomach growled, demanding to be filled.

"Kalia's going to kill me," Alex said aloud as he sat up again. For some reason, the thought made him smile. He rose to his feet slower this time and waited until his head stopped spinning. He took a few testing steps. He felt so much better than he had when he went to bed that he could barely believe it. His shoulder no longer ached, and even though he was tired, he felt almost normal.

Footsteps sounded down the hall and the door to his room opened before he could sit back down.

Cassie looked surprised to see him standing.

Alex froze midflight back to his bed. "I thought you were Kalia," he said.

"Why would Kalia be in here?" Cassie asked.

Alex shrugged sheepishly.

Cassie shook her head. "I was just coming to see if you wanted some lunch."

"I thought I missed it." Alex had completely lost track of

time. He looked around, but there was nothing to help him except the light that pooled through his window to create a rectangle on the soft beige carpet. Even Kalia had failed to mention what class she was hurrying to.

"It's just after two," Cassie explained. "Jaze asked Cook Jerald to keep a plate for you. He figured you'd be famished when you woke up."

Alex was grateful for the dean's foresight. "He was right."

"I'll bring it up," Cassie offered.

Alex shook his head. "I need to move around. I think it'd be good for me."

She looked him up and down worriedly. "Are you sure?"

"Trust me," Alex told his sister. "I know what I can do."

"I'm not so sure about that," she replied, but she sighed and led the way to the door.

"Shouldn't you be in English?" Alex asked as he followed his twin down the stairs.

"Grace won't mind if I'm late, especially if I tell her why."

Alex thought of Kalia's warning. "Don't mention that I went to eat."

Cassie looked at him with an expression that said she wondered if he had gone crazy. "Why not?"

Alex knew the look would only intensify if he explained. "Just don't, okay? Tell them you brought me the food or something."

Cassie looked completely baffled. "You want me to lie about where you ate your food?"

Alex shrugged. "I want you to not tell anyone that I left my room. It's not that difficult."

"Did you hit your head when you fell off that cliff?"

"Probably," Alex replied.

Cassie just shook her head and led the way to the Great Hall.

143

Alex sat down to wait while she went to get his food from the cook. He rested his elbows on the table. A thought occurred to him. Alex looked around, wondering where the secret entrance would be. He made a mental note to start exploring the passageways behind the walls so that he could learn them as well as Brock.

Chapter Fifteen

"Wake up, Alex."

Alex startled at the sight of red eyes peering down at him. He blinked, and realized it was Professor Kaynan.

"Are you coming or what?" Kaynan asked with a half-smile.

"Coming where?" Alex asked groggily.

"We tracked down the numbers," Kaynan replied.

Ice ran through Alex's veins. He sat up quickly and pulled on a shirt and socks without a word. Kaynan was already waiting in the common room when Alex reached it. The sound of snoring came from further down the hall. Don snorted and muttered in his sleeping before the sound of him rolling over drifted to them.

"What time is it?" Alex asked.

"About one-thirty." Kaynan replied, holding open the panel beside the fireplace.

Alex followed Kaynan inside. His wolven eyes adjusted easily to the sudden darkness. The soft fall of the professor's footsteps was the only sound in the tunnel that led below the Academy. "So the numbers lead to an address?" Alex asked.

Kaynan shook his head. "I wish it was that simple, and so does Mouse. The numbers led to a dead end. Burner phones. But Mouse was able to track down the purchase location, then pull up the credit card number used to buy the phones. The credit card had already been cancelled. However, Mouse worked his magic and was able to find an address behind the card."

"Let me guess," Alex said. "It was a dead end."

"Now you're getting it," Kaynan replied, throwing a smile over his shoulder. "Mouse's team didn't find anything at the address, but he did find a reference to a small business that used the address for a supply drop."

"What business?"

Kaynan grinned. "That's the ironic part. It's a silver refining company."

"Oh, great," Alex grumbled.

Kaynan huffed a laugh as he pushed open the panel to the small surveillance room below the closet. "Yeah, I know. You werewolves and your silver allergies."

"You're not allergic to silver?" Alex was amazed.

Kaynan shook his head. "One of perks of being made into a werewolf instead of born." His voice took on a forbidding tone. "Dark red fur, eyes that haunt even the bravest man's nightmares, and the ability to get shot by silver without dying."

"You've almost died a few times, need I remind you?" Jaze said from his seat at the table when they turned the corner. The rest of the professors were there waiting for them.

Kaynan shrugged. "So I figured Mouse's life was worth more than my measly existence. I don't see Lyra complaining."

Lyra shook her head, her blonde braids sliding across her shoulders. "I'm forever in your debt."

"You weren't even there," Kaynan pointed out.

"Yeah, but I wouldn't have my Mousy if it wasn't for you." She kissed Professor Mouse on the cheek.

Mouse's face turned red and he adjusted his glasses, but he didn't pull his hand out of his wife's grasp.

Alex didn't know how he felt about the professors' open displays of affection. Usually they were so quiet about their relationship. Both came across as shy and reserved, yet it was obvious by the smiles they exchanged that they were very happy with each other.

"Anyway, as I was saying," Kaynan continued, "The silver business happens to have a very well-known investor."

"Drogan," Alex guessed.

Kaynan nodded. "Correct. Now we're on our way to the last address Drogan used to collect his return on the investment. It's a solid lead."

"How's your shoulder?" Lyra asked.

Alex tested the range of motion. "Good. It barely hurts."

Lyra nodded. "The power of the moon is amazing."

Caden appeared from the panel that led down to the cavern. He carried a vast array of weapons.

"Weapons for the masses," the human said, passing them around. "We have your standard Glocks, a couple of Colts, and a Kahr PM9 with an extra clip for Lyra." Caden winked at her. "I included the tritium night sights. I think you might need them."

"You realize you're talking to a werewolf, right?" Brock asked, climbing through the panel after his cousin. "They can already see in the dark."

"It makes aiming easier," Caden argued. "That way she doesn't have to worry about sights and shooting and all that."

"You're probably just making her nervous," Brock pointed out.

"I'm really fine," Lyra said, accepting the small handgun.

Caden nodded. "See, she's fine. You don't have to worry." He grinned at Lyra. "And it's all because of the tritium night sights."

Brock rolled his eyes and Mouse chuckled. It was the first time Alex could ever recall hearing the quiet professor laugh.

"Oh, I almost forgot," Caden said. He took a gun from his pocket and set it on the table in front of Alex. "A Glock nine millimeter for the kid."

The professors immediately began to argue the decision.

Alex sat back as far away from the gun as he could get. It looked innocent enough, but getting shot definitely gave one a certain respect for firearms, kind-of like the way getting stung by a bee made one more cautious around them, only about a thousand times worse.

"I don't think that's necessary," Chet said from his seat near Jaze. "He has anger issues."

"Oh, *he* has anger issues?" Dray replied, his light eyebrows lifted.

"I don't think students should have guns at school," Lyra said. She gave Alex a warm smile. "No offense."

"I agree," Alex replied.

Kaynan was busy arguing with Colleen. "If he needs to defend himself, it could be necessary."

"But he's too young to be going anyway," Colleen pointed out, her violet gaze passionate.

"It's not as if he's going to kill anyone," Vance said.

Jaze stood. The professors immediately quieted. "Alex, pick up the gun," Jaze said in a level voice.

As much as Alex didn't want to, he knew Jaze had his best interest at heart. Alex picked up the Ruger. It felt heavier than he had expected, and the metal was cold. The touch of it sent a prickle along his arm.

Jaze leaned his hands on the table and looked at each professor in turn. "You know why Alex is here. You agreed that he should be included in our team."

"We didn't know..." Colleen began. At Jaze's searching look, she let out a breath and nodded. "We agreed."

"It's going to be dangerous. Alex knows the risks as much as any of us. He's bled for this cause." Jaze met Alex's gaze. "Are you ready?"

Alex looked at the gun in his hands. He took a steeling breath, then nodded. "I'm ready."

"Let's go."

At Jaze's words everyone stood. Alex fell in behind the dean as he led the way through the passage to the cavern below. To Alex's surprise, everyone filed into the huge helicopter near the southern wall. Mouse sat at the controls and pulled headset over his ears. Brock sat beside him and did the same.

"I told you a helicopter would be handy," Mouse said.

"Sure, rub it in," Kaynan replied into a headset as Alex took a seat next to him.

"How does the helicopter..." Alex's words dropped away when Mouse pushed a button.

The ceiling of the cavern above Alex split in two and lifted away from them. Mouse started the rotors. Jaze slid the door shut as the helicopter lifted into the air. They rose into the night sky. Alex leaned across Kaynan to see the greenhouses Dray was building. The path between them split neatly in two with the sidewalk on one side. The greenhouses stood elevated above Dray's gardens. As soon as the helicopter cleared the ground, Mouse pushed another button and the greenhouses slid around and lowered back into place.

"I'm not sure how that's going to affect the equilibrium of the plants," Dray said over the intercom.

Jaze laughed. "I think they'll survive."

"Last time we give Mouse free reign over the blueprints," Brock said.

Everyone laughed.

"We'll be there in fifty-four minutes," Mouse said quietly from the front seat.

The group quieted. All eyes turned to Jaze. He tipped his head to Brock. "What have we got?"

Brock spun in his seat as if he had been waiting for the question. He held up a small screen that showed the layout of a house.

"Heat surveillance reveals at least two-dozen individuals."

The small sounds of surprise that went up from the group let Alex know that the amount hadn't been expected.

Brock met Jaze's gaze. "I think this may be it."

Jaze nodded. He reached over and tapped Mouse on the shoulder. "Call the GPA and the Black Team. Have them meet us on the perimeter. We'll move in on my cue."

Mouse nodded. He switched his headset to a different channel. Alex could hear him relaying Jaze's words over the sound of the rotors.

He sat back in his seat. The ground raced by in dark patches below. Only the occasional road was visible now that they had left the city limits. He had no idea where they were going or what they would find. His heart began to race.

"Alex."

He looked up to see everyone watching him. "You okay?" Jaze asked. The dean's dark brown eyes studied him.

Alex nodded.

Jaze gave him a reassuring smile. "You'll be my shadow in there. Shoot only if absolutely necessary."

Chet slapped Alex's knee. "Don't worry. The rounds are loaded with sleeping agents. They won't kill if you don't shoot someone in the head." His gaze darkened. "The GPA has strictly forbidden us to start our own private war, a point I still feel we need to argue strongly."

"The bullets won't hurt anyone?" Alex asked, surprised.

Chet gave him a wry smile. "Oh, they hurt. Believe me." He tipped his head at Kaynan. "Right, Red?"

Kaynan lifted his teeth in a mock snarl. "Next time you aim that gun anywhere but at an Extremist, you'll be out for a week."

Chet winked at Alex. "I accidentally shot him on a

mission a few months ago and he hasn't let it go."

"You shot me in the butt," Kaynan replied. "It hurt like the devil and my leg was numb for weeks. Grace had to dig out the shell."

Chet winced dramatically. "My bad."

Kaynan grumbled something Alex couldn't make out over the intercom.

"Anyway," Chet said. "As I was explaining," he shot Kaynan a silencing look. "Shoot an attacker in the chest if you can. It'll knock him out immediately. Limbs take longer to have effect. If you shoot someone in the head, you probably will kill them because like Kaynan said, there is still a shell. It's thinner than the usual bullet, but has quite an impact."

"I'd be glad to demonstrate," Kaynan grumbled.

Mouse's voice came back over the intercom. "Agent Sullivan's on his way. The Black Team will be on their heels. ETA eighteen minutes."

"Thank you," Jaze said.

"Who's the Black Team?" Alex asked Kaynan. He forgot everyone could hear him over the intercom. When all of the professors looked at him, he tried to hide his embarrassment.

"The Black Team is my external werewolf task force," Jaze explained. "They're our backup in case things get out of control."

"If we're right about this location, things will definitely get out of control," Colleen said.

She didn't look the least bit concerned. In fact, to Alex, she appeared as if she was looking forward to the confrontation.

She met Alex's stare. A hint of red touched her cheeks as if she guessed his line of thought. "Sometimes it feels good to have the chance at a little payback. The General and Drogan have killed too many of our friends."

Everyone in the helicopter nodded in agreement. Silence fell. There was a camaraderie within the professors that Alex hadn't noticed before. They truly were a pack. They cared about each other and those they had lost, and they fought together for a common goal. Reassurance filled him at the fact that he had so many strong individuals ready to face Drogan with him.

Chapter Sixteen

The address led to a large cabin in the middle of a pine forest. Mouse set the helicopter down about a mile from their destination. The others were to meet them on the hike in. Lyra stayed at the helicopter to protect it in case Drogan's men located it.

"Be careful," Mouse said.

She nodded. "You, too."

She threw her arms around his neck and gave him a kiss at the last minute as if she couldn't help himself. "Be safe," she said.

"I will," Mouse promised.

He caught up to the rest of the group.

"Still got it, huh?" Kaynan asked.

Mouse's cheeks were red and he adjusted his glasses, but he didn't say anything in response to Kaynan's ribbing.

"Okay, let's focus," Jaze said. "The GPA and the Black Team will meet us at the perimeter. Kaynan, Chet, take the lead. Dray sweep right and Colleen take left."

Everyone fell into their places and the group took off at a fast walk, their senses alert.

"Where's Vance?" Alex asked Jaze quietly.

The dean kept his gaze on the trees. "Watching over the Academy. We never leave it unprotected." He shot Alex a smile. "Though he had some words about staying behind."

It wasn't hard to imagine the huge werewolf's frustrated rant; Alex had experienced plenty of those during gym class. "Who's the GPA?"

"The Global Protection Agency," Jaze answered. "They've been our allies throughout the genocide, helping us free werewolves and get them into hiding."

That surprised Alex. "But I thought the government was

on the Extremists' side."

Jaze shook his head. "Don't believe everything you hear. There are good and bad guys on every side. Not everyone out there wants werewolves eradicated. It's just that some organizations have to act more quietly than others. We still have friends." His gaze tightened. "Just a lot fewer than we thought when we started out." He fell quiet.

Alex followed in silence. He concentrated on walking the way Rafe had taught him so that no sound alerted their enemies of their approach. He noticed that all of the professors did the same. It was strange and surreal to see them out of the Academy. It was as if the title of professor fell away, and all around him were warriors ready for battle. Each held their weapon as though ready to use it.

Kaynan had his wristband off. The metal was straight and the blade glinted in the moonlight that filtered beneath the trees. Though Alex's heart thundered at the thought of the unknown that lay ahead of them, a surge of anticipation raced through his veins. He was finally able to fight back, to help others, and to stop Drogan from waging his war of death and destruction on the werewolf race.

"We have no indication that Drogan will be there," Jaze said softly. "But if this is really one of his houses, I want you to be prepared for what we might find. Drogan hates werewolves, and does everything he can to make life unbearable for those he finds. It might not be pleasant."

The thought made Alex's stomach clench. "I'll do whatever I need to," he answered.

Jaze nodded. "I know you will."

The pride in Jaze's tone filled Alex with reassurance. He was about to reply when Chet held up a hand. Everyone held perfectly still. A few seconds later, forms dressed in black appeared from the trees around them. The breeze carried their werewolf scent to Alex's nose. He glanced at Jaze. The werewolf leader motioned them forward without a word. The Black Team fell in around Jaze's pack. If they questioned Alex's presence, no one said anything.

The house was visible through the trees. Two windows showed lights while the rest were black rectangles against the midnight surroundings. Alex could see forms standing on either side of the porch. Brock crouched behind a low-sweeping pine and pulled out the screen. The Black Team and Jaze's pack stepped closer. Jaze pointed to the upper level of the huge cabin and indicated the Black Team. They nodded and faded back between the trees.

Brock handed Jaze something. He slipped it into his ear. "We're ready," he whispered.

"We're in position," a voice on the other end replied.

Jaze gave a quick, swirling signal with his finger and the werewolves moved out.

Alex crouched low behind Jaze. The rest of the professors had split up between the trees. It felt like he and Jaze were the only two in existence, creeping up on the house to take it on by themselves. He held the gun tight in his right hand. Chet had shown him how to take off the safety. The werewolf said that was all he needed to know. Alex felt like he probably needed to know a whole lot more.

Jaze paused at the edge of the tree line. Nothing moved; not even a breath of wind stirred the trees around them. The sentries on the porch were motionless. Only the glint of starlight against the guns in their hands reminded Alex of the threat they posed. He knew their bullets wouldn't be filled with sleeping agents.

Jaze held something above his head. He clicked it on, then off. The small light shone across the clearing. Jaze paused, and did it again. A sentry turned his head toward the light. Two dark forms broke from the trees and reached the porch before the guards noticed them. One tried to shout. Two small pops sounded as Kaynan reached the end guard and covered his mouth. Both sentries fell to the ground.

Jaze crossed the lawn at a run. Alex was unprepared for his sudden movement and was slow to start, but he reached the dean before Jaze was at the porch. Jaze put two hands on the top rail and leaped the railing without slowing. He landed soundlessly on the porch next to Kaynan and Colleen. The dean turned and caught Alex's hand; he pulled Alex over effortlessly.

Kaynan was already at the door. He worked the lock for a moment. It gave a quiet click and the door swung inward. At Jaze's motion, everyone hurried inside.

The lights went out. Alex wondered who had cut the power. Sounds could be heard on the second floor. The Black Team had made their entrance. Jaze's pack split up as if they had done the same thing a million times. Alex stayed close to Jaze. He heard yells from above followed by three gunshots. Someone cried out. Alex hoped it wasn't one of their team.

Jaze began systematically checking the rooms. The cabin was huge. Branching off from the living room where they entered were two separate halls. One led to the kitchen and a dining area while the other led to bedrooms. Jaze motioned for Alex to stay to the side and he opened the first door.

A man fired in the darkness. Jaze ducked inside. A scuffle sounded, then a thud. Alex peaked in just as Jaze came back out. The dean looked barely ruffled as he went to the next room. A similar scuffle followed. Alex was about to look inside when movement caught the corner of his eye.

He straightened up and his heart froze at the sight of two men running down the hall toward him. One was lifting a gun. The scar from the bullet wound in Alex's thigh throbbed angrily in remembered pain. Alex knew he was about to be shot.

Without even knowing he was doing it, Alex lifted his gun and fired two bullets. Both men halted. The one who had been about to shoot him tried to raise his gun again, then his legs gave out. Jaze reached the door just as both men fell motionless to the ground.

The dean gave Alex a short nod. Pride filled Alex's chest at the respect in Jaze's eyes. Alex knew if he hadn't been there, Jaze might have been shot. He followed Jaze down the hall and kept an eye on both ends as Jaze took care of the men inside the bedrooms.

Jaze and Alex reached the end of the hall and circled back to the kitchen. Colleen and Dray were already there.

Jaze touched a finger to his earpiece. "We have four caged Oscars in rooms two, three, five, and six."

"Got it," the voice on the other end replied.

Colleen and Dray exchanged a glance.

"What's an Oscar?" Alex asked in the quietest whisper he could manage.

"The objective," Dray replied in a hushed voice. "Werewolves."

Jaze led them down the hall. They found Chet and Kaynan near the stairs. Kaynan held up four fingers; Chet held up another three.

"Seven more in the basement," Jaze said into his earpiece.

"Got it," the voice replied.

Alex's mind reeled at the thought of eleven werewolves in cages in the house.

"It's clear down there," Kaynan said. "We took half a dozen men down. No sign of the General or Drogan."

"Do a final sweep. Free the werewolves. We'll meet you

on the porch," Jaze instructed.

He hurried back up the stairs with Alex close behind. Colleen and Dray met them in the kitchen. Several werewolves Alex didn't recognize huddled behind the pair. They looked beaten and exhausted.

"Agent Sullivan's bringing the vans. Take them out front."

Jaze and Alex were about to head up the next flight of stairs when Mouse came running in.

"It's wired to—"

"It's wired to blow." The voice that repeated Mouse's frantic statement sent a chill rushing down Alex's spine. He searched the ceiling for the source. An intercom next to a small camera sounded again. "Leave the boy, Jaze. You can have the rest of the werewolves, but leave him or I'll blow the place with your entire team inside," Drogan said in a tone that left no doubt he would do exactly as he promised.

Jaze glared at the camera. "You know that's not going to happen."

"I can get the boy one way or another," Drogan replied. "While I relish the thought of bringing down your crew after all the trouble you've given me, I need to know for sure that Alex is dead. Either you do it yourself while I watch, or you leave him and let me finish the job. Digging through debris promises to be a messy business, especially if I have to sort through all of your bodies to do it."

Alex felt numb. The sound of Drogan's voice and what he was asking stole Alex's ability to move or think. To him, there was only one choice.

"Go," he said.

Jaze stared at Alex. Emotions ran through the dean's gaze so quickly Alex couldn't catch them. He could hear the werewolves behind Colleen and Dray drawing in ragged breaths. They had just been given freedom only to have their death presented to them. He couldn't let that happen.

"I'll stay," Alex continued. "Get them to safety."

Jaze's jaw clenched. He looked from the fifteen-year-old werewolf to Mouse. Jaze gave the barest nod. Mouse's gaze flicked to Dray. Dray glanced down the stairs.

"Why are you waiting around like helpless idiots," Kaynan yelled in a voice Alex barely recognized. The professor burst up the stairs and tackled Dray around the waist, shoving him back into the other werewolves.

In the chaos, Mouse disappeared. Alex was watching the brawl with his heart in his throat, then glanced over to see the absence space the small professor had occupied. He couldn't understand what was happening.

"You've got to go," he said urgently to Jaze. "Get them out of here."

"Shape up," Jaze barked.

Kaynan and Dray stood. Both looked sheepishly at Jaze.

"We have a decision to make," Jaze said, avoiding looking at Alex.

"You better make it..." Fuzz took over the sound from the intercom.

"We only have a few minutes," Jaze told them. "Get everyone out now." He put a hand to his earpiece, then dropped it again. "I forget this thing doesn't work. Colleen, Kaynan, get the Black Team and any werewolves they found out of here. Kaynan, take your group out front to Agent Sullivan. Mouse's block won't hold forever. We need to get as much distance between ourselves and this house as we can."

"Got it," the others replied. They burst into action.

Jaze ran back down the hallway. Alex followed close behind. A man dressed in a black suit left the second room with a pair of bolt cutters. Werewolves followed close behind him.

Jaze and the man shook hands.

"We have five minutes, Agent Sullivan," Jaze said.

"That's all we need," the agent replied.

Alex smelled that the man was human.

Jaze held open the door and motioned the werewolves out. Alex followed them to the vans that took up the cabin's substantial driveway. Werewolves that had been freed piled inside. One werewolf, a young man a few years older than Alex, met his gaze. There was such pain in the haunted depths of the werewolf's eyes that Alex could barely breathe until the young man looked away.

"Where are they taking them?" Alex asked when the van door slid shut.

"Our safe houses," Jaze replied.

He put a hand to his ear. Static was crackling in it.

"Let's move!" Jaze shouted.

Jaze's pack hurried out the front door. The members of the Black Team followed directly behind. Five more werewolves were escorted to the last van. The vehicles began to pull away.

"Come on, Alex!" Jaze commanded.

Alex realized he was standing on the driveway watching the retreating vehicles. The rest of Jaze's pack was heading toward the tree line. The Black Team was nowhere to be found.

"Check," Jaze heard the voice say in the dean's earpiece.

Jaze's eyes widened. "Run!" he yelled.

Explosions sounded from inside the house. Jaze ran behind Alex as he dashed to the tree line. Alex knew he was faster as a wolf. He tore off his shirt and phased midstride. His paws hit the ground. He galloped to the trees and ducked beneath the brush just as a huge explosion shook the earth.

Jaze's black wolf form ghosted at his side. The dean took over, leading them slightly south back toward the helicopter.

When they reached the clearing, the blades were already spinning. Kaynan stood just inside the helicopter also in wolf form.

"Jump," Chet yelled.

Alex gathered his legs beneath him and leaped. He landed inside the chopper and slid over just as Jaze landed next to him. Mouse looked over his shoulder.

"Good to go," Lyra called.

Mouse lifted the helicopter into the air.

Chapter Seventeen

"Alex, get Chet to the medical wing," Jaze said as soon as Alex had on the clothes Brock had given him.

"Chet was shot?" Alex asked in surprise.

"It's just a graze," the black-haired Alpha argued. He took his hand away from the wound across the top of his shoulder. It dripped down the front of his shirt.

"Just the same, have Meredith check it out and clear you." He gave Chet a serious look. "That's an order."

Chet blew out a frustrated breath and nodded. He followed Alex up the stairs to the pathway.

"I'm not sure why he's having you go. You're the foolhardy one who wanted to die back there for the rest of us," Chet grumbled.

Alex glanced back at him. "You think Jaze is mad about that?"

Chet shrugged, then winced. "I'm mad about it. You're a kid with your whole life ahead of you. Let one of us worn out grumps die instead."

"Drogan didn't ask for you," Alex replied.

Silence answered the statement. Alex took the next left and led the way up the long ramp. They arrived at the panel where Alex had first found the underground cavern. He put his hands to it and it slid open.

Meredith was already waiting next to a bed and a table of instruments. Relief filled her eyes when she saw Alex.

"Mouse called up," she explained at his surprised expression.

"I can't believe he woke you up for this," Chet grumbled. He shook his head and took a seat where Meredith indicated.

"Oh, I wasn't asleep," Meredith replied. "I couldn't sleep while you guys were out risking your lives. I wanted to make

162

sure someone was here if medical attention was needed." She gave them both a warm smile.

"Well, thank you," Chet said with slightly less frustration. "It's really not that bad."

Meredith pulled back the collar of his shirt to reveal a deep gash across the werewolf's shoulder. "It's not healing yet. Looks like you have some silver in it. Jaze was right to send you up. Take off your shirt."

Chet did as he was told. He dropped the shirt on the floor and stretched his arm as though it pained him.

"Want to help?" Meredith asked.

Alex glanced at Chet. "Uh, okay," he said, uncertain he wanted to deal with the Alpha's anger.

"It's alright," Meredith reassured him. "He won't bite."

"I might," Chet replied sullenly.

She handed Alex a small tray with swabs on it. She then took one of the swabs and a pair of tweezers. Alex watched as she searched carefully through the wound. The fact that it was still gaping and hadn't started healing said she was right about the silver shards. A few seconds later, she pulled out a tiny sliver.

"Meredith, have you seen..." Cassie's voice died away when she saw Alex and Chet. "What is going on?" she asked.

The two werewolves exchanged a glance. "Uh, well, it's not what it looks like," Alex said.

Cassie put her hands on her hips. "It looks like you went off with Jaze and Chet on some sort of mission and got shot at."

Alex tried not to smile because he knew it would make her even more furious. "Okay; it's exactly what it looks like."

"How could you, Alex?" she demanded. "I've been so worried about you with Drogan's attacks, and now you have to go off trying to get yourself killed?"

"It wasn't like that," Alex protested.

Meredith took the tray from his hand. "I've got this," she said quietly. "Go talk to your sister."

"I really don't want to," Alex replied under his breath.

Meredith motioned with the swab. He sighed and followed Cassie out the door.

Cassie turned around after they reached the end of the hall. Alex was surprised to see tears in her eyes. "Seriously, Alex, why do you have such a death wish?"

"I don't," Alex told her, but the fire had left him at the sight of her hurt expression. He sat down on the stairs and motioned for her to take a seat next to him.

She did, but scooted to the far side of the stairway. "I can't take it, Alex. I worry about you so much. You have no idea."

"I have some idea," Alex replied quietly. He glanced sideways at her. "My biggest fear is that if we don't stop Drogan, he's going to get you. I'm not going to fail you, Cass."

She rested her chin in her hand. "But you're not careful. If the same thing happens to you, think of where I'll be. We're all we've got."

Alex shook his head. "That's not true. We have Aunt Meredith, Jaze, Nikki, and baby William. We have the Academy. We have a lot to live for."

"Then why risk it?" Cassie asked in a voice just above a whisper.

Alex leaned his head against the railing. "Because if I don't do something, I'm going to go crazy. I can't sit around being a target waiting for Drogan to get lucky."

"So you went after him?"

The pain in Cassie's voice made Alex's throat tighten. He shook his head. "I went with Jaze to free werewolves. He said when he felt the same way I did, the only way he could get over it was to help himself by helping others. It felt good, Cass." He met her gaze, hoping she would understand. "Freeing them made it easier because I'm doing something, really something, that is helping other werewolves and defeating Drogan at the same time. I'm fighting back."

"But what if you leave me alone?" Cassie asked in a voice so soft he barely heard it.

Alex let out a breath. "You're not alone, Cass. You have Tennison."

Her head lifted and she met his gaze. Her eyes said that everyone had been right. She loved Tennison. "Alex."

He gave her a small smile. "It's alright. As long as he takes care of you. He knows your twin brother will throw him off that cliff if he ever does anything to hurt you, right?"

She nodded with a smile of her own. "Right. But he's so sweet to me."

"He better be," Alex replied.

"He is," Cassie reassured him.

"Get some sleep so you can heal," they heard Meredith say from down the hall.

"I will," Chet replied. He walked out of the medical wing looking somewhat less grumpy than when they had entered. He spotted the twins and lifted his good arm. "Thanks, Alex. Have a good night." He glanced out the window at the rising sun. "What's left of it."

"You, too," Alex replied.

"Goodnight," Cassie said.

Chet smiled at her and disappeared down the professors' hallway.

Meredith poked her head out of the doorway to the medical wing. "You guys okay?"

Alex nodded, but Cassie shook her head. "Alex is an

idiot," she said.

Alex tried not to let her words bother him, but coming from his sister, they cut straight to the core.

Meredith read it on his face. "You guys better come back here."

The twins walked sullenly to the medical wing. Meredith led them to a room they hadn't visited before. It had couches and a refrigerator.

"This is where we take breaks if things get stressful," Meredith explained.

"Fitting," Alex said quietly.

Meredith surprised him by giving them both a hug. When she stepped back, her eyes glittered with tears as she smiled down at them. "I know how Cassie feels, Alex. I felt the same way the entire time you were gone."

"You did?" Alex asked softly.

She nodded. "Of course I did. You're my family. I couldn't bear to lose you after all we've gone through." She took a shuddering breath. "When I found out you were both still alive after everything, it was like I was given my heart back. Seeing you with Rafe in the forest felt like a dream. I couldn't believe...I didn't dare believe that it was true, that you were really safe."

"That's how we felt when Jaze told us who you were," Cassie told her. There were tears in his sister's eyes, but Alex was glad to see the smile on her face. She had been through so much. He didn't want her to cry anymore.

He nodded. "We lost everyone, or we thought we had. Finding out you were our aunt took away the fact that we were orphans. We had somebody."

Tears rolled down Meredith's face. "I have somebody too, now. You two are my everything."

Cassie gave her a tight hug.

Alex followed. "I was careful," he said. He ducked away and sat on one of the couches. He needed them to understand. "I can't stop helping Jaze." Cassie looked like she wanted to argue, but when she met Alex's eyes, she fell silent. "I can't help it. I need to go with him. I need to free werewolves and do what I can to stop Drogan and the General. If I don't, I'm going to go crazy."

"You're already crazy," Cassie said, but her words were tempered with a small smile as if she was trying to understand.

Alex nodded. "I know. Sometimes I feel so pent up that I'm going to explode if I don't do something. Going with Jaze to free Drogan's prisoners helped with that, even if it was dangerous."

"Maybe because it was dangerous," Meredith said, taking a seat next to Cassie. At the twins' stares, she lifted her shoulders in a small shrug. "When Mindi and Will moved away, I had no one. I didn't dare follow because I didn't want them to be found. It felt like someone was watching me all the time. I got paranoid and careless because I got tired of living like that. I left the city and moved around, but I couldn't shake the feeling." Her voice tightened. "Then I got caught."

Alex sat up straighter. "Who caught you?"

She shook her head. Dark shadows passed through her light blue eyes, memories that made a shiver run down her spine. She pursed her lips tight, unwilling to let them free. "It doesn't matter now," she said quietly, pushing the emotions away. "What matters is that we're here, together. We may have been through a lot, but we're not alone, any of us." She held out her hand. "We're a team, now."

"A pack," Cassie said, setting her hand on top of Meredith's.

Alex smiled. "A pack," he agreed, putting his hand on his sister's.

Meredith nodded. "And a family. Alex, we're going to worry about you." Her gaze was frank and honest. "You can't ask us not to. We care about you, and so we'll always worry when you're gone."

He opened his mouth to protest, but she cut him off with a shake of her head.

"But we won't ask you not to go." She looked at Cassie. "We'll try our best to understand and not hold you back."

Cassie nodded a bit reluctantly. She let out a small breath and looked at her brother. "Just be careful. I know the risks you take here."

"It's different out there," Alex told her. "Everyone's careful. Jaze sees to it. You should see them work. It's like a machine. Everyone knows where to go and what to do. Each person has a place."

"You do, too?" Cassie asked, her eyebrows pulled together with worry.

Alex thought of taking down the two men in the hallway. He had saved Jaze from getting shot. He nodded. "Me, too. Jaze needs me." The last sentence made him smile just a bit. Knowing he had a place calmed the agitation in his chest. He was making a difference.

"Just be careful," Cassie made him promise. "And stay away from guns. I don't need my brother getting shot again."

"I'll be careful," he said. He made sure not to agree to the gun part because he had already broken it. If Meredith and Cassie knew, they would probably petition Jaze to keep him from leaving the Academy ever again.

Meredith went to the refrigerator and brought back three bottles of orange juice. "It's almost breakfast time," she said with a warm smile. "Want to go eat together?"

Alex nodded even though the only thing he wanted to do was collapse onto his bed and sleep. He followed them wearily into the hall.

Tennison stood from where he had been leaning against the wall near the stairs. The lanky werewolf's pale eyes lit up at the sight of Cassie. She ran over to him and slipped her arm through his.

"I wasn't trying to pry," Tennison explained. "I just thought you might be getting hungry."

"You're right," Meredith said.

Tennison gave Alex a searching look. "Are you okay, Alex? You look exhausted."

"I'm fine," Alex replied, though he could barely keep his eyes open.

"Have you been up all night?" Tennison asked.

Alex pushed down his surprise at the werewolf's questioning. Apparently being a relationship with the Second's sister gave him stronger footing. "I have," he admitted.

"You should probably get some sleep," Tennison replied. "You look like you're about to fall over. We can bring you up some breakfast if you'd like."

"I, uh." Alex was caught off-guard by the werewolf's concern. "Um, okay?" he said as more of a question than an answer.

Tennison nodded as if everything was decided. He sniffed the air. "Smells like waffles or pancakes today. Have a preference?"

"Um, waffles," Alex replied, trying to regain his bearings.

"And scrambled eggs," Cassie told Tennison. "He likes cheese on them."

"Waffles and cheesy scrambled eggs." Tennison nodded. "Got it. Get some sleep, Alex."

The trio left Alex standing by the stairs wondering what had just happened. Part of him was grateful for the chance to sleep while the other was still trying to catch up with everything he had experienced in the past few hours.

Meredith looked back at him when they reached the door to the Great Hall. She lifted a hand with a warm smile on her face as if she guessed his confusion.

Alex waved back and started wearily up the stairs, still trying to figure out what had just transpired.

Chapter Eighteen

The chill that cut through the air made Alex glad he was in wolf form. The cold breeze couldn't get beneath his dense undercoat. He glanced back at Kalia. She pushed her way through the trees after the pack looking miserable. She pulled her white coat closer around her body. Her face was barely visible through the fur-lined hood and the light blue scarf that set off her eyes like shards of ice amid the white world around them.

Cassie padded next to Kalia. Her big paws allowed her to walk over the snow while Kalia had to struggle with each step. Sympathy filled Alex's chest. He allowed the rest of Pack Jericho and Pack Torin to pass him while he waited for Cassie and Kalia to catch up. Caitlyn pranced at Cassie's side, her white fur nearly blending in with the snowy landscape. Tennison walked behind the trio, his gray coat a dark shadow as he followed in their wake.

With the coming of winter and the restlessness of the students, Jaze couldn't keep them inside the walls any longer. The greenhouses had been completed, and there wasn't enough plant identification in the winter for Dray to keep them occupied. Jaze had reluctantly agreed to continue sense training with Colleen as long as they brought additional protection with them.

Professor Gem loped along the perimeter of the packs, her light gray coat easy to identify with its black stripes. Dray ran next to her, racing his wife as they enjoyed the chance to stretch their legs outside the Academy. Kaynan and Grace ran on the other side. Grace's small gray shoulder brushed Kaynan's huge dark red one as they traveled. Somehow, it allowed the blind werewolf to see as they loped across the ground at speeds she otherwise wouldn't have been able to meet without her husband.

The werewolves gathered around the cave Colleen and Rafe used as a go-between from their home further in the forest. Rafe's wolves already lounged around the cave. Alex sat down near them. Kalia hung back, eyeing the wild wolves nervously.

Colleen came out of the cave in her human form dressed in warm clothes. "Okay, class. Today we're going to learn scents associated with tracking in the snow. As you know, many of the animals we've become accustomed to in the summer vanish in the winter, and a variety of creatures with affinity to the snow take their place. Migratory paths..."

Alex's attention drifted. He watched Kalia lean against a tree and cross her arms. A second later, a clump of snow fell from the branches and landed on her head. She stomped angrily and shook her head in an attempt to dislodge the snow from her white-blonde hair. The werewolves ignored her as they concentrated on Colleen's lesson.

Kalia looked completely out of her element. She wasn't able to phase to wolf form, so the lesson didn't apply to her, but Jaze had asked her to accompany her class in case she ever did phase. His suggestion had riled her to the point that she glared at anyone who dared to look her way. Even Colleen pointedly gave Kalia space as she taught.

Kalia brushed the last of the snow from her hair, then shoved her hands into her fur-lined pockets and stomped away. Everyone let her go. They were deep in the forest and activity from Drogan and the General had quieted enough that it was no longer a huge concern, at least for someone who wasn't Alex or Cassie.

Cassie was occupied entertaining Caitlyn who had a hard time concentrating on Colleen's lesson with the fun of snow filling the clearing. The little wolf stuck her head into a drift, then pulled it back out. Snow covered her nose and eyelashes. Cassie gave a snort of laughter. Caitlyn wiped her head against Cassie's side.

A few minutes later, a tingle ran down Alex's spine. He rose soundlessly, his thoughts still on the path Kalia had taken. She couldn't have gone far. Even Kaynan and Mouse didn't appear too concerned. Kaynan nodded at Alex as he passed; he and Grace turned their attention back to Colleen. Alex padded softly down the trail Kalia had left.

She was apparently making her way back to the Academy. Deep boot prints showed where she had stumbled off their path into snow drifts. He imagined her muttering about the ridiculousness of a class in the middle of the forest at the beginning of November. Her honey and clover scent clung to the snow and the trees she had touched.

Alex's ear caught a faint sound. He paused with one paw in the air. He scented the breeze, but it was blowing in the opposite direction than he needed. His senses strained and his ears perked forward as he attempted to hear it again.

There it was. A tremor ran down his limbs at the shuffle and grunt. Two heartbeats later, Kalia screamed.

"Alex!"

He was already running. His paws barely touched the ground before they lifted again. He flew over a log and rounded the bend where the trees were so close they obscured any sight beyond. He burst into the small clearing near the partially frozen stream.

Kalia's face was white and eyes wide as she stared at the massive grizzly bear. A half-eaten fish lay at its feet. She must have startled the bear in the middle of its lunch when she reached the clearing. The grizzly rose onto its back legs and let out a roar. The anger in its beady eyes was unmistakable. It was a hungry animal, trying to finish what might be a final meal before hibernating, and the small human had interfered. The bear dropped back down with a massive thump and charged.

Alex was between the bear and Kalia in an instant. A growl tore from his throat so loud the bear slowed in its charge. It stared from Alex to Kalia. Alex could smell the sharp, mossy scent of the fish behind it. He willed the bear to go back to its meal and forget them.

The bear let out a deafening roar. Kalia gave a little cry of fear behind Alex.

Alex took a step forward, his gaze locked on the bear. Every inch of his fur stood up. His teeth were bared, his eyes unflinching. He growled again, softer this time.

The bear didn't move.

Alex's heart pounded. A hum sounded in his ears. He willed the bear to listen. He knew he didn't have a chance against a hungry grizzly, but there was no way he would back down with Kalia's life on the line. That was never a choice.

He took another step forward. His paw crunched in the crust that had formed along the top of the snow from the repeated heating and cooling of the tempestuous winter days. The bear grunted, its shovel face swaying from side to side. The massive hump above its shoulders moved back and forth as it picked up its paws.

Alex couldn't tell if it was about to charge or retreat. He hoped the animal had the sense not to attack a wolf and risk possible wounding before seeking its den for the long winter's rest. He hoped the scent of fish would lure it back.

The bear gave another grunt. Alex answered with a snarl. There was no way the bear was going to get past him.

The bear swung its massive head around and ambled with its great, rolling walk back to the half-eaten fish. It scooped the meal up and swallowed the fish down in one gulp before continuing its trek along the stream.

He heard Kalia fall to her knees. In seconds, Cassie was there. Kalia threw her arms around Cassie's light gray form and cried into her fur. Cassie gave Alex a searching look. He lowered his head and raised it again, indicating that he was alright. She closed her eyes for a brief second in gratitude.

A quiet huff caught Alex's attention. A glance to his left showed the entire class on the edge of the clearing. Professors Grace and Kaynan stood at one end with Professors Dray and Gem on the other. Colleen and Rafe watched from the middle. Alex knew he couldn't have stopped the bear if the animal had chosen to charge, but it was reassuring to know that he wouldn't have been the only one to try. More than a dozen wolves might have given the animal a reason to second-guess such a foolhardy decision. At least Kalia might have survived.

***

"You realize that was a grizzly bear, right?"

Alex glanced at Kalia.

They sat on the floor of his room, their backs to the walls opposite each other. The rest of the school day had gone by in a blur. Whenever Alex thought of the encounter, a thrill of excitement and fear ran down his spine. Kalia might have been attacked; he might have been killed. For the remainder of classes, everyone was talking about the bear.

He heard Terith say, "Did you see Alex face down that grizzly? It was the size of a house!"

Her brother Trent replied, "Its paw was bigger than his head. He would have died for sure."

The only thing Cassie had said when they got back to the Academy was that it was the most foolish thing she had ever seen him do, but she was glad he was brave enough to save Kalia. No one had any doubts what would have happened to Kalia if Alex hadn't been there.

"I knew it was a grizzly," Alex answered quietly.

He had to look away from her gaze. She kept searching his face as if wondering why he would do such a thing. There was a hint of uncertainty in her eyes. He knew she thought he was crazy. The way she was looking at him, it felt like she could see his soul. He rubbed a hand across his eyes. She didn't want to see what he buried deep inside.

"Why would you do that?" It wasn't an accusation; it was said with wonder. "Why would anyone?"

"Cassie calls it my death wish," Alex admitted.

Kalia tipped her head to one side; he could feel her gaze on him. "That does make sense with all you've been through."

He shook his head. "It's not like I want to die." He

hesitated, trying to explain how he felt. He was at a loss until he remembered Jaze's words. "It's as if in helping others, I find myself."

She nodded slowly. He looked at her, wondering if she truly understood. "Sometimes I feel like I don't exist."

His heart gave a little backflip. "Exactly. I feel like I'm just floating, just surviving, until either Drogan or one of the other freak accidents around here succeed in destroying me altogether. But when I'm with Jaze trying to save werewolves, or with you and the bear..."

"You feel like you're real," Kalia said softly.

Alex nodded.

"You help Jaze rescue werewolves?"

Alex nodded again. He knew he probably shouldn't have said it, but it was true, and in that moment, he felt like he couldn't hide anything from Kalia.

"Is it scary?"

"Sometimes," Alex admitted. "Sometimes it's horrible. The things Drogan and the General do to werewolves are completely wrong. That's why I help. I can make a difference, helping to get werewolves out of their clutches." His voice quieted. "I can avenge my parents and Jet, if only a little bit."

"I'll bet they're proud of you," Kalia said.

Her words gripped Alex's heart. He watched her, willing himself to believe what she said, daring to accept it as truth. "You think so?"

She nodded. "I'm proud of you."

Tears burned in his eyes. He gritted his teeth and glared at his knees that were bent in front of his chest, willing himself to maintain composure.

Before he knew it, she was by his side with an arm around his shoulders. "It's okay to cry," she whispered.

He shook his head, but the tears were already falling. He

inhaled a breath, trying not to let it burst into a sob.

"They see everything you do," she said, her voice gentle. "They know how hard you try."

"H-how do you know?" he asked.

"You can feel it," she breathed. "Close your eyes."

When he didn't listen, she repeated herself. "Close your eyes, Alex. You have to trust me."

His defiant heart gave a little stutter. His breath caught in his throat. "Why should I trust you?" he whispered.

"Because I trust you," she replied as softly.

He inhaled her clover and honey scent as he closed his eyes. For a moment, he was painfully aware of her arm around his shoulders, of the brush of her hair across his neck, and of the soft sound of her breath near his ear.

"Let yourself accept that they are proud of you," she said.

He didn't want to. He had put up the walls so firmly, yet they were crumbling with every word Kalia said. Hiding from the pain had been the only way to exist. Pretending he didn't care if he and Cassie were alone, telling himself it didn't matter that their home was an Academy in the middle of a forest instead of a house with a living room, pictures on the walls, and memories in the kitchen; it was the way he protected himself. She asked him to let that loose, to allow himself to accept what had happened. He didn't want to do that.

"I've seen you talking to Jet's statue," she said.

He nodded, his eyes shut tight.

"You know he is a part of you. He's a part of what pushes you so hard because he knows what you can become."

"What can I become?" Alex asked.

"The best of us," Kalia replied.

Alex opened his eyes and stared at her. Her light blue eyes were inches from his. They were filled with honesty and compassion.

"You were willing to die for me," Kalia said. "I've never known anyone like you." She let out a slow breath. A hint of something touched her eyes. Her lips pulled up in a gentle smile. "You have so many things you are willing to die for." She paused, then said, "Maybe you need something to live for instead."

She pressed her lips against his. The kiss was quick, barely a whisper of her lips against his. The next moment she was standing. Red colored her cheeks. She touched her lips with one hand. He couldn't read her expression. She turned and left the room.

Alex could taste her kiss. His heart thundered in his chest. He let his head fall back against the wall and relived the moment a hundred times. He couldn't believe it had happened; perhaps he had imagined it. Yet her scent lingered, and her kiss still hinted on his lips. At the end, when he gave up exhausted from his thoughts racing in circles and getting nowhere, a smile spread across his face.

Chapter Nineteen

Alex led Kalia to the train tracks. It was strange being there in human form. He had walked the pathway so many times as a wolf that he could have followed it blindfolded.

"I'd like to see you try," she said when he told her.

Alex laughed and shut his eyes. "Seriously, I can't believe you don't smell the trail. Even in human form I—" Alex let out a yelp of pain when something smacked his face. He opened his eyes to see the offending pine branch complete with the scratchy needles that had no doubt left an impression on his cheek.

Kalia giggled helplessly. "Guess you can't smell everything she said.

Embarrassed, Alex tried not to laugh, but he couldn't help it. "In my defense, as a wolf I would have been able to pass underneath that," he stated, glaring back at the branch that hung innocently across the trail.

"Blindfolded, huh?" she pressed.

"Oh, be quiet," he chided.

She laughed again.

"So you run along here for fun?" she said.

Alex shrugged. "I guess it's more like conditioning. I'm trying to get stronger."

"For what?"

"For Drogan," he replied.

Kalia fell silent for a few seconds. When she spoke again, her tone was sober. "You're trying to condition your heart."

Alex didn't answer. He hated that she knew about the way his heart stuttered. Weakness wasn't something werewolves shared. "I can't help it," he admitted quietly. "And it could get me or any of Jaze's pack killed if I can't do what I need to when we go out."

Kalia glanced at him, her gaze unreadable. "Has your heart always done, uh, whatever it does?"

Alex shook his head. "Not always. I think I did it."

Kalia stopped and gave him a straight look. "You think you injured your heart?"

Alex walked past her a few paces, then turned and crossed his arms, studying the snow at her feet. "Jet saved Cassie and me the day our parents died. We wouldn't be here if it wasn't for him." He kicked at the snow with the toe of his sneaker. "He took us to a safe house and promised us he would be back." He glared at the small pile of snow. "But he didn't come back," he said quietly, kicking the snow away. "When Jaze told us Jet had died, I didn't know what to do. I wanted to fight, to cry, to scream, and to die myself, because we had lost everyone and everything."

He looked at Kalia, willing her to understand. "We had no home, no relatives. We barely even knew Jaze and the others. We were alone." His voice grew softer as he remembered. "I woke up late that night at Two and found the training room. I pulled a practice dummy into the middle of the room and hit it so hard." His knuckles throbbed at the memory. "The wood broke. I kept smashing it, driving it into the floor. I imagined that it was the man with the mismatched eyes, Drogan. I kept seeing him kill my mom and dad. I couldn't stop myself."

He fell silent, lost in the memory.

Kalia touched his arm. The feeling of her fingers on his skin jolted him back. "What happened?" she asked quietly, her eyes searching his.

He let out a shuddering breath. "They found me there in the morning. My knuckles were bloody from beating the dummy into splinters and I was unconscious. I woke up in the infirmary with Cassie sleeping in a chair next to the bed.

She had tear stains on her cheeks as if she had cried herself to sleep." He grimaced. "I made myself promise then that she would never cry for me. I would be the brother she needed. I would make up for everyone else who had left us behind. I would be strong for her."

When he stopped speaking, Kalia said, "And that's when your heart started to stutter."

He nodded. "When I climbed off the bed, I almost fell over. I knew something was wrong, but I didn't want anyone to know. Cassie found out eventually. She tries to take care of me." He cracked a smile. "Guess I'm not doing so such a great job at the strong brother part."

"I think you're doing amazing," Kalia said.

A train horn sounded. Alex's head jerked up.

"Is that it?" Kalia asked.

"Yes."

"I want to see you race it."

Alex fought back a smile. "You do?"

She nodded enthusiastically. "I do. I want to see how fast you are."

"I, uh, I've got to phase first."

A hint of red brushed across her cheeks. At that moment, with her icy blue eyes, her pale blonde hair escaping the white fur of her hood, and her rosy cheeks, Alex realized she was beautiful. "I won't look," she promised.

He stared at her, wondering what she was talking about.

"Are you going to phase?" she asked with a hint of confusion.

Alex nodded quickly. He stepped behind a tree, cursing himself for acting stupid. He stood with the tree blocking his view of her for a moment to gather himself and collect his thoughts.

At that moment, a buzzing hum cut through the air. The

familiar sound sent adrenaline rushing through Alex's limbs. He jumped out of the way as a missile smashed into the tree.

"Alex!" Kalia yelled.

He found her in the next second and caught her hand. She ran behind him back into the forest. The sound of the tree falling and pulling others down with it crashed behind them. Alex didn't dare to look back. They were gunning for him, and Kalia was with him. His presence put her in danger.

"We can't stop," he called to her. "We've got to run to the Academy."

She nodded, her eyes wide. Alex slowed.

"What is it?" she asked in fright.

"Your eyes," Alex said. "They're gold."

"They're—" Kalia grabbed her head in both hands. A cry of pain tore from her. She hunched over, unable to move.

"We've got to run," Alex told her. He looked over her shoulder, expecting Drogan's men to appear through the trees at any moment. He had seen how many soldiers Drogan could send after him. He didn't dare to entertain hopes that they would give up after the miss.

"I can't..." Kalia said. Her fingers were white where they gripped her head.

Alex slipped an arm beneath her legs and another behind her shoulders. She held onto him as he stood up and ran.

He heard the hum of another missile. He dodged through the trees. The missile slammed into a trunk near his head. The force of the explosion knocked Alex and Kalia backwards into the snow. Alex gathered Kalia up again and ran as fast as he could.

His heart stuttered. His legs faltered. He gritted his teeth and forced them to hold. He cut through the forest at an angle, aiming for the Academy wall instead of the gate. If he couldn't get away, maybe he could give Kalia a chance to escape.

"Get ready," he told Kalia as they neared the huge brick wall that towered above them.

"I'm not leaving you," Kalia protested. She groaned and buried her face against his neck.

"You don't have a—Boris!" Alex spotted the Termer Alpha near the gate. Several werewolves were already out, searching for the source of the explosion.

Boris' eyes widened when he saw Alex carrying Kalia.

"What on earth is going—"

"I'm a target. Kalia's having a headache. I've got to go."

Alex set Kalia into Boris' arms.

He spun back around, suddenly free. He didn't have to worry about Kalia, Cassie, or any of the students. If Drogan was after him, he was going to give the Extremist what he wanted, complete with fangs and a thirst for revenge.

"Alex!"

He paused at Jaze's voice.

The dean reached the gate; it was clear by his rapid breathing that he had run the entire way.

"I've got to go," Alex said. His heart thundered in his ears. Instinct screamed for him to find the source of the danger to the Academy and end it. He was tired of running and being fired upon. He wanted to end it once and for all.

"Drogan's not here," Jaze said, grabbing Alex's arm before he could take off.

"But he shot at me. He almost killed us!"

Alex didn't want to believe Jaze's words. He wanted to fight back. He could attack Drogan in the forest and stop the threat.

"The missiles were long-distance. Mouse's drone is tracing them to the source," Jaze said. The dean looked around at the students who stared at him as if he was speaking another language. He gave Alex an urgent look. "Come to my office, now."

It was an order from the Alpha who was his leader. Alex nodded reluctantly.

The other professors had caught up to them. "Kaynan, Vance, take the north perimeter. Chet, Dray, sweep south. Colleen, send Rafe's wolves down the road so we'll have a warning if they try for a ground attack." The professors left without a word

The dean looked around at the students who watched with wide eyes. "The rest of you need to stay within the walls," Jaze instructed. "Boris, Torin, you're in charge of making sure all of the students get back inside." The two Alphas nodded. Jaze noticed Kalia in Boris' arms. "Take her to Meredith and Lyra. They'll see that she's comfortable."

Alex followed the dean wordlessly into the Academy.

Cassie and Tennison were walking down the hall. She spotted Alex amid the crowd of students. "Is everything okay?" she asked, rushing to his side.

Alex nodded. "I'll talk to you guys later," he promised quietly.

She let him go.

Alex hated the worried look that crossed her face every time she thought something was going on with him. He hated more the fact that she was usually right to be worried.

The rest of the students fell away when they reached the dean's office. Jaze shut the door and turned back to Alex with a shake of his head.

"You weren't supposed to go outside the walls alone."

"I wasn't alone. Kalia was with me," Alex pointed out.

Jaze speared him with a look. "Alex, you endangered Kalia, you endangered yourself, and—"

"And he showed us the holes in our defense system."

Both werewolves looked at Jaze's chair in surprise. The chair spun around, revealing Brock with an ice cream cone in his hand.

"We needed to know," Brock said.

An expression close to rage filled Jaze's usually calm face. "You knew Alex was going out there?"

Brock rose from the chair as if he realized it had been a bad idea. "Well, uh, the cameras, you see, and..." His voice died away. He licked the ice cream cone.

The phone on Jaze's desk rang. Brock reached for it, but glanced at Jaze and stopped. Jaze picked it up.

"Can you help me with William for a minute?" Nikki's voice asked on the other end of the line. "He spit up and it's all over our bed."

"I'll be right there," Jaze promised. He hung up the phone and stood there for a long moment looking out the windows.

Alex barely dared to breathe. He preferred it if Jaze had forgotten he was there.

"We'll talk about this later," Jaze told them both in an even voice without turning back around.

"Okay," Brock said quickly. He headed for the panel in the wall.

"Let me know as soon as Mouse finds the location of the shooters," Jaze said.

"Will do," Brock promised. A drop from his ice cream cone fell to the floor. Brock paused beside the open panel. He glanced at the drop, then at Jaze's back, and hurried through the panel. It slid shut behind him with a quiet shush.

Jaze crossed to the door without looking at Alex. "I'm going to take care of my family," he said. "When everything, including myself, has calmed down and we have more information, we'll regroup." He met Alex's gaze. "Until then,

186

Stay. Inside. The Academy." His strong words left no doubt about the Alpha command that filled them.

"I will," Alex replied.

Jaze nodded and left through the door.

Alex sank onto one of the chairs that ringed the dean's desk. Until that point, his limbs had held up despite the strain he had put on them. He had carried Kalia from the train tracks to the Academy even with his heart faltering. The adrenaline had begun to fade once they reached the Academy. Alex hadn't been sure during Jaze's short phone conversation with Nikki if he could stay up, but he didn't want to cause a scene, even with only two people.

He let his head fall back and concentrated on what was happening inside of him.

His heartbeat sounded almost normal. He could feel the blood pulsing through his veins, carrying life-supporting nutrients and oxygen to his limbs, organs, and brain. The rhythmic whump-whump was occasionally followed by the slightest stutter, something that hadn't been there before. It would go away, he told himself. He hoped he was right.

When he could manage, he pushed himself to his feet and left the office. He could hear the sounds of the students eating in the Great Hall, but couldn't muster the energy or appetite to join them. Instead, he made his way to the medical wing, hoping to find that Kalia had already left.

The second he set foot in the white-curtained room his nose told him Kalia occupied, a hand grabbed him by the throat and shoved him against the wall.

"What happened out there?" Boris demanded, his face inches from Alex's.

Alex struggled to breathe. His strength hadn't returned enough to free him from the angry Alpha's grasp.

"What happened?" Boris growled.

Alex pulled at the Alpha's hand. His heart skipped several beats, protesting the lack of oxygen. Boris finally relented and let him down just enough for his feet to touch the floor. Alex gasped in a breath; it rattled through his bruised throat.

"We were shot at," he managed to get out.

Boris looked over his shoulder at Kalia. "She didn't get shot."

Alex shook his head quickly. "Her eyes turned gold, I think from the rush of what was happening, and one of her headaches hit her."

"How did she get back here?" Boris asked.

"I-I carried her," Alex said. He couldn't keep up pretenses any longer. He let his legs give way. Boris stepped back and Alex slid to the ground. He leaned his head against his knees and willed his heartbeat to steady once more.

"How far was it?" Boris asked after several minutes had passed.

Alex blew out a slow breath. "By the tracks."

Several more minutes of silence filled the room. Only the steady beeping of the heart monitor on Kalia's finger dared to continue. Alex wondered vaguely what it would sound like if he put it on his finger instead.

Boris grabbed Alex by the shoulders and lifted him into a chair.

"You look like you could use Lyra's help, too," the Alpha said quietly.

Alex shook his head tiredly. "I just need to sit here a while. I'll be fine."

Boris looked like he wasn't so sure.

Alex heard the Alpha's stomach growl. After everything that had happened, eating seemed so trivial and meaningless that Alex couldn't help the chuckle that rose from his chest.

"What are you laughing at?" Boris demanded, his voice

less harsh than before.

"You're hungry," Alex said, still chuckling.

"Yeah, so what?" Boris asked defensively.

Alex shrugged. The laughter faded away. "I guess after everything, I couldn't imagine eating."

Boris snorted. "I never stop. I don't know how Cook Jerald keeps up with us all."

"If you saw the delivery trucks that come before the term starts, you'd know."

"There's a lot of them?" Boris guessed.

Alex nodded. "Hundreds."

Boris huffed a small chuckle at the exaggeration.

Alex waved a hand. "Go eat. I'll watch over Kalia."

Boris looked torn. He glanced in the direction of the Great Hall, then back at his sleeping sister. "Lyra said there's no telling when she'll wake up."

"So don't worry," Alex replied. "I'll make sure she's okay."

Boris' stomach growled again. He finally sighed. "Guess I'd better. I get cranky when I don't eat."

Alex rubbed his neck. "You better eat something then. I don't think I could handle more crankiness."

Boris nodded and walked to the door. He paused before going through it. "Alex?"

"Yeah?"

Boris gave him a small smile. "Thanks for carrying Kalia back here."

"Anytime," Alex replied.

He listened to the huge Alpha walk up the hall. The beeping filled him with a breath of relief. His heartbeat steadied as if the rhythmic sound of Kalia's pulse calmed his heart as well as his thoughts.

Chapter Twenty

Meredith's voice awoke Alex. "Jaze asked me to send you downstairs," she said, peeking into Kalia's room. She gave Alex an apologetic smile. "Sorry for waking you."

"It's alright," Alex replied. He stretched, feeling much better after his short nap despite the uncomfortable chair he had fallen asleep in. "I'd better go see what he wants."

Meredith gave him a warm smile. "I'll let him know you're on your way down."

Alex watched Kalia for a moment. Her steady breathing and the quiet beeping gave him the reassurance that she would be alright if he left. He crossed the hall to the panel and put a hand to it like he had when he first smelled Brock's meatball sandwich wafting up from below. The panel slide open to reveal the tunnel.

"Where are you going?"

Kalia's voice made Alex's heart leap. He looked back to see her leaning against the door frame. Her white-blonde hair was mussed and exhaustion still showed in her gaze, but the color had returned to her cheeks.

Alex realized she was looking at the tunnel. "Oh, uh, to Jaze," he said.

"I'm going, too," she said, giving him no choice in the matter.

Alex wasn't sure how the dean would feel about him showing Kalia the entrance to their secret hideout. Kalia crossed the hall. She stumbled slightly and righted herself with a hand on Alex's arm.

"Will you show me the way?" she asked.

Her voice was softer than normal, less demanding. She watched him with her bottomless blue eyes, her light eyebrows pinched together with worry or pain, he didn't

190

know which. Alex couldn't have refused her anything.

"Of course," he replied. He stepped into the darkness and led her through the door.

The panel slid shut behind them, sealing out the light.

"I guess this is where it comes in handy to be a werewolf," Kalia said.

Alex nodded, realized she couldn't see him, and said, "It helps to see in the dark."

"Just don't try to guide me with your eyes closed."

Alex grinned at the memory of running into the tree branch. "That was pretty stupid."

"Not as stupid as you trying to carry me all the way to the Academy. We just got done talking about your heart," Kalia reminded him.

Alex searched for a change of subject. "How's your headache?"

"Much better," Kalia replied with relief. "A bit of it is lingering, but I barely notice."

"I'm glad," Alex replied.

He was careful to lead her around the corner, then down the stairs.

"Where are we going?" Kalia asked after walking beside him in silence.

"The bat cave," Alex answered. He gave a little chuckle. "Jaze hates it when I call it that. I really think they should call it the Wolf Den. It's the command center for all of Jaze's rescue and monitoring activity. He keeps an eye on all the werewolves in the nation, and spends a lot of time rescuing those who are captured by Extremists or are in danger."

"I didn't know he still did all that," Kalia said with amazement.

"Me, either," Alex replied. "Now that I get to go with him, it's amazing to see how much he takes care of. He carries so much on his shoulders, but he never lets it show."

"He's here," Brock said, swiveling in his chair in the great cavern to face Alex.

Jaze turned from where he stood next to the human. His brow furrowed slightly at the sight of Kalia.

"Alex brought a date," Brock said proudly.

Jaze and Alex shot him matching looks.

"It's not a date," Alex replied. "Kalia saw me entering the tunnel and asked if she could come."

"That's where you say no if it's not a date," Brock pointed out.

Jaze gave a small shake of his head. "It's a little too late for foresight," he said. The dean smiled at Kalia. "Welcome to our headquarters. I'm glad you're feeling better."

Kalia was busy gaping at the vast cavern. "I, uh, yeah, thanks," she replied, taking in the equipment and vehicles. Her gaze stopped on the helicopter. "Alex was right. This is like the bat cave."

Brock burst out laughing. Jaze rolled his eyes. "Thanks, Alex."

"Are you sure you won't let me call it the bat cave?" Alex tried to press.

Jaze shook his head. "We're not bats."

"We could dress up like Batman," Brock offered.

"You're not helping," Jaze replied.

Brock sighed and took a bite of the donut that sat on the plate next to his station.

"The Wolf Den, then," Alex conceded.

Mouse appeared out of the tunnel Alex and Kalia had just exited. "I have some information. You're not going to like this," the small werewolf said. "We might want everyone to know what's going on."

"Call a meeting upstairs," Jaze instructed.

Mouse nodded and disappeared through the tunnel again.

Jaze led the way up to the smaller command room. He motioned for Alex and Kalia to take a seat at the table. Kalia looked torn between amazement at their surroundings and exhaustion from her headache. Alex's heart went out to her.

"It's a lot to take in," he whispered.

"It's amazing," she replied. "It's like finding out our dean is a double agent, only he's not, he's doing exactly what we know he did before the genocide and during, except that he's still doing it when I thought he was just a stuffy old dean."

"I'm not that old," Jaze spoke up.

Kalia's mouth shut quickly as though she was suddenly aware she had said everything within the dean's earshot.

"It's alright," Jaze told her with a kind smile, taking a seat across from them. "I may be a bit stuffy."

She shook her head quickly. "Not stuffy, really. You're just more, reserved, unapproachable."

Jaze's eyebrows rose. He looked at Alex. "Am I?"

Alex shrugged. "Not to me, but I've known you for years. You're just Jaze."

Jaze let out a half-snort, half-laugh. "Just Jaze, huh? That sounds pretty simple."

"It should be," Nikki said, walking into the room. "But it never is."

Jaze rose and gave her a hug and a quick kiss. "How's William?"

"Gem's got him. She's having a blast. He likes to pull her pink hair," Nikki replied.

Jaze smiled as his wife took a seat at his side.

"Another shooting?" Chet said as soon as the door closed behind him. "How are they finding Alex? Have they shot at Cassie?"

Jaze shook his head. "Apparently they've settled for trying

to take out one at a time."

The rest of the professors were filing in. If anyone found it strange that Kalia was sitting at the table, they didn't say anything. Meredith took a seat next to Alex. She patted his arm.

"We'll figure this out," she said.

"Yeah, if we can find out how they're locating him," Chet replied.

"Maybe they have snipers waiting day and night," Vance suggested, taking a seat on Jaze's other side.

"Perhaps there's some form of facial recognition," Brock suggested.

Kaynan sat down on Kalia's other side. "That wouldn't make sense. The first time Alex was shot at, he was in wolf form. This time it sounds like he was human." He glanced at Alex for confirmation.

Alex nodded.

Mouse and Lyra were the last professors to walk through the door. Mouse pulled out a chair for Lyra and made sure she was comfortably seated before he said, "Heat signature recognition."

Everyone exchanged glances and looked as lost as Alex felt. Apparently none of the other professors had heard of it before either.

Mouse tipped his head toward his wife. Lyra took up the explanation. "Apparently Drogan's missiles have the capability of recognizing Alex's individual infrared heat signature. That's why they almost hit him in his wolf form and his human form."

"But why would they miss?" Vance asked. "If they can lock onto one person, why wouldn't they follow him until it was a direct hit?"

Mouse spoke up. "Reflections. Drogan's using an

advanced version of the Javelin Heat Seeking Missile, but it's almost impossible to separate direct infrared emissions from the reflections of a person's heat signature. Trails, if you may. That's why the missiles hit close." He nodded toward Alex's shoulder. "Too close, but didn't quite reach him. If Alex had held still a moment longer in each instance, he probably would have been killed."

"So you're saying that they have a way of identifying Alex's individual heat signature in whichever form he is in even amid all of our students at the Academy?" Jaze asked.

Mouse nodded. "It seems that way." He took Lyra's hand. "We're already looking for a way to counteract it, but it may take us a while."

Alex felt sick. "If they know where I am, then I'm a danger to everyone here. No one's safe around me."

"We'll figure it out," Jaze reassured him. The dean looked at Vance. "Christmas break starts next week. We have to assume Drogan has the Academy scoped out and will be ready to try again. Alex isn't safe here until they can figure out a way to thwart the missiles. Can he go to your place?"

Vance was quiet for a minute as he thought it over. He finally shook his head. "While I understand your consideration of the overwhelming security at my mom's house, I couldn't put Alex through that. Mom insisted on rebuilding the guest wing and it'll be difficult to keep the crews tight." He gave Jaze a searching look. "We also know the place is being monitored by more than just our allies since she funded the repairs here last year. I don't think it's a risk we should take."

Jaze nodded. He was about to suggest something else when Kalia spoke up.

"What about my house?"

All of the professors look at her. She shrunk a little bit in her chair, but kept her gaze on the dean. "You know my mom and dad. Our house always has like thirty security agents all over the place. I can't even sneak out of my room without someone running to my mom. It's ridiculous." She looked at Alex. "But ridiculous might be what we need right now."

"You want me to go to your house during Christmas break?" Alex asked incredulously.

Kalia nodded. "Mom and Dad won't care. They barely know I'm there anyway." She seemed embarrassed that the admission had escaped her, but she turned her unwavering gaze back to the dean. "Alex would be safe."

Jaze looked at Mouse and Lyra. Mouse lifted one shoulder. "It's not a bad idea. When the vehicles come to pick up the students, Alex could escape through them to the car. It's impossible for thermal imaging to pick up through the tinted glass. If we got him out of here, he could be safe until we figure out how to defend against the missiles."

"I'll make the call to Mrs. Dickson," Nikki offered. "I have a feeling she won't be thrilled about us sending another werewolf to her house."

"Just don't mention that he's a werewolf," Kalia suggested. At Nikki's confused look, Kalia explained, "Tell her he's in danger, that I offered for him to come back with us, and that he'll be returning after the break. You can even tell her I'll return to school without a fight." She flushed with embarrassment at everyone's attention and lowered her gaze. "That may actually be the selling point."

Jaze nodded. "We'll try it. Thank you, Kalia." He looked straight at Alex. "Until then, stay within the walls. The full moon won't be until the break, so you can practice some discipline until then, alright?"

Alex nodded.

Jaze rose. "It's settled. Nikki will call Kalia's mother, Mouse and Lyra, continue searching for a way to thwart these things, and Vance and Kaynan, I want an exact location of where they were shot. We need to know the distance from which we can expect further attacks."

"Will do," Kaynan replied. He and Vance left through the side panel.

"How's your headache?" Meredith asked Kalia quietly.

"Better," Kalia replied. She waved a hand, indicating the room. "This is all a bit overwhelming."

Meredith nodded. "Trust me. I understand. Why don't you two go get some food? Dinner is over, but I'll call over to the kitchen and ask Cook Jerald to warm something up."

Kalia and Alex looked at each other. "Are you hungry?" they both asked at the same time.

Alex grinned and nodded. "Starving."

"Me, too," Kalia replied. "Who would have thought getting shot at would make me have such an appetite."

"I would," Alex told her. "Last time, I think I ate more than Trent and Don combined."

"No way," Kalia said with a laugh.

He nodded and led the way to the door. When he pulled it open, he glanced back to see Meredith, Jaze, and Nikki watching after them. Alex let the door close.

Chapter Twenty-one

"You sure you're going to be okay here?" Alex asked for the thirtieth time.

Cassie nodded. "I'm sure. I'll stay inside and play with baby William." She glanced over her shoulder to where Tennison was waiting on the steps. "Besides, I don't dare leave Tennison. If he starts sleepwalking again, it could be bad."

Alex decided not to point out the fact that Tennison hadn't slept walked since the night they had followed him. It was clear that leaving Tennison would be extremely difficult for her. Drogan's men hadn't shot at Cassie as of yet. He kept telling himself that if she stayed inside, Jaze would make sure she was safe.

"Promise me you'll be careful," he said.

"I promise, Alex. You be careful, too."

"I will," he promised.

Cassie wrapped her arms around his neck and gave him a tight hug. "This is our first Christmas apart."

"I know," Alex replied. His throat was tight as he held out the little box he had kept especially for her. "Merry early Christmas, sis."

Her eyes lit with astonishment. "Really, Alex? When did you get this?"

Alex shrugged, happy to see that he had caught her by surprise, a hard thing with a twin. "Open it so I can see if you like it."

She quickly undid the paper and opened the tiny jewelry box. Inside was a necklace with a little golden wolf hanging from a chain. The wolf had a small blue gem for an eye.

"It's beautiful!" she exclaimed, giving him another hug. "How did you get it?"

"Nikki helped me," he replied. He chose not to mention that Mouse had put a tracking device inside the wolf so they could make sure Cassie was inside the Academy at all times. If she left it would set off a warning signal on one of Brock's computers. He felt slightly bad for impinging on her privacy, but he was willing to do whatever it took to keep her safe.

"Thank you so much," she said, hugging him one last time. "I love you, Alex. Be careful."

"I love you too, Cass. Take care of yourself."

"I will," Cassie promised. She stepped back and looped her arm through Tennison's.

"I have a gift for you, too," Professor Mouse said quietly, appearing from seemingly out of nowhere.

Alex stared at him. "A gift?"

Mouse gave a small smile. "I guess it's not as cheery as a necklace, but it could save your life." He opened a plain gray box to reveal a tiny piece of metal.

"What is it?" Alex asked, accepting the box.

"It's a tracking device as well," he said quietly, tipping his head meaningfully toward Cassie, though there was so much commotion in the hallway she couldn't hear them.

"How does it work?" Alex asked, eyeing the object curiously.

"It has an adhesive on the back. Stick it to one of your molars, then be careful not to eat on that side. If you get caught, chomp on it. It'll send a signal traceable from the next country if needed."

"You want me to stick it to my tooth?" Alex repeated.

Mouse nodded. "It's harder to find that way. So many people have fillings that'll set off a tracker that most don't scan the mouth. There won't be a signal to pick up unless you bite it, so it'll be pretty much untraceable. Trust me."

Alex did as instructed and stuck the small device in the

crevice of his last top molar. He bit down carefully to make sure he had the device in a good place. It was back enough to miss his normal bite, but if he shifted his jaw slightly to the left, he could hit it.

"How's that feel?" Mouse asked.

"Good, I guess," Alex replied. "Thanks."

"Take care of yourself," the professor said with a small smile.

"It's time," Jaze called from near the door.

Termer students were hurrying out to the waiting cars. Jaze held out a coat. Meredith had sewn a heat-reflective blanket inside. If he kept to the middle of the mass and wore the coat only long enough to reach the cars, it would hopefully hide his heat signature until he was securely in the vehicle.

Kalia stood next to Jaze with a small suitcase in each hand that contained the possessions and clothes each of them would be taking home for the break.

"Ready?" she asked.

Alex nodded. "Let's do this."

Tennison and Cassie watched side by side as Alex shrugged into the coat. He zipped it up with the realization that he hadn't worn a coat for as far back as he could remember. He had always phased when he was cold. Extra protection against the weather hadn't been needed.

"Good luck," Jaze said with a warm smile. "We'll see you after the break."

Alex turned to go, but the dean touched the arm of his coat. "Be careful," Jaze said. He gave Alex a fatherly smile. "Make sure you get back to us."

"I will," Alex promised.

He took one of the suitcases from Kalia and walked through the door Kaynan held open.

"Enjoy the sunshine!" the red-eyed werewolf called after them.

Alex waved a hand.

"I can't believe we have to take you home with us," Boris grumbled from behind Alex. "I don't see why you can't stay here with the rest of the stinkin' Strays."

"You know very well why, Boris," Kalia replied. "So just shut up and accept it."

"You're lucky I'm not your Alpha here," Boris growled. "Or I would make you pay for that."

"You would try," Kalia replied.

Their arguments faded from Alex's hearing as he passed Jet's statue rising from the snowbank in the middle of the courtyard. Alex realized that he had never left the Academy for more than a day. The knowledge that the black wolf was always just outside the Academy watching over everything had given him a sense of security. He was leaving that all behind.

Alex set a hand on the statue. The metal was so cold it stung his fingertips. He looked up at the silver seven emblazoned on Jet's shoulder. His breath made a puff of white fog in the air as he set a hand on the seven.

"Are you coming?" Kalia asked. There was a hint of urgency in her voice.

Alex broke away from the statue with the realization that he was supposed to hurry so the coat didn't heat up and give him away. He followed Kalia and Boris quickly to the limousine that waited at the front of the courtyard.

"Come on, let's get moving," Kalia's mother said without preamble.

The driver set their luggage in the trunk while Alex ducked after Boris and Kalia into the vehicle. He stared at the spacious interior.

"Scoot over so Mom can get in," Boris growled with annoyance. "You'd think you'd never been in a limo before."

"I haven't," Alex replied. He ignored their surprised stares and took a seat near the front.

Kalia's mom slid onto the seat and the driver shut the door. Mrs. Dickson immediately pulled out a phone. She started talking almost before the person on the other end answered.

"Welcome to our lives," Boris stated dryly.

The limousine pulled out of the courtyard.

***

Alex didn't know what to expect, certainly not the sweeping white mansion with huge columns and finely manicured lawns as well as a white wall almost as big as the Academy's surrounding it. After the long hours of travel, they had left the Academy locked in winter far behind; sun peaked behind clouds and grass carpeted the far-reaching landscape, giving a perfect contrast to the spotless white along with black shutters, a black door inlaid with intricate glass etching, and the low green bushes on either side of the widespread stairs.

Two men stood at the top of the stairs at the door. They wore black suits and white gloves. Two more waited near the curved driveway where the limousine driver pulled in. A quick glance through the back window showed four men walking the perimeter and two at the gate who had questioned them regardless of Mrs. Dickson in the back seat. She seemed perfectly content to ignore everything that went on besides the person talking on the other end of the phone.

"Come on," Kalia said, climbing out the door as soon as it was held open by yet another white-gloved individual.

Boris was out next. Alex followed more slowly. He glanced back at Mrs. Dickson. She didn't even seem to notice that the vehicle had stopped. He stepped out and saw that Kalia was already halfway up the stairs. A servant carried her luggage and followed her to the doors that were now held open.

Alex reached for his bag.

"I've got that for you, sir," a servant replied.

"I can carry my stuff," Alex told him. It seemed pointless to have two people climb up the stairs when only one needed to.

The servant smiled. He was about twice Alex's age with short black hair and a small mustache that twitched in humor.

"I could use the exercise," the man said, though he was thinner than Mouse.

"Let him carry your bag, Alex," Boris instructed with an exasperated shake of his head. "It's not a big deal."

The big Alpha trudged up the stairs with a servant half his size following behind carrying his suitcase.

"But why?" Alex asked when Boris was at the door.

The servant shot a glance to where Mrs. Dickson was still waiting in the car. Her hand waved animatedly as she spoke so quickly Alex could barely make out what she was saying.

"Why do it for yourself when someone else could do it for you," the servant stated in a voice low enough for only Alex to hear.

At Alex's surprised look, the servant winked. "I'm Henry," he said, sticking out a hand.

Alex felt a hint of relief at the first sign of a normal human interaction at the house. "I'm Alex," he replied.

"Now, about that bag, Alex," the servant said. He took the luggage from Alex and gestured toward the stairs.

"I have a feeling I'm not going to understand this place," Alex said under his breath.

Henry shrugged. "Luckily, it's not a necessary part of your stay here."

Alex reached the doors. The servants on either side nodded at him in a gesture that was close to a small bow. "Uh, thank you," Alex said. The servants smiled and he stepped inside the house.

The grandeur of the exterior was outdone by the interior. A majestic, sweeping staircase ran on each side of the entrance hall. Marble floors, statues in cleverly designed nooks, and black and white as far as Alex could see made up the furnishings.

"Your room is this way, sir," Henry instructed.

Alex realized he was staring. He hurried after the servant up the right side staircase. He wondered where Kalia was. It seemed he had already lost her, something that felt very possible in the huge house.

Henry opened the fourth door on the right side of the hallway.

"This is the guest wing, sir. This room will be yours for the duration of your stay."

Alex stared at the huge, sweeping ceiling and vast space of the bedroom that would have taken up the entire Pack Jericho common room along with his room.

"Are you sure this is right?" Alex asked, amazed. "Isn't there somewhere, uh, smaller I should or could stay in?"

Henry shook his head with a warm smile as if Alex amused him. "I hope it doesn't disappoint you to hear, but this is the smallest room in the house, sir."

Alex shook his head in astonishment. "That's incredible. I wonder how big the biggest room is."

"That would be the basketball court, sir. It has an adjoining swimming pool and hot tub. I could give you a tour if you would like," Henry offered.

Alex let out an accepting breath. "Might as well. Good thing I can always find my way back here if I get lost."

At Henry's questioning look, Alex remembered that he wasn't talking to a werewolf. His interactions with humans had been limited to Nikki, Kalia, and Professor Thorson. Now Brock and Caden, he reminded himself. He forgot that a human's sense of smell wasn't nearly as keen as a werewolf's. He also didn't know if Henry knew he was a werewolf. Given Kalia's brief description of the fear of werewolves at the Dickson household, he doubted the servants knew of it.

"Uh, good sense of direction," Alex said.

Henry nodded. "At least I won't have to worry about finding you lost in some far quarter of the house, sir."

"You'd need to find me?" Alex repeated. "Why?"

"I am your personal assistant, sir; your servant, if you will. Your needs are mine to fulfill, and I am personally responsible for your wellbeing," Henry replied.

Alex studied him, not sure if having a manservant follow him around would be a good thing. "Does everyone here have a personal assistant?"

Henry smiled, his mustache twitching with humor. "In a manner of speaking, yes. Mrs. Dickson has four personal servants, as well as two maids, a seamstress, and a butler."

Alex dared to ask, "For the entire house?"

Henry's smile deepened. "No, sir. For herself. There are thirty-four servants at the Dickson household, as well as a dozen or so others for hire depending on the season."

"Why does the season matter?" Alex's head was reeling with the thought that it took so many people to run one house.

"Gardening, spring cleaning, clearing walkways of snow, trimming hedges, caring for the pool," Henry listed. He shrugged. "There are hundreds of odd jobs Mrs. Dickson hires out for. It gets a bit hard to keep track." He flicked his hand toward the door. "Shall we see to that tour?"

Alex was tempted to refuse. There was too much to take in as it was. Between the servants, guards, and Kalia's family, he had never been surrounded by so many humans. He had already started to regret taking up Kalia's offer about spending Christmas at her house.

Henry read his hesitation. "It might feel good to stretch your legs after the long ride. Besides, once you get the hang of this place, you'll see that it's not so bad.

Chapter Twenty-two

Everyone dressed up for dinner. The concept made Alex want to laugh and cringe at the same time. He tried not to fidget in the dress shirt and slacks Cassie had thankfully insisted he take. There was seldom an occasion to dress up at the Academy. Students were allowed their own form of worship, and there was even a small chapel room at the end of one of the classroom wings, but Alex only went there when Cassie dragged him for Christmas.

He missed Cassie terribly. It had only been one night, yet they had never been so far apart. He was grateful Cassie had Tennison, but looking around the table at the faces of strangers, he realized he had no one.

"How do you like our humble residence, Mr. Davies?" Mr. Dickson asked.

Alex's head jerked up at being addressed. "It's, uh, nice," he replied.

The Dickson family laughed. Small, twittering laughter came from Mrs. Dickson; she held a napkin daintily in front of her lips to hide her smile. Boris gave a deep, throaty guffaw that made Alex's cheeks burn. Alice and Jordy, Kalia's younger siblings, giggled because everyone else was laughing. Mr. Dickson fought back a smile that showed humor in the depths of his eyes. The one that got to Alex the most was Elizabeth, Kalia's older sister. She practically fell off her chair.

"It's, uh, nice," she imitated, covering her mouth with dainty white fingers that Alex doubted had ever seen hard work.

Alice and Jordy broke into giggles again.

Mr. Dickson took a calming breath, but he couldn't fight the smile that stole across his face when he asked, "If this house is just *nice*, you must come from quite the establishment, Mr. Davies," he said with a meaningful look at Alex's department store shirt.

"Dad," Kalia scolded. She sounded thoroughly dismayed at her family's rudeness to her guest.

Mr. Dickson lifted his hands. "I'm just saying, Kali. Your young man here must have quite the upbringing if this house doesn't awe him the way it does the rest of our friends."

Kalia gave him a stern look. "Maybe grandeur doesn't impress everyone," she retorted.

Mr. Dickson chose not to respond.

Mrs. Dickson cleared her throat gracefully and asked, "So Alex, where did you say you grew up?"

Alex shifted uncomfortably in his seat. "I didn't say," he replied.

It was obvious by Mrs. Dickson's silence and persistent attention that she wouldn't be satisfied until she had the answer.

Alex glanced at Kalia. Kalia lifted one shoulder.

"I grew up at the Academy."

Silence fell around the table. Gazes shifted from right to left. Boris looked at Kalia; the discomfort of their expressions let Alex know just what a mistake he had made.

"Is that Jaze Carso still the head of the establishment?" Mr. Dickson asked.

Before Alex could nod, Kalia cut him off with, "Dad, don't go there."

Mr. Dickson threw up a hand. "Kali, I just don't understand why *he* has to be the one to run that place. What kind of an example is he setting for those kids?"

"Adam, it's not our place to question," Mrs. Dickson said quietly, resting a hand on his arm.

"They're a bunch of murderers, Marnie. And we're sending our kids there. How is that supposed to help anything?" he demanded.

Mrs. Dickson shook her head. "It's the only place they're safe."

"What if by the time they come back, we're the ones not safe?"

Mr. Dickson's question hung in the air. Alex didn't dare even swallow the bite of heavily spiced fish that was in his mouth. He couldn't believe what they were accusing Jaze of. He didn't know whether he should say something. He couldn't let it sit, not with Jaze's reputation on the line. They should know how much Jaze put himself out there to protect werewolves.

Alex swallowed and spoke quickly before he second-guessed his decision. "Jaze puts his life on the line for—" He caught Kalia's quick shake of the head and remembered at the last minute that her parents didn't allow them to use the word werewolf, "For people like your children," he finished. "He leaves his family and confronts dangerous situations on a weekly basis."

"If only we could hope someone would end his life," Mr. Dickson replied.

Alex stood up so quickly his chair screeched back. He didn't know what to say. His instincts demanded that he defend the one who had done so much for he and Cassie, yet instincts also dictated that attacking someone in their own home was not smart or polite.

Mr. Dickson's eyes widened. Alex followed his gaze and glanced down. He realized he was holding a spoon in one hand and his fork in the other. Both utensils were bent by his clenched fists. He dropped them. They clattered on the table, the shapes of his fingers imprinted in the fine silverware.

"Please excuse me," he muttered before rushing from the table.

"Alex," Kalia called after him.

"Let him go," he heard Mr. Dickson reply as he hurried to the front of the house. "I'm not so sure inviting him here was such a good idea."

A servant opened the door when he neared. Alex stormed outside and rushed across the lawn. He wanted to phase, but knew with the heavy security around, he would be shot on sight. He ached to run away, to leave the Dickson residence behind and never look back. To hear what they thought about Jaze and the rest of the professors at the Academy made a knot in his stomach. The taste of fish refused to leave his mouth.

Familiar footsteps ran across the lawn. He carefully composed his expression and turned with his arms across his chest.

"I'm so sorry," Kalia said. "I can't believe he said that."

Alex kept his gaze on the white walls and black shutters of the mansion. "I guess it's good for me to know what he thinks."

She shook her head. "Not like that. He can have a little decorum."

Alex's lips twitched into a smile. "One of your fancy words again."

She let out a sigh. "I have a few other choice words I'd rather use."

Alex's eyebrows rose. "Oh, really?"

She nodded, opened her mouth, then shook her head with a little stomp of one foot. "I'm out of practice. Apparently the Academy has been good for me at least in one way."

Alex let out a small laugh. He turned his attention back to the house. The sound of the guards walking the wall a few hundred paces behind them was loud in the night. Alex could see the silhouettes of other guards checking the grounds near the house. The front door was opened by the servant. Mr. and Mrs. Dickson walked out. They paused on the porch and stood arm in arm, conversing quietly as if they didn't notice Kalia and Alex on the vast lawn.

Alex shifted his attention back to the white walls. "It's amazing how something so beautiful and grand can be so cold and unfeeling."

"I know what you mean," Kalia replied.

Alex glanced at her out of the corner of his eye and realized she was watching her mother as Mrs. Dickson made her way carefully over the wide expanse of grass toward them.

Kalia leaned closer and said in an undertone, "Just for your information, Jet may have been personally responsible for killing two of my uncles along with three cousins."

Alex could only stare at her. "You didn't think to tell me that *before* dinner where I just proclaimed my loyalty to Jaze and his cause?"

She lifted an eyebrow. "Would it have made a difference?"

Alex sputtered. "Well, no, but, uh, but I would have at least been a bit more prepared for your father's Jaze bashing fan club."

Mrs. Dickson reached them. "Are you two enjoying a little fresh air?"

"Any air is better than being in that house one more minute," Kalia replied.

Mrs. Dickson's gaze showed no reaction to her daughter's comment. She shifted her eyes to Alex. "I hope you found your accommodations suitable."

"Uh, more than suitable," Alex replied, remembering his earlier understatement that had been taken so badly. "Thank you for your hospitality." He studied the ground at her feet. "I, uh, would like to apologize for dinner."

She waved her hand as though brushing away the conversation. "Don't bother. That's the most lively I've seen Adam since he and Kalia went at it at the beginning of the school year. It's funny how he argued so hard for her to go then, and yet his opinion flips when it's the most inconvenient for him to be disagreeable."

"Yeah, funny," Kalia muttered.

"Thank you for allowing me to stay here," Alex told Mrs. Dickson. "I promise to induce fewer outbursts."

"And take away my enjoyment of our meals?" she said in a tone that was so heavily laced with sarcasm Alex couldn't tell what part she was serious about. She turned away with a flit of her fingers before walking back across the grass.

"She doesn't act like she lost someone she cared about," Alex noted quietly.

Kalia shook her head, her shoulder-length blonde hair brushing back and forth. "She doesn't. They were Dad's brothers, and she despised them. He did, too, if the truth was known, but like she said so poetically, it's convenient for him to be offended and cause arguments. He revels in drama."

"Why not just say the word werewolf?" Alex asked. "That's got to be dramatic."

Kalia shook her head quickly. "The last time Boris did, Dad almost shot him, for real." The note of fear in her voice let Alex know just how traumatic that had been. She let out a shaky breath. "My parents may be harmless on the surface, but they still have their Extremist side tucked away beneath."

After a few minutes of silence, Alex asked, "Do they know which one carries the werewolf gene?"

Kalia's eyes drew up at the corners in the hint of a satisfied smile. "No. They're too afraid to check. Neither wants to carry the guilt."

"Of having werewolves for children," Alex finished.

"Of having beasts." Kalia's eyes flashed gold.

"Kalia..." Alex tried to warn her.

Kalia let out a cry of pain and hunched over with her head in her hands. Alex looked around quickly. Mrs. Dickson was already back inside the house. Her husband was nowhere to be seen. The guards acted as though they couldn't care less about Kalia's troubles.

"I've got you," Alex said softly.

He picked up Kalia in his arms and carried her into the house. The servant at the door opened it without question. Once inside, Alex ran into Henry at the bottom of the sweeping staircase.

"What is going on, sir?" the servant asked. Alex had to give him credit for showing more alarm than the two guards on the porch and the servant at the door.

"She has a horrible headache," Alex explained.

Kalia held her head in both hands as if it was about to split open.

"I appreciate that you are trying to help her, sir," Henry said. He tried to figure out a way to take her from Alex, but maneuvering his arms didn't seem to gain him any purchase.

"I'm alright, Henry. I just don't know where her room is," Alex told him.

"Oh, uh, right," Henry stammered. He hurried up the stairs ahead of Alex and led the way along the hall. "This is her room, sir."

Henry pushed open a door to reveal a room that made Alex's look like a kennel. Beside her huge four poster bed, private bathroom complete with a four person jetted bathtub, and recessed vanity, there was a sitting area with comfortable couches, a fireplace, bean bags, and enough recliners for a dozen friends.

Alex took Kalia to the bed and set her gently on top of the carefully folded bedspread.

He knelt down near her face. "What can I get you?" he asked.

Kalia shook her head, then winced, her eyes squeezed shut.

Alex didn't know what to do. He looked back at Henry. "Do you have anything for headaches?"

"Yes, sir. Right away, sir." Henry rushed from the room looking frazzled.

Alex hated seeing the pain that filled Kalia's face. He would do anything to take it away, yet he felt helpless.

"Hold me," Kalia said in a small voice. She opened her eyes just enough to give Alex a pleading look. He was shocked to see that her irises were still golden. The headache was lasting longer than the others he had seen.

Alex climbed carefully onto the bed. Kalia scooted higher so that her head could rest against his chest. He ran his hand up and down her arm, hoping it helped.

"It's not going away," Kalia said with alarm in her tight voice.

"Your eyes are still gold," Alex told her.

Kalia gave a little sound that might have been either from pain or dismay.

"It's okay," Alex said softly. "You're going to be alright. Just hang in there."

When he fell quiet, Kalia said, "Keep talking. Your voice helps."

Alex's heart gave a loud thump at that. Put on the spot, he tried to think of what to say.

"Please?"

Kalia's pleading voice cut to Alex's core. He took a

calming breath. "I'll tell you about the Academy before the students came. I don't know if you want to hear it, but I don't know what else to say." He thought back. "When Cassie and I lost our mom and dad and Jet, we were taken to the Academy with the first group of orphans from the genocide. Torin was there, along with Trent and Terith. Torin was already a bully." Alex gave a wry smile, remembering. "That first morning, Torin tried to force Trent to make his bed. Trent refused. I think Torin was about to kill him when I stepped in."

"What happened?" Kalia asked in a whisper.

"He gave me the worst beating of my life," Alex replied. "He had rage issues. I think he would have killed me if Vance hadn't interrupted."

"That's horrible," Kalia said, a bit stronger.

Alex shrugged. "I guess that's what happens when kid werewolves are displaced and lost. You have to take out your frustrations somewhere. I just happened to be the first thing that stepped in Torin's way."

He tried to ignore Kalia's scent. It tickled his nose, filling his senses with honey and clover. He reminded himself that she was hurting, which was the only reason he was holding her.

"What else?" Kalia asked.

Alex thought quickly. "The Academy was much smaller back then, just a fragment of what it is now. They built one of the dorm wings and the classrooms. Apparently they were busy building the rest of the underground, too. I never knew it was there until this year."

"It's incredible," Kalia agreed.

Alex smiled. "You sound like you're feeling better."

Kalia nodded, lifting her head from Alex's chest. Their eyes met, and he was relieved to see that hers were blue again.

"Thank you," she said. She lowered her lashes, her cheeks coloring red. "I'm sorry."

Alex shook his head quickly. "You have nothing to be sorry about. I was glad I could help. It's a horrible feeling, knowing there was nothing I could do to stop the pain."

"You definitely helped," Kalia said.

Alex slipped off of her bed. He stood next to it with uncertainty.

"I think I'll get some sleep," Kalia told him, the blush still coloring her cheeks. "I'm always exhausted after a headache."

"You should sleep," Alex agreed. He glanced back at the door to find Henry watching them both; the servant held a glass of water and several small pills sitting on a tray. "Uh, Henry is here if you need some medicine."

"I think I'm okay," Kalia replied. Her eyes were already closed and the words slurred slightly.

"Goodnight, Kalia," Alex whispered.

He made his way to the door. He and Henry watched her for a moment until he realized how creepy it would be if she awoke to find them still there.

He left the room and Henry followed, leaving the tray with the water and medicine on one of the lavish end tables that decorated the room.

Chapter Twenty-three

"Mr. Dickson requests your company," Henry told Alex after Kalia's door shut behind them.

"My company?" Alex was surprised. "I got the feeling Mr. Dickson didn't especially like me."

"He sent me to find you," Henry replied, leading the way down the stairs and along another hallway Alex hadn't been. "That's why I met you at the door. He's been waiting for a few minutes." There was a hint of trepidation in his voice as if in fear of Mr. Dickson's retaliation if they were late.

Henry opened a door to reveal a massive study. Books lined the walls all the way to the vaulted ceiling. Other shelves held collectibles that looked as though they had been gathered from across the world. A huge window took up the entire wall opposite the door. In front of it was a large, polished desk that made up the only furniture in the room. Despite the late hour, Mr. Dickson sat behind it reading a book. He looked up at their entrance. Disapproval at their tardiness was evident on his face.

"Thank you for taking time out of your busy schedule to see me, Mr. Davies," Mr. Dickson said in a cold voice.

"I'm sorry it took us so long. Kalia had a headache and I was helping her to bed," Alex explained.

Mr. Dickson was quiet for a moment. He finally nodded and indicated the single chair on the other side of the desk.

"Please, take a seat."

Alex glanced back at Henry. The servant gave him an uncomfortable look before leaving the room and shutting the door quietly behind him. Alex gathered his nerves and crossed to the chair. His footsteps echoed against the walls, making him feel even smaller.

He took a seat on the thinly cushioned wooden chair and

waited. Mr. Dickson studied him closely, his hands linked together and elbows resting on the arms of his lavish leather chair. Alex felt every inch of his features scrutinized.

"I have need of your," Mr. Dickson cleared his throat, "Talents tonight."

"I don't understand," Alex replied.

Mr. Dickson lifted his lips in a humorless smile. "Why do you suppose I would allow my daughter to invite someone of your bloodline into my home?"

Alex shifted uncomfortably on the chair. "I thought you were being nice."

Mr. Dickson gave a small chuckle. "Nice. Well. Yes. I suppose there is that." His gaze was bland when he met Alex's. "You must realize by now that there are not too many nice individuals left in this world toward those with your unfortunate traits."

"Whether they are unfortunate or not is up to me to decide," Alex replied in a steady voice. He tried not to let show how much Mr. Dickson's conversation bothered him.

"Yes, well, so be it." Mr. Dickson waved his hand as though he couldn't care less. "I called you here because I am in need of your assistance and if you value your relationship with my daughter and son in any way, you would do best to accompany me."

A tremor of concern ran down Alex's spine. "Accompany you to do what?" he asked carefully.

Mr. Dickson straightened a stack of papers near his elbow. He then lifted a manila envelope. "I am a criminal defense attorney, and I have gotten to the point where I need to let go of a few clients. Some of those clients don't take kindly to being let go, if you know what I mean."

Alex realized what Mr. Dickson was saying. "You need me to be your protection?"

Mr. Dickson smiled. "I have plenty of bodyguards, Alex, but I can't involve them in these matters. What I need is for someone to discreetly manage my safety during these interviews. It should be simple, really." His gaze narrowed. "I have a strong feeling that Jaze Carso is teaching you much more than academics at that Academy. It's time to prove yourself, my boy."

"And if I refuse?"

Mr. Dickson's lips pressed together in a tight line before he said, "Then I'll have to invite Boris along instead. I'd prefer to keep my son out of my business, but if you insist on taking the coward's way out, I will have no choice."

Alex's stomach clenched. He was being blackmailed into acting as Mr. Dickson's personal security. He had no idea what kind of men Mr. Dickson was dealing with. He didn't want to mess with them, but he didn't want Boris too, either.

"Need I remind you that one word from me and you'll be back at the Academy? From what I hear, it is a dangerous place for you right now."

The knot in Alex's stomach turned to steel. He didn't want to bring the danger that followed him back to the Academy where his family and friends lived. If he wanted to stay, he had to do what Mr. Dickson asked.

"Okay," Alex quietly agreed. "I'll do it."

Mr. Dickson nodded. "I knew you would make the right choice." He rose and pulled out a cell phone. "We'll meet you out front," he said into the receiver.

Alex followed Mr. Dickson to the hallway. He saw Henry at the top of the stairs. The manservant gave him a questioning look. Alex shrugged, feeling as confused as he no doubt appeared.

A limousine was waiting for them out front. The driver held open the door and they were helped inside. Mr. Dickson didn't say a word during the drive. If meetings with his clients at such a late hour were unusual, he didn't let on. Alex was left to his own thoughts as the driver made his way through the darkened streets of the city.

The car pulled to a stop near a small park lined with trees. No one was in sight. Mr. Dickson climbed out of the car when the driver opened the door, then motioned for Alex to do the same.

"Wait in the limo," Mr. Dickson told the driver. The man nodded and retreated to his station.

Alex relished the light of the almost full moon as it settled on his shoulders like a comforting blanket, calming his nerves. A few minutes later, Alex caught the scent of several men. He watched as shadows separated from the darkness of the trees and made their way toward the pair.

"Just hold your ground," Mr. Dickson said under his breath.

Alex didn't know if Kalia's father was talking to him or just thinking aloud.

"Strange time for a meeting, don't you think?" A man wearing black slacks, a blue button-up shirt, and a black baseball hat said.

"As good a time as any," Mr. Dickson replied.

"That's what I told him," an older man with wiry gray hair replied, nudging the younger one in the side.

The four men with them were huge. Alex wouldn't have been surprised to find out they had bears in their ancestry. None of the other men spoke; they didn't need to. It was clear by their humorless stares and crossed arms that they would mean trouble if things went other than the way their bosses wanted.

"I appreciate you coming out," Mr. Dickson said. He handed each of the two men a piece of paper from the envelope.

"What is this?" the older man asked.

The younger one read through the page quickly. "You're dismissing us as clients?" he exclaimed.

Mr. Dickson nodded. "It's a matter of protocol," he replied. "Donny Junior, you've skipped your parole and refused to appear in court even after I told you it was mandatory." The older man gave the younger one a hard look. "And Donny Senior, I hear rumors that you've gotten more guns."

It was clear by the older man's silence that the rumors were true.

Mr. Dickson shook his head. "I warned you both that violation of the limits of your release terms would mean a dismissal of my services. I already put my neck on the line for you two, and you've thrown that away with your actions." He pointed at the papers they held. "Those documents state exactly what I am telling you. I dismiss you from my services and I will no longer be acting as your attorney."

Donny Senior's face hardened. "I say when you're done with us, Mr. Dickson, and you are not done with us."

He motioned and the four men stepped forward. Mr. Dickson fell back behind Alex.

"I'm sorry, Adam, but I think you should reconsider your decision," Donny Junior said.

"I don't reconsider decisions like this, Donny. You're too big of a risk," Mr. Dickson replied.

"I think you might," Donny Senior told him flatly.

The four thugs closed in. Alex raised his fists.

Donny Senior laughed. "What is this? Some kind of juvenile security in training?"

"He's all the security I need," Mr. Dickson replied.

One of the men reached over Alex intent on Mr.

Dickson.

To Alex, time slowed.

Alex's body fell into the training cadence Chet had worked so hard to teach the students. He bent one knee and drove his fist into the man's groin. When the man bent over, Alex slammed both fists into the man's back. He fell to the ground with a cry of pain.

"What is this?" Donny Senior demanded, all humor vanishing from his voice.

"Like I said," Mr. Dickson repeated. "He's all the security I need."

"Finish them," Donny Junior growled, lifting his lips to show gold-plated teeth.

"Where do you find these guys?" Alex asked.

"I've rethought my profession many times, believe me," Mr. Dickson replied tightly.

The three remaining thugs crowded in.

Alex sidestepped a punch and brought both arms together in a scissor hold that snapped the man's elbow. He dropped and spun, kicking the legs out from beneath the thug. The man landed heavily on his back. Alex jumped over him, barreling a two-legged kick into the next man's chest. The thug fell backwards into the last man. Alex rolled when he hit the ground and came up in a defensive crouch.

The first man was back on his feet. His face twisted in rage.

"I'll kill you!" he yelled.

The man planted his feet and swung boxing style. Alex ducked inside the man's reach and jumped up, smashing the man's nose with the top of his head. The thug staggered backwards as blood flowed down his face.

Another tried to pin Alex in a bear hug. He stomped down on the man's instep, slammed his elbow into the man's groin, ducked under his arms, and drove the same elbow into the man's back to send him crashing to the ground.

"Alex!"

Mr. Dickson's strained cry caught Alex's attention. He turned in time to see the other two thugs advancing on the man. One thug held his elbow.

Alex crossed the space between them in less than a second. He jumped and spun. His foot connected with the back of both of the men's heads before they could reach Mr. Dickson. Donny Senior's warning cry called behind them too late. Both the thugs stumbled, then collapsed to the ground.

Alex's heart stuttered. He landed and his knees hit the pavement. He knelt there for a moment willing his heart to cooperate.

"Alex, behind you," Mr. Dickson warned.

Alex glanced back to see the man with the broken nose running toward him with a crowbar.

Alex caught the crowbar at the last second as it barreled toward his head. He spun to the side, using the momentum the thug had already built to drive the crowbar into the ground. He rolled over the man's back and slammed his elbow into the side of the man's head. The thug fell to the pavement in a motionless heap.

All four thugs were on the ground, two of them moaning and writhing in pain.

"I think we're done here," Mr. Dickson said, straightening his tie.

"This is bad business and you know it," Donny Senior protested.

Mr. Dickson closed the space between them. "Bad business is getting your little gun trade noticed by the feds in the first place. Bad business is raising up your son to follow in your footsteps even though you know it's going to get him killed." He looked back at the fallen thugs. "Bad business is not knowing when to call it quits. Well I know when to call it quits, and you'd best be accepting my resignation this time."

Donny Senior looked from Mr. Dickson to Alex, then back. He finally nodded and held out a hand. "Thanks for all you've done."

Mr. Dickson accepted the handshake. "Just make sure it's worth it. I don't think any other attorney is going to save your hide if you get taken in again. Do your family a favor, Donny. Retire, and make sure Junior here does the same." Mr. Dickson tipped his head toward the road. "Come on, Alex."

Alex followed slowly after Mr. Dickson. Tingles ran up his spine, giving him the sensation that he was being watched. He looked back to reassure himself that the thugs were still down. It looked like the Donnys were going to have a heck of a time getting them back on their feet.

"You didn't turn into a wolf," Mr. Dickson noted, his attention on the pair of headlights coming toward them.

"You protect your family your own way, and I protect mine," Alex replied quietly.

Both of them were silent all the way back to the house. Mr. Dickson didn't speak again until they climbed out of the car.

"Thanks, Alex. I appreciate not having to involve Boris in this," Mr. Dickson said.

Alex gave him a steady look. "Like you told Donny Senior, it might be time to call it quits."

Mr. Dickson cracked an actual smile at that. He chuckled as he made his way up the steps. "Sage advice, my boy. Sage advice." He went inside.

Alex took a few minutes to collect himself before following.

Chapter Twenty-four

Alex lay on his bed. He couldn't sleep. Thoughts of the Academy, of Cassie, and of the fight kept circling through his head. He wanted to go home. He missed the Academy, the familiarity of the forest, being with his sister and pack, and the professors. He missed baby William, and he missed Aunt Meredith.

It was amazing to know that with Aunt Meredith there, they were no longer orphans. Jaze and Nikki had done so much for them, but there was a great difference between them and baby William. Even though Alex regarded him as a brother, he knew deep down that they didn't share blood. Blood between werewolves was a powerful thing. It was nice knowing that he and Cassie weren't the only ones left in their bloodline.

Aunt Meredith was so kind. It was as if she, too, felt the relief of not being alone. He felt better knowing that she and Cassie were together. Cassie also had Tennison. Alex's heart twisted as he wondered whether she missed him as much as he missed her. She was probably busy having fun and keeping Tennison from jumping off cliffs in his sleep. Alex snorted and rolled over. If anyone could help Tennison, it was Cassie.

Someone banged on his door. Alex sat straight up.

"Alex, open the door," Boris growled.

"Now what?" Alex muttered.

He climbed out of bed and made his way to the white panel door. He turned the lock and opened it just a crack.

"What do you want?"

Boris shoved the door open, propelling Alex back into the room.

"Think I couldn't protect my dad?" he demanded, charging in with his eyes wild and fists clenched.

226

Alex held up his hands against the Alpha's onslaught. "I was just doing what he asked me to."

"Yeah? Did you forget that family takes care of their own?"

Boris grabbed Alex by the front of his shirt and threw him against the wall.

Alex hit the floor and came up with his fists clenched. Boris tried to grab his shirt again. Alex ducked under his hand and rolled, landing a punch to Boris' kidney before dancing out of the way.

"I knew you shouldn't have come here," Boris growled, his icy blue eyes filled with fire.

He lunged. Alex jumped back, but tripped over a lamp table. Boris grabbed him by the arm and flung him into the mantle above the fireplace. Fancy vases and statues fell to the floor with a crash. Alex landed on his feet. Fire filled his limbs. He could no longer think past the red that took over his vision.

A sudden rush of strength fueled Alex's body. An animalistic roar of rage left his mouth as he charged at Boris. The Alpha's eyes widened as Alex rammed into him like a bull, slamming the Alpha to the ground. Alex punched Boris' face and chest. He felt the Alpha's nose break beneath his fist.

"Your dad wanted me to go because I'm expendable," he shouted. "If I didn't, he said he'd send me back to the Academy where I'm a threat to everyone I care about." The words pounded through Alex's chest with every beat of his heart. "He asked me to protect you. He made me fight them because he cares about you and I have no one out here."

Alex's heart skipped a beat before he hit Boris' face again. He tried to lift his fist, but it refused to cooperate. Darkness swarmed his vision. His heart skipped two more beats. He slid to the ground and lay on his back, gasping and trying to will his heart to respond. The fight had been too much. After defending Mr. Dickson, then being attacked by Boris, his heart had finally had enough.

"Alex?" he heard Boris ask. The sound was muted and heavy as though it came from miles away in a fog.

Someone shook his shoulders. Alex couldn't respond. Fingers pressed against his neck. A heavy fist slammed against his chest. Alex thought vaguely that Boris' attempt to kill him when he was already down was a coward's decision.

Alex's heart gave a weak beat in response to the blow. He felt the life-giving blood surge through his body. It was all he could do to lay there and hope it would beat again. It did.

"Alex." Boris' voice was stronger this time.

Alex forced his eyes to open.

Boris was kneeling beside him, his blue eyes wide and blond hair a mess. Blood smeared below the Alpha's nose where the break was already healing. Alex could feel his own injuries mending.

"Alex, are you okay?" Boris asked.

Alex took a testing breath. His heartbeat sounded normal. He nodded. "I think so."

He tried to push himself up to a sitting position. Boris grabbed his arm and helped him.

"What was that?" Boris demanded.

Alex was quiet for a few minutes. He didn't know how much he wanted to admit, but it was obvious he had to say something. He let out a slow breath. "My heart acts up sometimes."

Boris silently took that in. The Alpha finally looked around the room. "We made a mess."

"I'm surprised nobody came to see what the noise was," Alex noted.

Boris shook his head. "They're used to me breaking things. They probably just thought you did the same." His voice lowered with a hint of self-loathing. "It's safer for them not to interfere."

"Are they afraid?"

Boris nodded without speaking.

"I should have insisted that you went with your dad instead of me," Alex admitted.

Boris shook his head. "It sounds like my dad gave you no choice if you wanted to stay here." True regret crossed his face. "You shouldn't have been put in that position."

Alex shrugged. "I didn't mind. Sometimes it feels good to hit someone."

Boris chuckled at that. "I know what you mean." He gestured to Alex's face. "You don't look so good."

Alex grinned, feeling blood in his teeth from when his face had hit the mantle. "You're pretty banged up yourself. You might want to hide from the servants for a while."

Boris laughed. "Just what I need. For them to be even more scared of me."

"You like people being scared of you," Alex said.

Boris nodded. "I do. It's something I can control. Here, I am constantly reminded that I'm something to be feared, that I'm different, that I'm a monster. At least at the Academy I can be myself and not feel bad about it."

Alex took a testing breath. He could tell that his bruised ribs were healing, but they ached with each inhalation. He glanced out the window at the almost full moon filling the air with shimmering light.

"We should go out there," Alex said.

"Why?" Boris asked.

Alex pushed gingerly to his feet. He wavered and caught himself against the wall. He waited until his knees were mostly steady before he headed across the room. Boris followed behind without further questions.

If the servant at the door thought it odd that the two bruised and bloody boys wanted to go outside at such a late hour, they weren't questioned. Maybe there were some benefits to the servants' detachment from those who employed them.

Alex led the way across the well-manicured lawn to a little rise. He sat down and Boris took a seat wordlessly beside him. After a minute, Alex settled onto his back. He opened his eyes a few seconds later to see Boris with a pensive expression on his face.

"Relax," Alex told the Alpha. "Try to enjoy something for a change."

Boris gave a snort of humor. "I enjoy things," he replied.

"Right," Alex said, closing his eyes again. "When was the last time you enjoyed something?"

He heard the Alpha lay on his back. "I enjoyed throwing you across the room."

Alex gave a wry chuckle. "I'm sure you did." He fell silent for a moment, then said, "You know you could have just asked me about going with your dad instead of attacking me."

Boris was quiet so long Alex didn't think he would respond until the Alpha finally said, "I'm sorry."

Alex fought back a smile. He stretched out, feeing the ache in his ribs ease. "You don't have to apologize. I think if I had a dad and he asked some stranger to go with him instead of me, I'd be pretty upset, too."

He glanced at Boris.

The Alpha was staring up at the lowering moon. There was a hint of wistfulness on his usually guarded face when he said, "Dad needed a werewolf. For the first time in my life since I found out what I was, I could have helped him. I guess it just made me mad that he would choose you instead."

Alex couldn't imagine what it must feel like for someone's own parents to despise and fear what they were. It was one thing for someone like Drogan to be fixated on wiping him from the earth; he couldn't even begin to understand what it would feel like if that person was someone who was supposed to love and care for him unconditionally.

"I should have insisted that he take you," Alex repeated with regret.

Boris shook his head. "It sounds like he gave you an ultimatum." He cracked a smile. "My dad sure likes his ultimatums."

Alex nodded. "He sure does." He sat up.

"Feel better?" Boris asked, eyeing him uncertainly as he sat up, too.

Alex stretched his arms out gingerly. "Yeah. Moonlight works wonders."

Boris glanced over at the orb that was almost lost behind the mountains on the horizon. "It does. I forget it sometimes."

The silence that settled over them was companionable. Crickets chirruped in the night that was much warmer than in the mountains where the Academy lay. Thoughts of Cassie and the place they had learned to call home filled him with longing. He remembered the cell phone Jaze had given him before he left.

He stood.

"Where are you going?" Boris asked.

"I need to call Cassie. She's probably missing me and I promised I'd call."

"It's late," Boris noted.

Alex shrugged. "She said to call whenever. I feel bad I

haven't called her before now."

"You've been busy," Boris replied with a hint of what Alex was surprised to recognize as humor.

Alex jogged to the porch. He looked back to see if Boris was following, but the Alpha had laid back down on the small rise in the grass. It was the first time he could recall ever seeing the Alpha look somewhat peaceful.

Alex stepped through the door, aware of how easy it was to get used to somebody at each doorway.

Henry met him in the hall.

"Hello, sir."

"Don't you sleep?" Alex asked in surprise.

Henry shrugged. "I sleep enough."

"I'm not sure about that."

Henry gave a smile that lifted his small mustache. "I could say the same about yourself. You look a bit worse for the wear." He gave Alex's torn clothes and bloody face a pointed look.

Alex smiled back. "You should see the other guys. I'm heading to bed. See you in the morning."

Henry gave a nod that was close to a small bow. "Same to you, sir."

Alex jogged up the stairs. He dug through his luggage for the phone, then collapsed on the bed. The battery showed low. He made a mental note to plug the phone in when he was done. He hit the speed dial for the number of the phone Mouse had given to Cassie.

"Hello?" she answered groggily after the second ring.

Alex felt bad about catching her asleep. "Hi, Cass. I'm sorry I woke you up."

"Alex, it's so good to hear your voice!" she exclaimed. "What have you been up to? I thought you would call before this. I was starting to get worried."

It felt so good to hear her familiar voice that Alex couldn't stop smiling. "I should have called sooner. I didn't want you to worry. Everything here is fine."

"Just fine?" Cassie asked, reading into his words like she always did. "What happened?"

Alex debated whether to tell her about acting as Mr. Dickson's personal bodyguard, or his fight with Boris, or the fact that their family was apparently responsible for wiping out most of Kalia's relatives. He went with, "Oh, you know. I don't really fit in here."

He could hear the smile in Cassie's voice when she replied, "You know we don't fit in anywhere."

He chuckled. "That's true. At least I haven't bitten anyone."

Cassie laughed outright. "So you're keeping the werewolf thing under wraps. Good call."

"I figured as much." Relief that she was alright was tempered with worry that the threat Drogan presented might still be following him. "Has Mouse figured out how to thwart the heat signature missiles?"

"I'm not sure, but I'll check with him in the morning," Cassie promised. "Meredith said to tell you hi and that she missed you when I got the chance to talk to you. She said she has a present for you."

"She didn't have to do that." The fact that their aunt had gone so far as to get him a Christmas present warmed him.

"I told her the same thing," Cassie said, "But she insisted, saying that she was so happy to have a family for the holiday this year that she wanted to spoil us rotten."

"That might not be a bad thing," Alex said.

Cassie laughed. "It might not. We need to get her something so she knows how much it means to us to have her here."

Alex smiled. "I was thinking the same thing. I'll figure it out. We can surprise her when I get back."

"Okay. I love you, Alex."

"Love you, Cass. Have a good night. Tell Tennison I said hi."

"I will," Cassie promised.

Alex hung up the phone feeling much better. At least one part of his life made sense and was safe. He was almost asleep when he remembered to plug in his phone. Cassie would surely be upset with him if he let it die and forgot to call her. He smiled. Sometimes it was nice having someone who cared so much. The smile stayed on his face as he fell asleep.

Chapter Twenty-five

"Is it supposed to be some sort of cruel irony that the full moon falls on Christmas Eve?" Boris demanded.

"It can't be that bad," Kalia replied, though she, too, looked anxious.

They had spent the entire day trying not to bring up the subject. Kalia's worried glances toward the door in the poorly used sitting room let Alex know she was still concerned about her father overhearing. The werewolves had been too restless to do anything remotely close to sitting.

"It is that bad, Kali. It's not like you know," Boris spat. At Kalia's hurt expression, Boris sighed. "Look. I know you're *caught in-between* and all," he said, waving his fingers. "But for those of us real werewolves, it's hard to think of anything but phasing tonight. Right, Alex?"

Alex wasn't sure Boris' explanation had helped Kalia feel any better. He gave her a forced cheerful smile. "There are benefits to not being able to stop moving. I fixed the squeaky door."

Alex opened the door to the closet and shut it again for emphasis. It gave a louder squeak than it had when he started.

Kalia rolled her eyes. "You took off the hinges, cleaned them, checked the alignment, refastened the screws, and it still squeaks. Did you think of greasing the hinges first?"

As if on command, Henry came into the room carrying a bottle of grease on a fancy silver tray that looked as if it should be used to carry fine Hors d'oeuvres or wine in fancy glasses instead. He offered it to Alex with a flourish.

Alex sprayed the grease on the hinges, then opened and shut the door again. To his dismay, it was completely silent. He sighed at Kalia's satisfied expression. "Okay, so the entire day was wasted." He gave Henry a weary smile. "Thank you for bringing the grease."

"You're welcome, sir," Henry replied before leaving the room.

"He apparently likes you," Boris noted, flinging himself into a corner couch with enough force to make it tip on two feet before it fell with a thud back to the floor.

Alex glanced to the shut door uncertainty. "He said he was a manservant and is doing his job."

Boris smirked. "Do you see any servants following me around? Our servants avoid Kalia and I like the plague until they absolutely have to be around us. Henry seems to actually like your company. It's odd."

Alex walked to the bay windows as he had done a million times that day. The sun was setting. Relief that he would soon be able to run in the moonlight filled his chest, then a nagging thought touched his mind. He turned slowly. "Where do you go during the full moon?"

He had a sudden cringing image of phasing in his bedroom and spending the whole time locked within the walls of the Dickson household afraid to make a sound in case the servants checked on him and were terrified out of their minds. The worst would be Mr. Dickson. For all he knew, the ex-Extremist still had weapons that would no doubt render a phased werewolf into a nonentity.

"We have chains in the basement," Boris said with a hint of dread in his voice. "Dad's too worried we'll kill the servants or terrorize the neighborhood. It's his requirement when we're home during the full moon."

Alex tried to keep his voice steady. "Even you?" he asked, meeting Kalia's gaze.

She nodded, her light blue eyes serious.

The dread in his stomach tightened into a knot at the thought of chains around his neck and wrists. He had heard of Jet and some of the other professors suffering such things, but never imagined he would also.

Something flashed in Kalia's gaze. It took him a second to recognize it as laughter. He glanced at Boris. The Alpha was watching him with an almost-straight face. Suddenly, Boris' grim expression dissolved into a huge smile.

"Gotcha," he crowed.

Alex looked at Kalia. She was smiling as well. For the moment, it looked as if the brother and sister were extremely pleased with their joke.

"You know that was mean," Alex said.

Boris laughed. "Yeah, but you should have seen your face. You tried to keep calm, but I could tell you were close to panicking."

Kalia grinned. "So close."

Alex hesitated, then nodded. "I was close."

"I told you," Boris hooted. "He'll believe anything." He gave Alex a closer look. "You must really think things are horrible here for us."

Alex forced a nonchalant shrug. "I don't know. Your siblings avoid you. Your parents blow up if you mention a word about werewolves, and you said yourself that you've hated what you are since you saw the disgust on your father's face the first time you phased."

He regretted the words as soon as they left his mouth. Sometimes being honest wasn't the most pro-life choice. Boris looked at his sister. Kalia's eyes were wide. Alex doubted she had ever heard Boris voice anything like that. He wished he realized Boris had spoken the words in confidence.

Alex's muscles tensed, ready to defend himself. It was so close to the full moon that he could feel the wolf pulsing beneath his skin. He could imagine the fur running up his arms. The sensation of his ears wanting to grow and become pointed tingled through the sides of his head. He could imagine his nose elongating, smells flooding it with so much information that to breathe was to understand life.

"Alex?" the note of panic in Kalia's voice brought him back.

Alex shook his head, clearing his thoughts. He realized both Boris and Kalia were staring at him.

"Sorry," Alex apologized to Boris. "I shouldn't have said that."

Boris shook his head without taking his eyes off Alex. "It's not that. You changed, uh, phased, but only part way. We were watching you and you became something different. It's like you were a wolf, but still a man."

Alex looked at Kalia for confirmation. "I've never seen anything like it," she said. There was the slightest tremble of fear in her voice.

"I thought I was imagining it," Alex told them, wanting to take away their worry. "I was afraid Boris was angry about what I said and might attack me."

"Wonder what gave you that idea," Boris replied with derision at himself. "But you didn't have to go all weird beast like that."

"I don't know what I did," Alex said honestly. "It didn't feel strange, just different."

"You had wolf ears," Kalia told him, the fear gone from her voice. "Your nose was bigger, and hair was starting to grow on your arms."

"Fur," Boris corrected. "Gray fur, like when you're a wolf. Only, you weren't."

Alex shook his head. "That doesn't make sense."

Boris glanced at his sister. "I guess we're lucky we weren't at dinner."

Kalia gave a half-smile. "Though I would give anything to

see Mom's expression if he did that during chicken manicotti."

She gave Alex a hopeful look.

"No way," Alex protested. "Whatever just happened, I'm not doing it in front of your parents. They're ready to kick me out as it is."

"Probably not the best idea," Boris added. He and Alex had agreed not to tell Kalia about Alex's bodyguard trip with Mr. Dickson. With her headaches, they didn't think she needed another stressor. Instead, Boris shrugged. "Anyway. Just don't do that again, whatever it was."

"I'll try not to," Alex replied, though it came out sounding more like a question than a statement because he didn't even know what he had done to make *it* happen.

"And to answer your question, we can do whatever we want," Boris replied. "The servants know something's up with us, well, me, but they don't know what. As long as I keep it that way, Mom and Dad prefer not to take an interest in what I do during full moons."

"So what do you do?" Alex pressed.

A smile crept across Boris' face that Alex was certain meant nothing good. "I'll show you when it's time."

Alex left them in the sitting room when it came closer to phasing time. His skin itched. There was no fighting the pull of the full moon, and he didn't want to. He longed to run in the night lit by the bright shimmering reflected light. His body ached for the rush of leaping logs and dodging trees intent on the scent of a deer or rabbit. He wished for the laughing of the brook that traveled through the forest to Dray's greenhouses that amazingly enough hid Mouse's helicopter. He wanted to follow the rise of the forest floor to the peak of the cliff that looked over the Academy, the same cliff Tennison had almost jumped off.

A shudder ran through Alex's skin, but it was different. He felt the same tingle that he had in the sitting room. His senses felt sharper. He could smell the oily scent of shoe polish applied too heavily to the spare penny loafers in the wardrobe. The whispered swish of a socked foot sounded rooms away as one of the inhabitants of the Dickson manor prepared for bed. There was a scent in the air he hadn't noticed before, a lemony pine that lingered on the bedframe as though used to shine the mahogany months before they started applying an orange-based cleaner instead.

Alex's head jerked up. He stared at his reflection in the mirror across the room. Familiar dark blue eyes looked back at him, the same color as Cassie and Jet's; but that was all he recognized. Instead of his normal ears, large, pointed ears with gray fur poked through his wavy black hair. A muzzle took the place of his nose and mouth. The nose twitched, and he smelled the scent of the boysenberry candle a servant had placed in an alcove further down the hallway.

Alex's heart stuttered. He grabbed at his chest. He winced and stared down at thick black claws that took the place of his fingernails. His knees gave out and he collapsed to the floor.

***

"I'm not sure what the protocol is for this," a voice said with uncertainty.

Alex opened his eyes to find Henry hovering over him.

"Protocol for what?" Alex replied. He pushed himself up to a sitting position.

Henry grabbed a pillow from the bed and propped it behind him.

"Well, sir." Henry glanced uncomfortably out the window. "It's close to nightfall. The crickets have begun to chirp louder."

Alex couldn't understand what Henry was trying to tell him. He also couldn't remember why he had been lying on the floor in the first place instead of using the perfectly good bed. He glanced up at the mirror across the room. The images of what he had seen flooded through his mind.

"Something's wrong," he said, rising quickly.

Henry grabbed him before the swarm of lightheadedness at the sudden movement made him fall again.

"Take it easy, sir. I'm sure we can get you outside in time," Henry replied.

Alex stared at him. "Outside?"

Henry nodded and spoke slowly as if Alex had lost more than a few brain cells when he fell. "The moon is rising."

The realization hit Alex. "You know."

"That you're a werewolf? Yes," Henry replied simply.

"But-but Boris said none of the servants knew. I'm supposed to keep his secret."

"And yours, I presume," Henry added. At Alex's nod, Henry gave a small smile. "Servants know a lot more than we let on; probably a lot more than Mr. and Mrs. Dickson suspect."

Alex gave him a searching look. "You're not afraid?"

Henry returned the look. "Should I be?"

Alex shook his head. "I'm not exactly used to being around humans, at least this many. Maybe I should be the one who's afraid."

Henry smothered a smile. "Don't worry, sir. Your secret's safe with me."

"Do me a favor?" Alex asked.

Henry bowed his head. "Anything."

"Call me Alex."

Henry nodded with another smile. "Allow me to show you a back passage outside, Alex. I assume we don't have much time to lose."

The telling shudder that ran down Alex's spine agreed. He followed Henry quickly to the door.

Chapter Twenty-six

Alex found Boris pacing the inside of the wall. At Alex's appearance, the black-coated Alpha gave a snort filled with impatience. Alex let his tongue hang out in the silly wolf grin that always made Cassie laugh. Boris shook his head and trotted away, leaving Alex to follow behind.

The guards were noticeably absent from the back wall. Alex wondered if that was luck or on purpose. Perhaps Mr. Dickson knew more about his son's activities than Boris realized. Alex followed Boris to the statue of a lion on the inside of the back gate. The Alpha leaped onto the lion's back, then up to the wall. The soft sound of wolf paws hitting the ground on the other side came to Alex's ears.

Alex leaped onto the lion's back, then to the top of the wall. He glanced back in time to see a silhouette in one of the windows. His memory of the night before said that it was Kalia's. He wondered how it must be to stay victim of the moonlight, yet unable to phase and enjoy it. He had no doubt Kalia was pacing inside like he and Boris had done in the sitting room all day. Perhaps it was their activity that had enabled her to stay still. With them gone, he wondered how she would maintain her sanity behind the walls.

Boris let out a huff of annoyance from below. Alex gave the silhouette one last look, then leaped down. In a flash of shadow, Boris was running. Alex followed him into the silvery moonlight.

Boris definitely had a destination in mind; it was obvious by the werewolf's unwavering direction of flight. They loped across a road and back into the underbrush that separated the ritzy part of town from the older establishments. Before long, Alex was following Boris down alleys and streets into a gloomy part of the city in which most of the businesses looked like they had been abandoned.

Broken windows, cushion-less couches soggy with countless storms, old televisions with the screens smashed out, and garbage bags ripped open by cats and even bigger rats littered the narrow streets. Boris continued to run without pausing as though he had followed the same route many times.

Alex began to catch the scent of other werewolves. He saw paw prints on the pavement before them. Werewolves in wolf form had crossed the same path. The signs Colleen had taught them in class let him know that the wolf trails were extremely fresh. Boris ran as if they were late; perhaps he truly did have something waiting for them.

The scent of werewolf became overpowering. Alex began to see shadows in the adjoining alleys, pacing figures who ran as they did, intent on the same destination. Foreboding filled Alex's chest. Instinct told him not to rush into something headlong that he didn't know he could get back out of. What if Boris was leading him into a trap? What if Boris' Extremist parents still practiced, and they knew Alex's connection with Jet and Jaze.

His steps slowed. He was about to listen to his instincts and turn around when he glanced back. The golden shine of six pairs of wolf eyes met his gaze. They were following him. He didn't know if he should fight or run. The spaces between the adjoining alleys had gotten longer. The scent of rot and the aged, baked wood of the old, collapsing buildings crowded his nose. The wolves behind him paced closer.

Boris gave an encouraging bark ahead. Alex had to choose between fighting the half-dozen werewolves behind him or catch up to the one who had led him there. Another bark sounded, more impatient this time. Alex snorted softly, clearing the scent of decay away. He trotted to Boris, leaving the other wolves to follow.

Boris turned at the middle of the long alley and disappeared. The glow of wolf eyes coming from the other direction made Alex hurry forward. He found storm doors flung wide open, revealing the poorly-lit basement of a huge warehouse. With at least a dozen werewolves in front and behind, Alex knew he didn't have a choice. He gritted his teeth and padded down the cement stairs.

Alex blinked, then blinked again. He paused at the top of the first landing and stared at the sight before him. Roughly fifty wolves lounged, ran, or tumbled around the huge basement. Machines that had once made up what appeared to be an old carpentry business were pushed to the sides to make room for the revelry. The sounds of barks, yips, and huffs filled the air.

The padding of paws on cement made Alex's ears flick back. He stepped to the side in time to avoid the werewolves he had seen in the alley. They shoved past him and trotted down the stairs without a backwards look. The wolves were a mixture of young and old, male and female. Alphas and the others mingled without conflict. It was a haven of sorts, a safe escape for werewolves looking to enjoy the full moon's forced phase without danger.

Boris caught Alex's stare. The Alpha gave a small huff of humor before turning to pace down the cement steps after the other wolves. Alex chided himself for his lack of trust of the Alpha and followed behind.

As soon as Alex's paws touched the floor, a shoulder slammed into his, knocking him to the ground. Alex sprang up with his fangs bared and a snarl rumbling from his chest, ready to take on his attacker. All around him, other huffs sounded, giving laughter to the situation. Alex focused on the wiry brown wolf who had struck him. The wolf appeared to be a bit older than him with dark green eyes. He waved his black-tipped tail as a slight apology.

Alex realized the attack had been nothing more than some sort of initiation. Apparently his bristling fur and bared teeth was what the others had hoped for.

Boris bumped Alex's shoulder with his own, tipping his head to the side to indicate the wolf. Alex followed his gaze to see the wiry wolf stretch his front paws forward as a puppy would to invite another puppy to play. Alex was torn between amusement and affront. He was no longer a puppy, and was still a bit ruffled by the unexpected attack.

The wiry wolf rose and shook himself. Boris and the wolf bumped shoulders as if they knew each other. Boris tipped his head with his ears forward to indicate that Alex should follow them. The two roamed around the machines to the center of the room. As Alex paced behind them, more wolves fell in, crowding each other. Boris and the wolf snapped at each other. Other wolves leaped at them. Soon, Alex watched an all-out good-natured wolf brawl spread across the floor of the warehouse.

Boris hit Alex's shoulder hard enough to send him sprawling, but this time Alex was ready. He leaped back to his feet and sprang over Boris before the Alpha could strike again. Boris turned in surprise. The wiry wolf tried to knock Alex off his feet again, but Alex jumped back. As the wolf followed, Alex continued back. The wolf was relentless, snapping at his paws and trying to make him stumble. The mock fights around them slowly stopped as others became interested in what was going on.

Alex couldn't shake the brown wolf. He was fast, but the brown wolf was taller and older. He had a longer reach and knocked Alex down more times than Alex got away. Alex was growing frustrated. He didn't know why he had become the wolf's target, but apparently their little tussle had the attention of the entire warehouse. Even Boris watched with an amused gaze as if Alex's discomfort didn't bother him.

Alex hated feeling foolish, especially if that was the brown wolf's only intention. He was worried his heart would skip a beat and he would end up sprawled on the floor like an idiot. For a wolf, a true wolf, the others' estimation of that wolf's power proved his standing in the pack. If Alex slipped up, he would be hard-pressed to gain the respect of the wolves in the warehouse. Pride and instinct refused to let him fail, yet the persistence and skill of the wolf that attacked him didn't leave room for any lapse of attention or strength.

Alex knew he couldn't depend on his heart to hold up under more strain. He had a sudden idea. The next time the brown wolf sprang at his paws, Alex leaped sideways and latched onto the back of the brown wolf's neck. He rolled over the wolf and jerked his head around. The momentum flung the brown wolf halfway across the warehouse.

The brown wolf hit the side of a round cylinder with enough force to dent it before he fell to the ground. Silence filled the room. Only Alex's rough breathing and ragged heartbeat met his ears. He held perfectly still, wondering if he had done the right thing, or if he had seriously offended who appeared to be in charge of the wolf gathering.

After a few seconds of intense silence, the brown wolf rose to his feet. He met Alex's gaze. The wolf's eyes were two different colors. For a second, Alex thought of Drogan. The Extremist leader's eyes were green and dark blue. Even a picture of the man had sent Cassie screaming with the memories of the terror he had caused.

Yet this werewolf's eyes were brown and green. He padded slowly across the floor, his gaze only on Alex. Alex stood perfectly still. He knew it would only take a bark of command for every wolf in the warehouse to tear him apart. Alex would fight; he would never give in to anything without a fight. Yet it was obvious it would be a very losing battle.

The brown wolf paused a few paces from Alex. Very slowly, as if time no longer mattered, the wolf pushed his paws forward into a long, stretching bow, the same invitation to play he had given at the beginning. The wolves around them began to break away, the tension dissolved. At Alex's surprised stare, the wolf's mouth opened into a yawn that ended in a bark. He rose and shook himself again. He finished crossing the space between them and butted Alex's shoulder with his head, a wolf's sign of acceptance. Wolves flooded over to them, swarming the brown wolf and Alex. Before long, it seemed he had met every werewolf in the warehouse.

***

"Not what you expected, huh?" Boris noted.

They sat on the landing where they had first entered. The hold of the moonlight had long since faded, and Boris had rustled them up some clothes from the apparently well-established stash in the warehouse. Other werewolves lounged around the room or went home. A few of the younger ones still played in wolf form between the machines.

"Not what I expected at all," Alex replied. "I thought you might be taking me off to slaughter."

Boris gave him a glance filled with laughter. "You're honest, at least." The Alpha was quiet for a moment with his gaze on the floor. When he broke the silence, he didn't look at Alex. "So why did you still follow me?"

Alex thought about it. "I'm pretty hard to kill."

Boris snorted a laugh. "That's an understatement."

A man with long brown hair and mismatched green and brown eyes climbed up the stairs to join them.

"Sorry about startling you there," he apologized, taking a seat a few paces away from Alex. He let his legs dangle over the edge of the landing. "It's sort of our tradition to haze newcomers." He fell silent, then gave a slight smile as he said, "I suppose it's a bit cruel."

"It's not that bad," Alex said.

Both of the other werewolves laughed at Alex's uncertain tone.

The brown-haired werewolf held out a hand. "I'm Red."

"Red?" Alex asked.

Red grinned. "I know. I had red hair when I was born. It eventually turned brown, but I was already stuck with the name."

"Nice to officially meet you. I'm Alex." He shook Red's

hand.

"That was a nice retaliation back there," Red said, nodding toward the warehouse floor where they had fought. "Nobody's flipped me like that before."

Alex glanced at Boris. "Even the Alphas?"

Red gave a slight lift of his shoulders, a shrug that said much more than his words. "There's a reason I challenge each wolf who comes in. I don't care for bullying or fighting on full moons. Each who makes it to my safe house deserves a night of freedom from pecking orders or rank fights."

"You don't allow rank fights?" Alex couldn't believe it.

Red smiled. "When you have enough Alphas willing to back up your rules, nobody messes with them. Trust me. It's nice to put all of that aside for a night."

Several werewolves walked up the stairs. "Excuse me," Red said. He walked with the werewolves to the door and talked with them quietly for a few minutes.

"He's a lone wolf," Boris told Alex quietly.

"He doesn't have a pack?" Alex replied.

Boris shook his head. "I don't know what happened to them during the genocide, but I know it was bad. Red runs by himself, but keeps this place as a gathering safe house for full moons and to house families on the run. He's a good guy."

Alex nodded. "I can tell." He asked what had been bothering him. "Why are all of these wolves here? There are kids that don't go to the Academy. It's safer there. Why don't their parents send them?"

Boris studied the wall across from them. "Not everyone's parents can afford to send them to the Academy."

That surprised Alex. "Jaze would take care of it."

Boris shook his head. "I don't mean financially." He looked at Alex. "You lost everyone." He said it as a fact. "I think you'd understand how those who have lost so much cling to what they have left. How do you tell parents who have lost some of their children to send away the rest, even if it means their safety? We hold those we love closest to us so we can protect them ourselves, not send them away."

The Alpha couldn't hide the bitterness in his tone. Alex remembered Kalia's arguments with her mother the first time they arrived at the Academy. She had been sent away with her brother, problems their parents didn't know how to handle. No matter how many toys, clothes, or nice furniture occupied Boris and Kalia's rooms, the objects didn't mean love. In fact, the emptiness of such things was even more pronounced to Alex now that he saw them through Boris' eyes.

"We need an Academy the parents can go to, also. Somewhere families can be safe together," Alex said quietly, thinking aloud. "Somewhere Drogan and the General can't touch them."

"Those are names not allowed here," Red said from behind them.

Alex turned quickly, worried about offending the werewolf who had been kind to them. "I'm sorry. They're a bit close to home."

"Drogan killed Alex's parents in front of him," Boris said.

The silence that hung in the air let Alex know Boris was letting him decide whether or not to tell Red he was Jet's brother. Alex chose for the time being to keep the information to himself. He wasn't sure why he felt that was the right decision, but since leaving the Academy, he had come to realize that the world wasn't quite as black and white as he had imagined it.

"I'm sorry to hear that," Red said. "There are many here who have suffered the same. You are among friends, and welcome to return at any time."

Boris and Alex knew a dismissal when it was given to

them. Weak sunlight filtered through the storm door to the alley.

"Have a merry Christmas, Red," Boris said, shaking the werewolf's hand.

"You as well," Red replied. He patted Alex's shoulder. "Take care of this one."

"I will," Boris promised.

Chapter Twenty-seven

"Is your family going to mad that you're late on Christmas morning?" Alex asked.

"Who says we're going to be late?" Boris replied. He dug through a pile of garbage bags near the entrance to the underground warehouse. A few seconds later, he pulled out a cell phone in a sandwich bag. Boris opened the bag and removed the phone. "It's a pre-pay," he explained as he dialed the number.

A few minutes later, a limousine pulled up to the mouth of the alley. The limo driver didn't look the least bit surprised to pick them up at such a dangerous part of the city in the early hours of the morning. The guards and then the servants at the door were equally expressionless upon the arrival of the two boys.

"Go get changed into something nice for breakfast," Boris said as he jogged up the stairs to his own room.

Alex did as instructed. A few minutes later, he had shrugged into his only dress suit Henry had already thoughtfully set out on his bed, and was back downstairs. To his surprise, Kalia was the only other person in the dining room. He took a seat across from her.

"Have a nice night?" Kalia asked.

The hint of longing in her eyes made Alex downplay the experience. "It was alright," he conceded. "Not like running in the forest."

"I saw how that went," Kalia replied. "It's a little more difficult with missiles chasing after you."

"Don't remind me," Alex said with a shudder.

She smiled. "I still haven't thanked you for carrying me back. I feel so bad about that. You were already a target. You didn't need to take care of me, too."

"I wasn't about to leave you there," Alex replied. The sunlight from the wide windows around the dining hall danced in her gaze. He was taken by the many colors of blue caught in her irises. "What kind of person do you think I am?"

"I'm really not sure anymore," Kalia replied.

She was staring at him with such an intensity that Alex felt she could see every bit of him, the fear, the defiance, the drive to fight Drogan, the reluctance to accept that he deserved to be alive when so many had already died. He felt as if all of his defenses crumbled away, as though her searching look rendered him completely bare. The sensation sent a shiver down his spine.

Alex was afraid to move, filled with fear that she would turn away from him after all she had seen. He was damaged. He was filled with the haunted memories of watching his parents die. He was full of holes, merely a shell of who he had been when Jet was still alive. He hated who he was, but couldn't find that carefree boy again no matter how hard he looked.

As if she couldn't help herself, Kalia reached out a hand and set it gently on his cheek. The heat from her fingers warmed his skin.

Alex closed his eyes, unable to meet her gaze anymore.

She breathed his name so softly he would have missed it if he hadn't had his werewolf senses. "Alex."

Alex gathered his courage and opened his eyes again. The understanding in her light blue gaze as she looked at him filled him with so many emotions he had to blink to keep the tears from falling.

"You don't have to hide yourself," she whispered.

"If I pretend to be whole long enough, I can almost believe it," Alex replied as softly.

"We're all searching for pieces of ourselves," Kalia told him. "But we can't do it alone. You have to let people in."

Alex shook his head. "Nobody should have to see what's inside me."

Kalia gave him a soft, sad smile. It filled her eyes with sorrow as though she wanted to cry for him.

"Merry Christmas!" Jordy yelled as he and Alice ran into the room. Their nice clothes were already wrinkled and Alice's had what appeared to be toothpaste on the collar of her dress.

Kalia and Alex sat back. Kalia gave him a quick smile as though they had shared something that meant a lot to her.

"Merry Christmas," Elizabeth said, following the children at a more sedate pace.

Kalia returned the greeting. Eventually, Mr. and Mrs. Dickson entered. As soon as they sat down, servants began to flood the room bearing trays of pancakes, waffles, ham, pudding, and spreads.

Boris slumped into his seat a few minutes later looking exhausted. "Mornin'," he mumbled.

"Did you forget something?" Mr. Dickson asked.

Boris looked down at the absent space beneath his chin.

"I have your tie, sir," Boris' man servant said, offering the already tied red and green object of discussion to Boris.

"Thanks," Boris muttered, slipping it over his head. "As if I need a noose around my neck to eat breakfast."

"Boris," his mother chided. She turned her attention to her youngest children. "Alice, what have you gotten on your lace? And Jordy, it looks like you've been wrestling with Todd again. I'll have him know that his job is to dress you, not entertain you."

"It's not Todd's fault he has to chase Jordy all over the nursery to get his clothes on," Elizabeth pointed out. She

255

gave a fake yawn, covering her mouth with a dainty hand. "I don't know how anyone can keep up with those two rascals."

Kalia caught Alex's gaze and rolled her eyes. Alex smiled in return.

Breakfast went rather quickly with the younger children begging their elders to hurry so they could run into the sitting room to see what presents waited for them under the tree. Even Kalia was caught up in the excitement. Alex trailed behind. He knew not to expect anything. He was a stranger to the house, and longed to be back with Cassie at the Academy where the familiarity of the holiday and a family to share it with was enough of a gift.

Mr. Dickson waited for him near the door to the sitting room.

"We didn't expect you to be with us," he began by way of explanation for the lack of presents.

"It's okay," Alex replied. "I really don't need anything."

"Just the same," Mr. Dickson said. "Here's a little token of my appreciation for the other night. This one can switch from manual to automatic. I'd recommend the automatic for starters."

He took Alex's hand and set something in it. Alex stared down at the set of keys on his palm.

"Take it for a joy ride," Mr. Dickson said.

Alex looked up at him. "You know I'm fifteen, right?"

Mr. Dickson shrugged. "Anyone who can take on four adult men by himself is old enough to drive in my book."

"What if I wreck it?" Alex asked.

Mr. Dickson chuckled. "I'll just report it stolen."

At Alex's hesitation, Kalia's father gave him a push toward the garage. "Go on. Be back by lunch." He paused. "Try not to destroy it. It's one of my favorites."

Alex walked numbly in the direction Mr. Dickson had

indicated. He pulled open the door to the garage. The lights turned on automatically and he stared. Henry had shown him the cars on their tour through the house, but at that time they were only vehicles, not something Alex had been given ownership of for the next four hours. He wondered which one Mr. Dickson had deemed fit for a stranger.

The key was red and had a horse on its hind legs in gold on the side. Alex may have been sheltered at the Academy, but he still knew the symbol for a Ferrari when he saw one. Sure it was a joke, Alex searched for a car to fit the symbol. With a start, he found himself staring at a bright red Ferrari that looked as though it had never been driven in its life.

The side garage door slid up. Alex squinted at the sudden sunlight. Boris stood near the door.

"I think this might be a mistake," Alex said uncertainly.

"Own it," Boris replied. "If Dad gave you the key, you can't go back inside until you've driven it."

Alex stared at him.

Boris indicated the car. "Drive, Alex," he said in a tone that left no room for argument.

Alex opened the door. He carefully sat down on the black leather seat afraid of accidentally scratching it. The crisp smell of a new car filled his nose. "You sure about this?" he asked.

"Is this your first time driving?" Boris asked with a smirk. At Alex's nod, he grinned. "Then I'm sure. Put the key in, turn it on. Okay, now push the start button."

Alex pushed the starter. The engine roared to life. He stared, amazing at the rumble that came from beneath the hood. He put his left foot on the left pedal and pushed it. Nothing happened. He put his right foot on the other pedal. The engine roared. Alex quickly took his foot off.

"You need to put it in gear," Boris explained, sliding into the passenger seat. At Alex's blank look, Boris pointed down.

"Put your right foot on the brake, the one on the left."

"Shouldn't I use my left foot because it's on the left?"

Boris shook his head. "You don't use your left foot at all."

"Why not?"

Boris stared at him. "You just don't, okay? Do you want to drive?"

Alex nodded.

"Okay, then put your right foot on the brake."

Alex did as instructed.

"Pull the paddle next to your right hand."

As Alex let off the brake, the car began to move forward. A smile crept across Alex's face.

"It's in automatic right now," Boris said, reaching for his seatbelt. "We'll work on manual shifting later. For now, I'm going to try to survive this. Put your seatbelt on. You may be a werewolf, but rolling a Ferrari is a bit more painful than you might expect."

Alex clicked the belt on and glanced at him. "You sound like you're talking from experience."

"Let's just say I'm amazed Dad's letting you drive the *new* one," Boris said, emphasizing the new.

Alex smiled as he drove carefully down the driveway.

"Jordy can run faster than this," Boris pointed out.

Alex stepped on the gas. The tires spun, then caught, jerking them forward with a speed that took Alex by surprise. It was only with his werewolf reflexes that he was able to keep the car from slamming into a tree. He pulled it back onto the long driveway with his heart thundering in his chest.

Boris gave a surprised laugh. "I can't believe you did that."

Alex didn't know if he referred to almost wrecking the car, or saving it. Either way worked. He gave a tight laugh. "I know, right?"

He turned his concentration to the road. As they drove through the city, Alex ignored the urge to brake with his left foot. Eventually, he got used to using the right for everything. They soon made it through the city limits and left the houses and buildings far behind.

"We should just keep going," Boris said after a long while of companionable silence had passed.

Alex glanced at him, wondering if the werewolf was joking.

"We could drive on forever, or until the gas runs out," Boris continued. He linked his fingers behind his head, his gaze out at the expanse of land that stretched on before them. "There's got to be somewhere in this world that isn't crowded with fences, buildings, or stop signs." He looked at Alex. "Or humans."

"It's not that bad," Alex said.

"Oh, really?" Boris replied. "You've been sheltered at the Academy the last seven years. You get one taste of my home life and you think that's it?" Boris' voice became passionate. "Don't you realize there's a reason all those werewolves go to Red's warehouse to phase? We're still number one on the humans' hit list. They fear us, and so they kill us. It's that simple."

Alex shook his head, surprised at the turn the conversation had taken. "I don't think it's that simple."

"Really?" The disbelief in Boris' voice colored the air. "Hasn't Drogan taken a personal interest in wiping you and your sister from this world?" At Alex's stunned look, Boris gave a humorless smile. "Students talk, Alex. A human has been trying to kill you, and yet you don't believe it's that bad? Maybe you need to value your life a bit more."

"But your parents are human," Alex pointed out.

"And they remind me of it every time I come home," Boris replied angrily. "We're different, Alex. We're beasts, and you don't believe humans see the need to wipe us from this earth even after the genocide and everything you've been through. I don't get it."

"It's not that," Alex protested. He waved his hand, indicating the town they were driving through. "I have a hard time believing that all humans want to kill us. I doubt it's their main agenda."

"You don't think they'd shoot you on sight if you phased in front of them?" Boris pressed.

Alex hesitated.

"See," Boris replied smugly. "We're monsters. Humans fear monsters. Humans kill what they fear. It's that simple."

Alex carefully turned the car around in a small church parking lot. He didn't trust his skills enough to do it on the main road, even with the lack of traffic that early on Christmas morning.

"I choose to believe there's good out there," Alex said quietly after a few minutes of silence had passed.

Boris snorted. "Good for humans; not good for werewolves."

"Believe what you want."

Several more minutes went by. Finally, Boris shook his head. "Seriously, dude. After all your family's been through, why keep believing that there's good left to be found? They killed your brother and your parents. Jet became a martyr for us, someone to rally behind because he wasn't afraid to lay down his life to protect those he cared about. Did the humans spare him? No."

Alex winced at the sharpness of Boris' tone.

"They slaughtered most of the werewolf race," Boris continued. "We need to be prepared to fight back and establish our place in this world. We shouldn't have to hide the rest of our lives."

"We should be able to live together in peace."

Boris stared at him. "Jaze thought so. Remember what happened when he told the world about werewolves? Even his allies turned against us."

"I don't believe every human had a gun."

"Yeah, well I believe that the ones who did more than made up for those who didn't," Boris replied. "That includes my family."

Alex stared at him. "My family killed your family."

"And vice versa, I'm sure," Boris said sullenly. "In war, all the sides begin to look alike, especially when you suddenly find yourself an ally for the other side." The Alpha looked out the window, the reflection of his expression dark. "I phased right after my seventh birthday party. It was a full moon that night. Luckily, Mom hadn't been thrilled with the idea of a sleepover and sent everyone home after Jonathan sleepwalked and peed in the fridge." He snorted. "Who would have thought such an act saved all their lives."

Boris glanced at Alex. "I have no doubts what my father would have done to protect his family against rumors that he had werewolves for kids. I thought he was going to kill me. I remember not knowing what was going on, then suddenly being a wolf. I stared up at him, filled with fear. He took a step toward the rifle he kept above the living room door." The bitterness of his voice twisted his face. "He actually took a step toward the gun. Then Mom set a hand on his arm. He took one last look at me and stormed from the room. That was the last time I ever felt like my dad really saw me."

"But he protects you," Alex said quietly. "He didn't want you to go the other night because he didn't want you involved in the trouble he had made for himself."

"He said that?" Boris asked with a brush of surprise in his voice.

Alex nodded.

Boris gave a noncommittal huff and leaned back against the seat.

"It must be nice living at the Academy," Boris said above the hum of the wheels over the pavement and the roar of the well-timed engine.

"Sometimes," Alex replied. He tipped his head to indicate the buildings flying past them. "But wolves weren't meant to stay behind walls."

"Beats getting shot at."

Alex nodded. The scar from the bullet wound in his thigh gave a reminding throb. "Yes, it does."

He pulled carefully down the Dicksons' driveway. Henry met them outside the garage.

"I'll park it, sir," he said, opening the door for Alex.

"I can try," Alex replied. At Henry's look, he laughed. "Just kidding. I've been lucky so far. I don't want to push it."

Henry winked. "This is my only chance to drive it, so you're doing us both a favor."

Alex grinned and stepped aside so the servant could slide onto the seat.

"One could get used to this," Henry said.

"I know what you mean," Alex told him. They both laughed.

Chapter Twenty-eight

Cassie ran outside the second the limousine pulled up in the Academy courtyard. Alex laughed when he stepped from the car and she threw her arms around his neck.

"I missed you so much!" she exclaimed.

"See," Boris said to Kalia as they climbed out behind Alex. "It's normal for brothers and sisters to actually get along."

"I like our way better," Kalia replied, punching Boris in the arm.

"Me, too," he said with a good-natured grin. "Should I flush your favorite shirt down the toilet?"

"If you do, your brush will follow," Kalia retorted.

Alex and Cassie stared at Boris. The big Alpha shrugged. "So I have a good brush." He ran a hand through his white-blond hair. "Got to keep this looking good."

Kalia rolled her eyes.

Alex laughed. "Let's get inside. I'm starving."

He and Cassie were about to hurry in when he noticed Kalia struggling with her suitcase.

He took it from her and hefted it easily with his werewolf strength. "After you, ladies."

Kalia and Cassie exchanged a look. Cassie laughed. "Apparently going home with you has been good for him."

Kalia smiled back. "We'll see how long it lasts. They're all animals out here." Both girls burst into laughter.

"Alright, alright," Alex told them. "Get inside."

They ran ahead of him as he and Boris carried the luggage.

"Girls," Boris said with a shake of his head.

Pack Jericho met them in the common room.

"Good to see you survived the holiday," Jericho told him,

slapping Alex on the back.

"You, too," Alex replied. "Any excitement while I was gone?"

"Trent managed to blow up a wall in Professor Mouse's chemistry lab," Terith told him.

"Terith!" Trent rebuked her. "You promised you'd keep that a secret!"

"The whole school felt it," Jericho replied to save Terith from her brother's wrath. "It took them two days to clean all the walls."

"What were you doing?" Alex asked. "We don't even have chemistry this term."

Trent gave an embarrassed shrug. "I was trying to perfect a formula for a high-nitrogen chemical fertilizer to use in Professor Dray's greenhouses. He said he would give me extra credit." Trent blushed. "But I had a little accident involving tipping over the Bunsen burner."

"He was flirting with Cherish," Terith put in.

"Raynen's Second, really?" Jericho replied interestedly.

Trent waved his hand. "That's beside the point! Anyway, the flame accidentally ignited the ammonium nitrate mixture and the rest is still being scrubbed off the walls."

"It stinks in there," little Caitlyn said with a giggle.

Alex grinned. "Sounds exciting. So Cherish, huh?"

"That's not the point!" Trent argued. Everyone laughed.

"Amos and Parker got into a fight," Jericho said. "Apparently Pack Boris had a hard time not fighting the entire holiday with their Alpha gone. Parker told Amos he couldn't have any of the cookies they were serving with Christmas dinner because he wanted Amos to clean the toilets in Pack Boris' quarters."

Alex tried to picture the huge werewolf fighting Parker. "I can guess who won."

Jericho nodded. "Amos broke Parker's other arm, then ate his own cookies and Parker's. I'm glad I don't have to sort that one out."

Alex shrugged. "Maybe Boris will let Amos be in our pack again next year."

"We can hope," Jericho replied.

Alex put his things back in his room. He stood there for a moment breathing in the familiar scents. It felt so good to be home.

Alex began to unpack his suitcase.

"Have you seen Jaze?" Alex asked when Cassie's familiar footsteps paused in the doorway along with another set he recognized.

"We haven't," Tennison replied.

Cassie smiled. "I'm sure he's enjoying some family time with Nikki and baby William during the holidays."

Alex nodded. "I can't blame him." He picked up something from his bag. "Want to go with me to give this to Meredith?"

Cassie's eyes widened when she took the object from Alex. It was a snow globe with a family of wolves inside. They lounged in a snow-laden forest. One of the pups was tackling another while the parents relaxed beneath the trees.

"It's beautiful," Cassie exclaimed.

"Think she'll like it?"

"She'll love it," his sister gushed. "Let's go give it to her."

"I'll catch you afterwards," Tennison said.

To Alex's surprise, Cassie stood on her tiptoes and kissed the skinny werewolf on the cheek. "Okay, see you soon."

She skipped out of the room ahead of Alex.

He looked at Tennison. The werewolf had the presence of mind to look somewhat abashed. "Uh, sorry about that. She's a bit free with her affection."

Alex tried not to let it bother him. "That's okay. I'm glad you two are happy."

Tennison nodded. "I'm not going to hurt her; don't worry."

Alex gave him a level look. "I'm trusting you."

Tennison nodded again. "You saved my life. I'm not going to stab you in the back."

"Thanks," Alex said, though worry for his sister still lingered around the edges of his mind.

"You coming, Alex?" Cassie called from the common room.

"I'd better go," Alex said. He hurried from Tennison, sure it would do him good to put some space between himself and his sister's chosen boyfriend for the moment.

He followed Cassie down the stairs to the medical wing. They found Meredith in the back mending a rip in a hospital gown. Meredith's smile lit the room when she saw the twins enter.

"No matter how careful you tell werewolves to be with these things, they just don't know their own strength," Meredith said, putting her sewing aside to embrace the siblings. "It's so good to have you back, Alex."

"Good to be back," Alex replied.

When Meredith let them go, Cassie cleared her throat pointedly.

"Oh, uh, we brought you a Christmas present," Alex said quickly.

Cassie put it in her aunt's hands.

Meredith stared down at the tiny scene. "It's beautiful!" she exclaimed.

The smile that glowed on her face warmed Alex's heart.

Meredith shook the snow globe, causing tiny flakes to dance through the water and swirl around the wolf family.

"It's perfect," Meredith said. Alex was surprised to see tears in her eyes. She pulled them both close again and gave them an even tighter hug.

"I made you this!" she exclaimed, letting them go as if suddenly remembering. She hurried to a cloth bag by the table and pulled out something long. She walked back to Alex and wrapped the scarf around his neck. "I know it's silly to make scarves for werewolves, since you don't get that cold and all, but I liked the colors and figured it was something. I'm not exactly sure what else you would like, so I guess you'll have to settle for this even though it's only a scarf and I'm sure there are many more things you would have liked. I just don't know enough about—"

"I like it," Alex said with a warm laugh.

"You do?" Meredith asked with a hopeful smile.

Alex nodded. "Very much." He wrapped the scarf made of black and silver thick, soft yarn closer around his neck. "It fits perfectly."

Aunt Meredith and Cassie laughed.

"That's the nice thing about scarves," Meredith said with a pleased smile.

Cassie grinned. "She made me one, too. I'll show it to you when we go back upstairs."

"Thank you, Aunt Meredith," Alex told her, giving his aunt another hug.

"You're welcome, Alex. I'm glad you're back," she replied.

***

Alex made his way to Nikki and Jaze's rooms. He found Nikki in the living room playing with baby William. Nikki gave him a big hug.

"It's great to have you back," she exclaimed.

"Thank you," Alex replied, ruffling baby William's hair. "Have you seen Jaze?"

Nikki shook her head. "They left a while ago on a mission. You could check with Brock."

Alex thanked her and slipped through the hidden entrance to the tunnel from Jaze's main living quarters. He worked quickly along the passage without the need of light. He was anxious to find out if Mouse had figured out a way to block Drogan's heat signature recognition technology so that the other students would be safe while he was at the school. If not, he was determined to leave again and return only when his presence wasn't a danger. His time out with Boris had let him know that there were indeed werewolves living successfully in hiding. If he had to, he would join them.

"Brock?" Alex called when he reached the small monitoring room.

The human was nowhere to be found. Alex left through the side tunnel to the huge security cavern.

"Brock!" he yelled.

There was no answer. A seed of foreboding began to sprout in Alex's chest. Whenever Jaze's pack was on a mission, Brock's job was to be their eyes and ears. He was always glued to the screens, yet he was nowhere to be found.

"Brock, come in Brock." Jaze's voice demanded.

Alex grabbed the small headset near the computer.

"Jaze, it's me, Alex."

"Alex, what are you doing there? You've got to find

Brock," Jaze said.

Alex scanned the monitors. They showed scenes from security cameras around a large facility he didn't recognize. None of the footage from the team's cameras came through.

"What's going on?" Alex asked.

"We're trapped, and there are other lives on the line. If you can't find Brock, I need you to call the GPA. You've got to send them to our location. I'll upload it to you now." Coordinates appeared on the screen.

"Got it," Alex answered.

"And Alex," Jaze began. The voice muffled. Several shots were fired. Static filled the air.

Alex's heart began to race. "Jaze?" he called. There was no answer.

Alex raced up the stairs. He burst into Pack Jericho's quarters. Cassie and Tennison were playing a card game on the floor while Jericho, Terith, and Trent were discussing night games diagrams at the table.

"Alex, what's wrong?" Cassie asked, alarmed at the look on his face.

"I need all of you to come with me and not ask any questions," Alex replied as he fought to catch his breath from the mad dash.

"Let's go," Jericho commanded.

Von appeared at the doorway to the hall. "What's going on?"

"Von, can you cover for us for a bit?" Alex asked. "We've got to go do something, and we might be a while."

"No problem," Von replied.

Kalia walked in from the girls' hallway. She paused when everyone looked at her.

"Uh, is everything okay?" she asked uncertainly.

"Kalia, come with us," Alex said.

At his tone of command, she fell in line behind the others. Alex raced back down the stairs. The sound of the six other set of footsteps filled him with certainty that he was making the right decision.

Alex led the way into Jaze's office and shoved open the door to the tunnel. The members of Pack Jericho stared at him with astonishment.

"I don't have time to explain," Alex said. He motioned them inside. Kalia, at least, had been there before. She helped lead the others down to the main cavern.

"Welcome to the Wolf Den," Alex said, shoving past his pack mates. He hurried to the surveillance wall, then turned to face them. "Jaze and the others are trapped on a mission. We need to get them out."

"Are you sure this is a good idea?" Trent asked.

Alex pointed to the helicopter. "Can you fly that?"

Trent swallowed noisily, then nodded. "I've been working with Professor Mouse on a smaller style, but the basic controls should be the same."

Alex nodded. "Then this is a good idea. Everyone to the chopper."

He grabbed Kalia's arm before she could join them. "Not you. I need you here."

"You going into danger," Kalia argued. "I'm not staying behind."

Alex pointed at the screens. "I need you to be our eyes and ears." He picked up the headset. "Someone has to let us know if we're walking into danger. Can you do that?"

Kalia hesitated. Her eyes roamed from the helicopter to the weapons desk on the other side of the room. "You're going armed?"

"Definitely," Alex told her.

"Be careful," Kalia said. To his surprise, she kissed him

lightly on the lips.

Alex stared at her in shock.

"Come back here, okay?" Kalia asked quietly.

Alex nodded numbly.

Kalia smiled. "Go then." She pushed him gently toward the weapons table.

"Come on, Romeo," Jericho called, already sorting through the guns, knives, grenades, and other equipment Alex didn't even know the name of.

Alex shook himself and jogged to the table. He picked up a Glock. "These guns are loaded with sleeping agents." He glanced at the others grouped uncertainly behind him. "Don't shoot anyone in the head."

"Got it," Trent said, reaching for a gun.

Terith grabbed his hand. "I don't think this is a good idea."

"Do you want to wake up tomorrow and find out that all of our professors are dead?" Alex asked. He felt bad about being so blunt, but he knew they were wasting precious time arguing.

Terith shook her head.

"Then choose a gun and get to the helicopter," Alex concluded.

To his relief, everyone obeyed. They piled into the helicopter and pulled on the headsets. Alex took the seat next to Trent. After verifying that everyone was buckled in, he gave Trent a thumb's up.

"It's great to have a helicopter in the basement of the Academy and all," Trent began. "But how do you expect me to fly through a cement wall?"

Alex leaned over and pushed the button Mouse had pressed. The ceiling opened. The others stared in awe as the greenhouses split and lifted to give them space to depart.

"Okay," Trent replied. "No more questions." He started the rotors. After a few minutes of double checking to ensure that he had the controls figured out, Trent maneuvered the helicopter into the air.

"I found Brock," Kalia called into their headsets during their flight.

"Where was he?" Alex asked, relieved.

"In the bathroom. There's a shoe streak across the floor. He must have slipped. His head has a huge gash in it and he's lost a lot of blood. Meredith's taking care of him."

"Good to know," Alex replied. "If he's conscious, ask him how to contact the GPA. We're going to need them."

"Will do," Kalia replied.

Alex turned his attention to the path they were taking. Night was starting to fall. He was grateful it would help cover their flight.

Chapter Twenty-nine

The coordinates led them to a short, squat building on the outskirts of the capital. Trent landed the helicopter with a jarring thud about a half mile from the complex.

"You call that flying?" Terith asked.

"I said I've flown before, not landed," Trent replied. "It's not as easy as it looks."

"Obviously," Terith retorted.

Jericho confronted the pack. "We're in a dangerous situation. Everyone have each other's backs and take care of your pack mates. If this doesn't work, we're going to all be in trouble."

Trent dug through the back of the helicopter.

"What are you looking for?" Alex asked.

Trent pulled out a huge pipe with handles.

"Are you kidding me?" Tennison exclaimed, backing away from the small werewolf. "You brought a bazooka?"

"A manportable recoilless antitank rocker launcher weapon, to be exact," Trent corrected him. "And yes, I brought it."

"Are you sure that's a good idea?" Jericho asked.

Trent gestured toward the wall. "How else are we going to get in?"

"The explosion will send everyone in the area to the site," Cassie said.

"In which case, you should probably be somewhere else," Trent recommended.

"That wolf's crazy," Tennison said as they hurried away from the determined looking student.

"Yeah, but he's also brilliant," Terith defended him. "Give us five minutes," she said into her headset.

"Got it," Trent replied.

"What do you see, Kalia?" Alex asked with a finger on his earpiece.

"The cameras are empty for the most part. I see a few guys on the second level, but other than that, nothing."

"That's what worries me," Alex replied.

He met Jericho's look. "Professor Mouse had a camera that read the heat signatures so we knew where every guard was. It would be handy about now."

"You've been out with Jaze's pack?" Jericho asked in amazement.

"A few times," Alex told him. "It was more organized than this. I wonder what went wrong for them."

"I hope we don't find out," Jericho replied.

Alex couldn't have agreed more.

"I got ahold of the Global Protection Agency," Kalia said into their headsets. "They'll reach you in about ten minutes. Agent Sullivan said not to act until they arrive. He doesn't want to risk anyone getting killed."

"I'd have to agree with him," Alex said.

His headset crackled and Trent's voice came over the intercom. "We're seriously waiting for them?"

"We need to," Jericho replied. "Rushing into things like this blindly will definitely get at least a few of us hurt if not killed. It'd be smarter to wait."

"Great," Trent muttered. "Just what I need, to stand in the snow with a bazooka on my shoulder waiting to become a target for the next ten minutes. Any chance they have this heat signature technology you've been talking about?"

The thought sent a chill down Alex's spine. "If Drogan has anything to do with the trap, there's a very good chance of that. Be ready to move."

While they waited, Alex sent Terith back to cover Trent. He sent Cassie and Tennison to take cover on the other side of the compound so that if one of the pairs got caught, the others wouldn't be compromised.

"The GPA has arrived," Trent said.

"Are you sure?" Jericho asked.

Trent's tone was thick with irony when he replied, "Unless men dressed in black wearing jackets that say GPA are here to trick or treat."

Alex put a hand on Jericho's arm to keep him from replying.

"Trent gets sarcastic when he's stressed," Alex said in an undertone. "It's his way of dealing with the pressure."

They waited for the black forms to make their way over.

Alex recognized Agent Sullivan from their first mission together. "You guys have a way in?" the agent asked, straightening his black suit as though the run through the snow had been a bit of an inconvenience.

"Trent's got a bazooka," Jericho told him.

Agent Sullivan rolled his green eyes. "Where did you get these boys, Alex?"

"They're a part of my pack," Alex explained. "Jaze's pack is made up of our professors, so they wanted to help get them out."

"Not that we enjoy school," Trent muttered on the other end of the headset.

Alex chose not to repeat the werewolf's words.

"Fine," Agent Sullivan said. He pulled out a small screen. "Who's your surveillance team?"

"Kalia," Alex said. "She's back at the command center."

"Another student?" the agent asked. At Alex's nod, Agent Sullivan sighed. "Fine." He typed something on the screen. "What channel are you on?"

When their headsets were synced, the agent said, "Kalia, I've sent you the live feed from our cameras. Are you getting it?"

"No, uh, yes. I see it," Kalia replied. They heard a quick intake of breath. "There are at least thirty people in that compound."

"It's alright," the agent replied calmly. "Some of those will be Jaze's pack. If we can free them, we'll doubled our force. What we need to do is locate them. Is there anything you know of that you can use to identify them?"

"Let me check with Brock," Kalia replied.

"Why isn't Brock there?" Agent Sullivan asked when Kalia's microphone clicked off.

"He apparently slipped in the bathroom and hit his head," Alex told the agent. "That's why we're here."

Agent Sullivan shook his head. "I wouldn't be surprised if the slip is food related. I've told that boy sandwiches will be his downfall."

Alex smothered a laugh with the realization that the agent hadn't meant to make a joke. Jericho nudged him in the side with an elbow. Alex sobered and turned his attention back to the compound.

"Okay," Kalia said breathlessly. "Apparently Kaynan has a tracking device on his wristband knife, whatever that means. Brock said to enter the sequence..." Her voice fell away as she followed whatever Brock had told her to do. "There!" she exclaimed. "They're in the top floor in the middle of the compound. By the looks of it, there are a dozen men guarding them, and others circling the hallways."

Agent Sullivan clicked off his headset so the others wouldn't hear. "This doesn't make sense," he said quietly. "Jaze knows better than to get himself caught like this. We have to assume he has ulterior motives in this one."

"What do you mean by ulterior motives?" Jericho asked.

The agent met both of their gazes. "We have to assume

that Jaze got caught for a reason. Perhaps he found something, or someone is there that he wants us to find."

"Drogan," Alex said. The name sent a shiver down his spine.

Agent Sullivan nodded. "Perhaps, or the General. Whatever the case may be, we're about to go into a firefight none of your friends are prepared for."

"They'll fight," Alex reassured him.

"They might die," Agent Sullivan replied.

Alex met the agent's stern gaze. He let out a slow breath, thinking it through. Alex finally nodded. He put a hand to his headset again. "Alright, Terith, Trent, as soon as the wall blows, get back to the chopper. Pick up Cassie and Tennison. We'll call you as soon as we need an airlift."

"No way," Trent argued immediately.

"We're not leaving you," Cassie echoed.

Alex met Jericho's eyes. The Alpha nodded. "This is your Alpha speaking," Jericho said over the headset. "You four will get to the helicopter and meet us when we're ready. That is an order."

Thought Alex knew how badly the others wanted to argue, they answered with silence.

Jericho locked eyes with Alex. "Do I need to order you, too?"

Alex returned his gaze. "Jaze is my family. The rest of the professors are, too. I'm not leaving them if I can help them get to safety."

"Fine," Jericho relented. "But we're going in together and getting out together. Understand?"

Alex nodded.

Agent Sullivan touched his earpiece. "Brace, open a door for us on the south side. I want silence. Thrash, cut the power as soon as the explosion hits. Trace, take team Bravo and sweep the north side. We'll be cutting around as soon as we're clear. On my five, Trent. You ready?" At Trent's affirmative, the agent said, "Five, four, three, two, one."

An explosion rocked the rapidly growing darkness. Immediately, red and white search lights and sirens cut through the night.

"Let's go," Agent Sullivan breathed.

They ran behind the agent to the south side. Instead of cutting through a door lock like Alex had expected, Brace had conveniently detached the entire door and left it leaning against the wall. Agent Sullivan shook his head with a small smile at the sight and led his team inside. Alex and Jericho fell in with Sullivan's men as they swept through the building.

The lights went out. Chaos erupted. Emergency lighting flickered on overhead as Agent Sullivan's men took down guards on either side of the hallway. Guns flashed. Acrid smoke from smoke grenades filled Alex's nose. His wolf eyesight was confused by the whirling emergency lights attached to the sirens that blocked out any chance to hear the enemies approach. Alex felt cut off, his senses delayed. The smoke thickened. Men yelled and guns fired. His heart beat a staccato rhythm in his chest, threatening to burst out of it.

"Alex, run to the left!" Kalia said into Alex's headset.

Alex covered his ear with one hand so he could hear her better and grabbed Jericho's arm with the other. Together, the pair dashed down the hall.

"Take the door to the stairs on the right," Kalia commanded.

"Agent Sullivan, this way," Alex shouted over the commotion.

Agent Sullivan fell in with most of his team after commanding a few to stay behind to protect their retreat.

Gunfire erupted above them on the staircase. The light

flickered off and on. Alex run up with the others close behind. He turned at the landing and fired above him. The bullet struck a guard in the chest. The man wavered, then fell forward over the railing. Alex and Jericho watched him slam to the ground below.

"So much for the sleeping agents," Jericho said as Agent Sullivan's team returned fire around them.

Alex and Jericho ran up with the humans.

"Through the door on the right," Kalia said.

Jericho hit it with his shoulder and it burst open to reveal a dark room filled with guards. Jaze's team was in the middle chained to chairs. Many of them were cut and bleeding. The lights flickered over their heads, revealing guards standing behind them with guns ready to use. Alex held his breath, worried he was about to see the second father figure in his life slain before his eyes.

"Fire," Agent Sullivan said quietly.

Glass crashed as the windows were shot from the outside. The guards around Jaze's team began to fall as Agent Sullivan's snipers took them down.

The guards returned fire, but they were quickly becoming outnumbered.

A form caught Alex's eye. He turned in time to see a figure disappear down a side hall. His gut told him it was Drogan. Alex charged across the room.

"Alex, where are you going?" Jericho shouted.

Alex dove through the door as a volley of bullets peppered it. He rolled up to his feet and continued running.

"Alex, go back!" Kalia said with distress in her voice. "What are you doing?"

"I've got to finish this," Alex told her. He tore out his earpiece and threw it to the ground as he ran. The sound of footsteps in front of him propelled him faster. He turned a corner, then another, following Drogan's scent as well as the sound of his retreat. Alex's senses locked on the man who had caused him so much pain. He had promised to avenge his parents and brother; he would stop the threat to Cassie and end the cause of fear in his life.

Alex charged down a flight of stairs and around a corner. The scent of panic along with Drogan's musky smell filled his nose. He ran into the dark room. The door slammed shut behind him. Alex dropped into a defensive crouched and turned, expecting to see Drogan standing at the door.

Instead, four men in thick vests and bearing defensive shields barred the way. They each held machine guns. The metallic scent of silver let Alex know that they contained bullets meant to kill werewolves.

Glancing around, he saw four more guards on each wall. That made sixteen guards with machine guns. He knew it was more than he could take down. Four thugs without armor had been hard enough. He didn't stand a chance against heavily armed, trained soldiers.

They advanced toward him. Alex looked around for an escape around. The wall of shields pressed closer on every side, creating a cage. Panic welled in his throat. He wanted to attack them, but he wanted to return to Cassie and Kalia, to return home to the Academy. Attacking would definitely get him shot. Even if each man only shot him once, he knew he couldn't survive sixteen silver bullets. He spun in a circle looking for an escape.

"Alex Davies."

Alex's teeth bared of their own accord at the voice.

A sound of footsteps followed. The men with shields shifted on the right side, revealing Drogan. He looked slightly ruffled from his flight, but gave a predatory smile as he studied his captive.

"Who would have thought you'd come searching for your beloved Jaze?"

"They're coming for you, Drogan," Alex replied, forcing his voice to remain steady. The gun felt heavy in his hand. He lifted it slowly.

"Drop the weapon, Alex. We both know it won't kill me."

"It will if I shoot you in the head," Alex replied.

The guards closest to Drogan shuffled their feet as if anxious to protect him, but he lifted a hand and they held their positions.

"Then my men will kill you and you'll have lost everything anyway," Drogan replied calmly.

"At least you'd be gone. The world will be a safer place," Alex growled.

Drogan's voice grew deadly. "Give me the gun, Alex."

Alex shook his head. "Never."

Drogan lifted a hand. Every gun in the room aimed directly at Alex's head. "At my signal, your face will no longer be in one piece. You sure you want your body to go home to your sister like that?"

Alex's hand that held the gun shook. He didn't want to give it up. It felt like the only lifeline he had. Yet there was no denying the cold attention of sixteen guns aimed with deadly accuracy at his head. He held his breath and opened his hand.

Drogan took the gun from him. "Good boy," he said. He lifted the weapon and fired it point blank at Alex's chest.

Alex stumbled backward with the force of the blow. He fell against the shields behind him as the sleeping agent swept quickly through his veins.

Drogan was about to win. Alex couldn't let that happen. He gritted his teeth and surged back to his feet. Drogan's eyes widened. He pulled the trigger two more times. Each bullet slammed into Alex's chest. Pain ricocheted through his ribs. He fell to the floor. The sleeping agent stole his ability to fight or think. He tried to force his mind to clear, but his eyes closed against his will.

"Werewolves," Alex heard Drogan mutter before his thoughts shut off to the world.

Chapter Thirty

"He looks like Jet," a voice said through the haze that filled Alex's mind.

Another voice laughed. The sound sent ice rushing through Alex's veins. "You know that's impossible."

"Yeah, but the resemblance is uncanny."

Someone slapped Alex's cheek. He jerked back more at the shock of it than the pain.

"Thought I may have killed you with all that sleeping juice," Drogan drawled, giving Alex a humorless smile. "Thought you might get off lucky."

Alex willed his gaze to focus on the man's mismatched eyes. "Where am I?"

Drogan shrugged. "Safe. Or not, depending on how you look at it." His gaze narrowed. "I'd go with not."

"Why keep me alive?" Alex asked. His head pounded and his wrists burned where they were fastened behind his back. He had no doubts the metal coating the handcuffs was silver. He sat in a hard-backed chair that felt flimsy beneath him. A lone light hanging from the ceiling lit the small cement room. Three guards wearing the same armor Alex recognized from before stood near the door.

"Who said anything about keeping you alive?" Drogan replied.

The man's fist slammed into Alex's cheek. Pain flared through his cheekbone so intense that Alex had to blink back tears. He tried to focus on Drogan's fist to see why it had hurt so badly. He had been punched many times during combat training, but nothing had felt like that.

Drogan grinned and flexed his fingers, revealing a set of brass knuckles coated in silver. "Smarts, doesn't it?" He hit Alex again.

Alex's head rocked back. His jaw slid to the left and he bit down, feeling his cheek slice open on the inside from his teeth. A different taste touched his tongue. A memory of a small square of metal in a plain gray box brushed his mind. He had gotten so used to the device he had forgotten it was there. He bit down on it hard. If he could stall Drogan, Jaze might find him in time.

"Why not kill Jaze?" Alex asked, shaking his head to clear his vision. The second blow had opened his cheekbone. He could feel the blood dripping from the wound.

"Oh, I wanted to," Drogan replied. His eyes narrowed. "I can't tell you how badly I wanted to. But there are others interested in your great leader's hide." He gave Alex a stare laced with steel. "But if they're that slow getting to us next time, I'll kill Jaze and the rest and tell my father they died in the firefight. Having them dead will make quieting this little rebellion that much easier."

"This rebellion is a lot stronger than you think," Alex told him, picturing the wolves in Red's warehouse.

"They're cowards," Drogan spat. "They've gone into hiding, fending for themselves and leaving the others to our mercy. If that's your rebellion, you've got a lot of disappointment coming your way."

"They'll beat you," Alex told him. "They'll win in the end."

"Like your brother, Jet?" Drogan's mouth cracked into a cruel twisted grin. "Oh, wait. My mistake. He's not your brother, is he?"

Alex followed Drogan's gaze to a smaller man near the guards at the door.

"He's not," the man confirmed with a chuckle. "That would be impossible."

Alex's heart burned with indignation. "Jet is my brother,"

he growled, trying to stand.

Drogan hit him in the chest so hard Alex fell over backwards, landing painfully with his wrists locked behind the chair. Drogan put a foot on Alex's chest and leered down at him. Alex's ribs ached from being shot. The shells were still lodged in his chest. He could barely breathe.

"It's about time someone told you the truth, boy." Drogan's eyes narrowed. "Your parents adopted you after you were given up by your birth mother. She apparently didn't like the taint of your bloodlines, and neither do I."

Alex spit out the blood that coated his mouth. He didn't want to know what Drogan was talking about, but the man's words ringed with truth. "What are you talking about?" he forced himself to ask.

Drogan's eyes narrowed. "My father has issues with werewolves. What I didn't know is that those issues also included him taking a female werewolf and using her any way that he liked before throwing her to the gutter to die." He shook his head and growled, "My father apparently forgot that werewolves don't die so easily."

Drogan picked up Alex and the chair in a fit of rage and threw him against the wall. Alex fell to the ground on his knees and face. He lay there struggling to breathe.

Drogan flipped him over. "That woman had twins." His lips lifted in a snarl. "My baby half-brother and sister who turned out to be filthy werewolves like their tramp of a mother." The man's green and blue eyes glittered in the half-light. He pulled out a knife. Alex's heart slowed when he recognized it as the same blade Drogan had used to slit his parents' throats. Drogan leaned down.

"I'm going to end your revolting lives so that my father doesn't find out he gave life to such vile offspring. When you and Cassie are out of the way for good, we can blow up your

precious Academy and I'll know for certain that you're dead."
The corners of his lips lifted at the thought. "I can't think of
a better way to get rid of several generations of cursed
werewolves."

Alex's mind reeled. He couldn't take in everything
Drogan was saying. It didn't make sense; yet the back of his
mind argued that it did. He could hear the truth in the
human's foul words. His soul rebelled against them.

Drogan's knife pressed against Alex's throat. Alex could
feel the burn of the silver-coated metal as the razor sharp
blade touched his skin.

"I can think of a better way to get rid of them," Alex said,
his voice tight.

The pressure against his throat lessened slightly. Drogan
grinned down at him. "Feeling like some revenge against your
classmates?" the human asked. He glanced up at the man by
the door. "What do you think, Jenkins. Should I slit his throat
or listen to him?"

Alex lifted his head just enough to see the man lace his
hands together as he thought.

"It couldn't hurt to listen," the man said. "Maybe his
ideas are more creative than yours."

Drogan leaned forward. "I'm all ears," he said.

Alex kept his voice carefully quiet. "I think you should go
to the school."

Drogan bent closer to hear him better.

Alex dropped his voice even quieter. "Go through the
front doors, up the stairs to the left." He spoke softer and
Drogan crouched lower. "Go to the end of the hallway and
open the window." Alex felt the weight of the knife lessen as
Drogan's interest was piqued. "Then jump out of it so the
wolves can tear you from limb to limb when you end up
broken on the ground," he finished with a shout so loud

Drogan jumped.

Alex jerked to the side and turned as soon as his knees hit the ground. The legs of the chair caught Drogan on the back of his legs and sent him tumbling to the floor. Alex spun sideways, slamming his shoulder and the top of the chair into Drogan's back before the guards could pull him off.

Drogan gave a shout of pain. Rough hands grabbed Alex and tore him away from the Extremist leader. He was thrown onto his back again. The clatter of the metal chair against the cement floor echoed through the room.

Drogan clambered heavily to his feet. He gripped the knife so tight his knuckles turned white. He limped back to tower over Alex.

"You think you're funny?" Drogan demanded.

Before Alex could move, Drogan slammed the knife into his stomach.

A ringing sound filled Alex's ears. The pain from the silver blade made his legs go numb. He could see Drogan shouting, but couldn't make out the words. Drogan looked like a mad man. Spittle flew from his lips and landed on Alex's cheek. Alex wished with one line of strangely coherent thought that he could wipe it away so he didn't die with Drogan's slobber on his face.

Drogan's eyes widened. He looked over Alex's chair to the door beyond. Alex wished through the hum that he could see who entered. Shots rang out. Drogan fell back clawing at his chest. Alex stared at the three pools of blood that began to flow down the Extremist leader's shirt. Drogan's eyes lock on Alex's. His legs buckled and he hit the ground.

"Alex, are you alright?"

Alex blinked, focusing on Jaze's concerned face. The werewolf motioned and Alex was lifted up to a sitting position. His handcuffs were unfastened.

Jaze touched the blood that coated Alex's cheek. He ran his hands quickly over Alex's sides and back. They paused at his chest.

"You were shot," he said. Before Alex could reply, Jaze tore open Alex's shirt. Jaze's brow furrowed as his gaze shifted from the bullet holes to the knife wound in Alex's stomach. Blood pooled down to Alex's pants.

"Lyra, Alex needs your help," Jaze said, looking past him.

She stepped quickly around the chair and knelt down in front of Alex. "These look like they're from one of our guns," the werewolf said, her gaze on the three bullet holes as she pressed bandages against Alex's stomach.

Alex thought wearily that they sure hurt a lot more than the tiny holes looked like they would.

"You've lost a lot of blood," Jaze said. "We need to get you home."

Alex nodded. "Home sounds good," he said, his words just above a whisper.

Jaze gave him a warm smile. "We almost didn't find you."

"You got Drogan," Alex said.

"You got Drogan," Jaze replied.

Both of them watched Kaynan and Chet lift Drogan and drag him not so gently from the room. A moan of pain came from the man.

"He's not dead?" Alex asked.

Jaze shook his head. "Sleeping agents." His voice said he preferred it to be different. "He'll be well sedated on his way to the GPA. We'll deal with him there."

Alex winced as Lyra pushed harder on his stomach.

"We need to get Alex to surgery. There are silver shards in the wound that will have to be removed so he doesn't get an infection," Lyra told Jaze.

Jaze nodded. "There's no time to waste." He shifted his

gaze. "Get him to the helicopter."

Vance knelt beside Alex and picked him up.

"Not again," Alex protested. "I can walk."

"I don't believe you," Vance replied.

Every step flooded Alex with pain.

"Just think of it as if you have your own personal servant," Vance told him.

Alex stared at the huge werewolf.

Vance cracked a smile. "Yeah, Jaze told me what horrible living conditions you were in over Christmas. Now I wish I'd sent you to my mom's."

Alex chuckled, then winced and doubled over at the pain through his stomach.

"Easy there, chief," Vance replied quietly. "Maybe cut down on the laughter until you don't have a gaping hole in your stomach."

"Good idea," Alex replied tightly.

Chapter Thirty-one

Drogan's words pressed against Alex's mind as the sedation from surgery wore off. The General, Jason Carso, was their father. If that was the case, everything he knew about his childhood was skewed. His parents, his relationship to Jet, even his revenge against Drogan.

His stomach twisted at the realization that Drogan was his half-brother. Being related to the man made him feel sick. Yet he and Cassie had Jet's dark blue eyes. There had been a kinship there he couldn't deny. There was no way it was true.

Understanding flooded him so sharply he couldn't catch his breath for a minute. His heart skipped several beats. The monitors that had been beeping quietly sounded an alarm. Footsteps hurried into the room. He heard voices talking as the monitors were quickly checked.

A hand touched his forehead, brushing back his tangled black hair. He opened his eyes to see Meredith looking down at him.

"Hi, Mom," he forced through his throat that was so dry his voice cracked.

Meredith's blue eyes filled up with tears. "Oh, Alex," she said softly.

"What does he mean?" Cassie asked from the other side of the bed. She looked from Alex back to Meredith. "Why did he say that?"

Alex took a shuddering breath and turned his head to face his sister. "She saved us, Cass. She gave us to her sister and brother-in-law after their baby was stolen." He took a shallow breath. "She was afraid the General would find her. She saved our lives." He winced at the thought that the General was their father. He took another breath and felt the pain in his ribs ease. "Meredith is our mother."

Alex's gaze shifted to the form standing in the doorway. Jaze watched him with sad eyes. At Alex's questioning look, the dean nodded, confirming Alex's words.

Alex slipped his hand under Meredith's. Tears streamed down her face. "My little boy," she said in a sob.

Cassie ducked under Meredith's arm. It was clear by her expression that Cassie didn't understand it all yet, but she trusted her brother. Alex gave her a weak smile. "It's okay, Cass."

She nodded. "I know it is. We're going to be alright."

Alex smiled and let his eyes droop shut. Memories of being a child at his father's knee filled with the wonder of the world held him. He saw Jet there, lying on the grass watching the moon and speaking of hope. Mom stood in the doorway with her soft smile on her face, her eyes so warm and deep like her sister who turned out to be their birth mother. They were family. Nothing could change that. If anything, he and Cassie had been given a gift. They had a mother again; they were home. Alex drifted off to a sleep that was filled with peace.

About the Author

Cheree Alsop is the mother of a beautiful, talented daughter and amazing twin sons who fill every day with joy and laughter. She is married to her best friend, Michael, the light of her life and her soulmate who shares her dreams and inspires her by reading the first drafts and adding depth to the stories. Cheree is currently working as an independent author and mother. She enjoys reading, riding her motorcycle on warm nights, and playing with her twins while planning her next book.

Cheree and Michael live in Utah where they rock out, enjoy the outdoors, plan great adventures, and never stop dreaming.

Check out Cheree's other books at www.chereealsop.com

***If you liked this book, please review it online so others can find it!

Look for Werewolf Academy Book 3: Instinct

77999603R00163

Made in the USA
Middletown, DE
28 June 2018